NIGHTMARE Sky

STORIES OF
ASTRONOMICAL
HORROR

EDITED BY
RED LAGOE

DEATH KNELL PRESS

NIGHTMARE SKY
STORIES OF ASTRONOMICAL HORROR

DEATH KNELL PRESS

www.deathknellpress.com

This book is for all the people who turn off their porch lights,
risking being trapped with monsters in the inky black of night,
so they can have a better view of the stars.

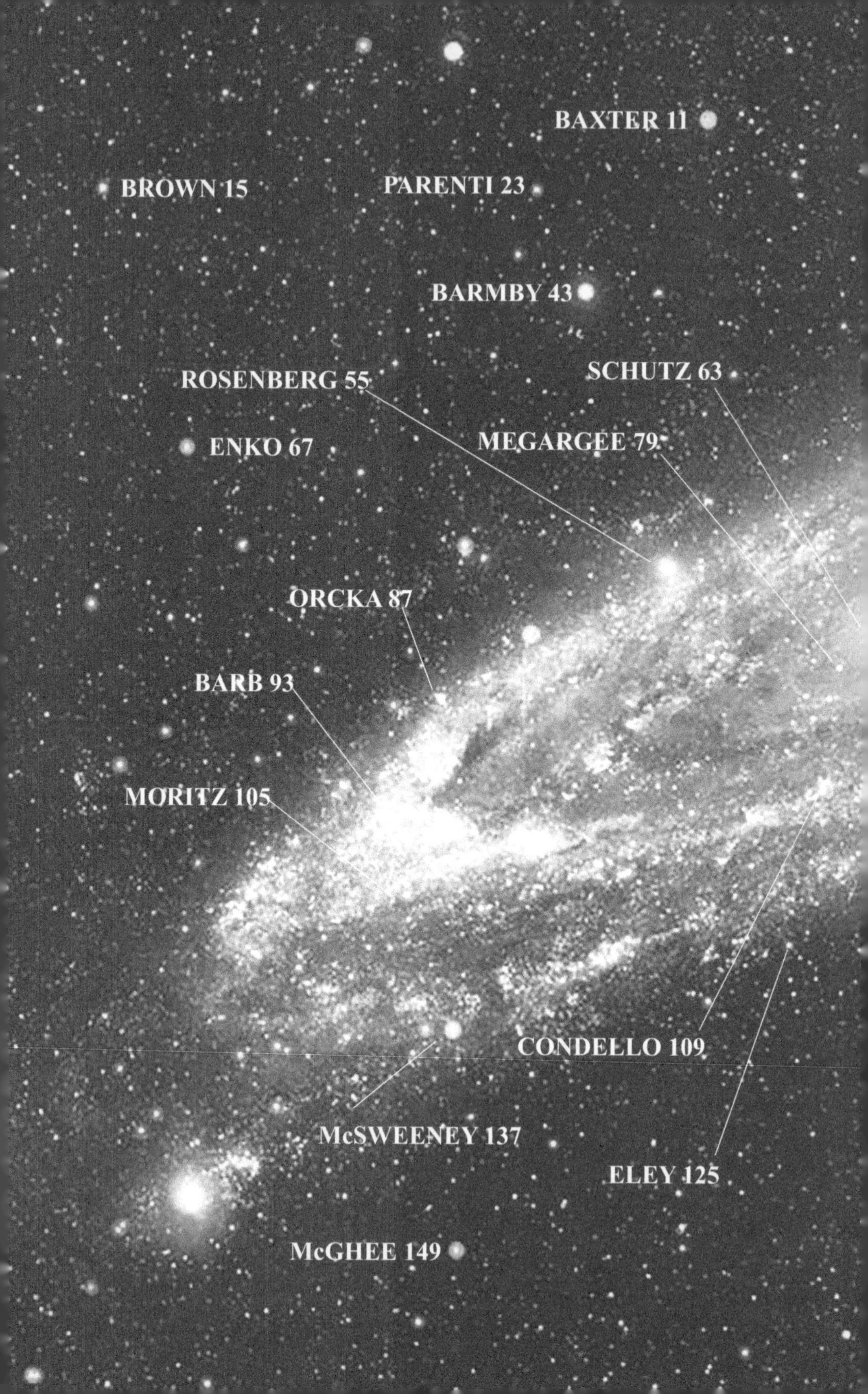

BAXTER 11

BROWN 15　　　　PARENTI 23

BARMBY 43

ROSENBERG 55　　　　　　SCHUTZ 63

ENKO 67　　　　MEGARGEE 79

ORCKA 87

BARB 93

MORITZ 105

CONDELLO 109

McSWEENEY 137

ELEY 125

McGHEE 149

DAVIS 157

RAGSDALE 159

MOHR 171

LOGAN 177

DALE 189

JIANG 195

BEIDEMAN 197

AYALA 201

OTA 213

GARCIA 223

MARGARITI 237

REYNOLDS 241

SEIPEL 249

STRICKMAN 259

TABLE OF CONTENTS

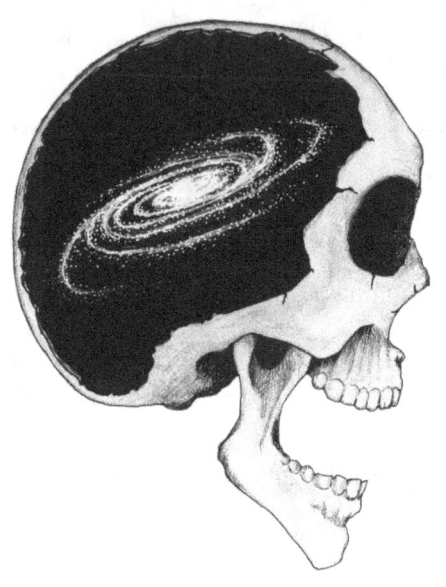

"We are base, vile creatures rutting in the muck we've created, our eyes looking up at a poisoned sky we've populated with ghosts to help us sleep at night, to allow us to come up with reasons to do the things we do."

— Gabino Iglesias, *The Devil Takes You Home*

FOREWORD

ALAN BAXTER

Awesome (*adjective*) – extremely impressive or daunting; inspiring awe—an overwhelming feeling of reverence, admiration, or fear.

That last one. The fear part. For me, nothing invokes reverence and *fear* like space. The beauty and wonder of the cosmos is undeniable, but the simply inconceivable size of it all terrifies me. Weirdly though, it simultaneously creates a kind of peace, because it reminds me we are less than dust motes. We are nothing. That in itself should be terrifying too, but maybe it's the horror writer in me who finds it strangely comforting. In the grand scheme of all things, we really don't matter. The earth won't notice when we're gone, other than it'll feel a lot better to have shaken us off. The universe? It already cares less about us than we care for the little guys we can't see living in our eyebrows (I'm not kidding – look up Demodex.)

The point is that space has this ability, perhaps more than anything else with the possible exception of the deep ocean, to fill us with both wonder *and* fear. To make us feel part of something magnificent *and* make us feel truly insignificant.

The thing about people though, is that we don't like feeling insignificant, so we insert ourselves into things. We try to mold things around us and make them ours, like dogs pissing on lampposts. But in the long run, that too is destined to fail. Entropy is the only certainty in the ever-expanding universe. (I know, there is a theory that it expands and collapses over and over again, but in our tiny blink-of-an-eye existence, that's kind of irrelevant.)

This whole situation creates a kind of dichotomy where we have to find personal peace with being awestruck at the fantastic thing of which we're a part while also reminded of our own inconsequentiality, and when we try to address that irrelevance, we are destined to fail. That's where the real fear comes in, I think.

So as we've always done, we fight our fears with our imagination. If anything is perhaps bigger than the universe itself, it's humanity's ability to imagine. The mind is a truly endless landscape, not beholden to physics, and arguably the best part of the mind is the dark places it can go. If we see a shadow, we tend to imagine something in it, unseen, patient, waiting…

The dark matter of our minds gives rise to some of our most powerful imaginings. Like space itself, the gaps between the matter—wide open, black and effectively endless, but not empty—are terrifying. Dark matter and dark energy are components of our existence that we're only just beginning to comprehend. I often think that what we may learn about those things might drive us deeper into insanity. I'd like to think they'll open panoramas of understanding, but I'm a horror writer, remember?

It's hard to go past that H.P. Lovecraft quote: "We live on a placid island of ignorance in the midst of black seas of infinity, and it was not meant that we should voyage far. The sciences, each straining in its own direction, have hitherto harmed us little; but some day the piecing together of dissociated knowledge will open up such terrifying vistas of reality, and of our frightful position therein, that we shall either go mad from the revelation or flee from the light into the peace and safety of a new dark age."

I'm hoping for the opposite, of course, while very much aware of the possibility that Lovecraft is right on that front. But I think we should voyage far. As far as we can. Of course, the more we explore, the more answers we get from science, the more prepared we are for what we might discover. Whatever it is, it'll be awesome.

Meanwhile, the gaps in our knowledge are populated by our imagination. And as space is teeming with dark energy, so too is our imagination, waiting to be unlocked. We confront many unknown possibilities through the telling of stories, and this book is full of them.

The stories in here are awesome in the more modern sense. They'll create their own vibrations of reverence and fear in your heart. Stories about people hungry for knowledge of the infinite, while it is hungry in its turn to swallow us whole, without even noticing. We don't stand a chance in the long run, but that only makes whatever fleeting impact we do make all the more important. Whatever we learn, whatever we create, might resonate for a while. And in the face of eternal entropy, what greater pursuit is there than to make an impact, to make a difference, even for just a little while?

Like this book. It will make a difference.

Alan Baxter

NSW, Australia 2022

STARGAZER

TIFFANY MICHELLE BROWN

I didn't see it when you first caught my eye and I swiped right on your profile, but how can anyone discern something so intimate through the veil of technology? It wasn't until we were seated in the hipster bar, the soles of our shoes sticking to the gummy floor, some Top 40 hit pulsing over the speakers, that I understood. That I saw what you possessed.

It's the reflection of the flame in her eyes, I tried to reason. But even with that logical explanation batting around in my brain, I had to lean closer. Further inspect the situation. I feigned complete interest in what you were saying—something about a dog park nearby, or maybe a dog bakery?—and shuffled forward in the cushy banquette.

Now I could see it clearly—an explosion of energy and matter nestled within your right eye. Gently revolving like that restaurant in Seattle where you spin and spin, but the movement is so slight, it's easy to forget you're going in circles. What I'd mistaken as reflected candlelight was, in fact, a smattering of stars burning against a backdrop of darkness. They winked at me. Danced brazenly in the cosmos within you.

There were swirls of color, blues and purples and reds I'd never beheld. Gaseous plumes that painted space with the deftness of a seasoned artist. I imagined throwing myself into the endlessness within your eye, no spacesuit, no oxygen, letting the galaxy do what it would with my corporeal self. It would be worth it, no matter the outcome.

You were mid-sentence when I reached across the table and held your chin in my palm. Your eyes widened, and that small movement gave me an even greater glimpse of the space-scape I'd discovered.

"Your eyes," I said, "are like nothing I've ever seen before."

We'd set up our second date before the fedora-clad waiter returned to ask about a second round.

For a handful of days after our first meeting, my memories were enough to tide me over. I'd remember the slow carousel of light and color that bloomed in your eye and completely lose track of time.

Once, I came back from the cosmos to discover I'd completely ignored three full episodes of the true crime documentary I'd begun watching. The TV remote was clenched in my hand, and there was drool on my chin.

Another time, a custodian at my workplace tapped me on my shoulder and asked if I wouldn't mind handing them the wastebasket lodged between my legs and my computer tower. It was 7:48 PM, well past the time I should have clocked out for the day.

My shower water ran cold. I burned meals in my oven. I traded sleep for journeys into the unknown. And while I lost time and my routine, my galactic meditations made me feel like I was part of something bigger than myself. Something infinitely more important than my day-to-day.

Toward the end of the week, it became more difficult to conjure up the images. They lacked wonder and vivaciousness. My existence began to feel… mundane. Trivial. Woefully colorless and uninspired. That night in the bar, I'd seen something beyond myself, and now everything else paled in comparison.

I called you, tried to keep my voice casual, asked if you'd like to go to dinner. Yes, we had plans that coming weekend, but I just really wanted to see you.

You couldn't do dinner, but you could do a drink. Same place as before,

9:00 PM?

I showered, shaved, ironed my shirt, even spritzed on some cologne, because I would not show up on the doorstep of the universe looking shabby and ungrateful.

Have you ever fucked under the stars? Experienced the wonder and awe of gazing up at the night sky while reveling in the pleasures of flesh and heat and connection?

When you took me to bed after our fifth date, I was giddy to discover you craved eye contact. You held my face between your smooth palms, your eyes wide and focused. With every pump of my hips, I felt something building, something greater than earthly pleasure. It was a connection to the great unknown. This feeling that if only I could get closer, all the secrets of existence would open up to me.

When I came, I pressed my forehead to yours, and I was damn near blinded by the light in your eye. When I could take no more, I rolled off of you and stared up, expecting to see the shitty popcorn ceiling of your apartment. Instead, the night sky greeted me. Pulsing. Twinkling. Beckoning. It was as if some power greater than us had removed your upstairs neighbors, the roof, the whole damn building. The cosmos opened up to me, shining light and power and wonder on our bodies.

Your voice brought me back to earth, and my skin quickly grew cold.

"I really appreciate that you like eye contact," you said, kissing my jawline, hooking a thigh over my stomach.

I turned my head to meet your gaze. "I like looking at you."

You leaned in to kiss me, but you didn't close your eyes until the very last second, granting me the opportunity to stargaze.

We started seeing each other every other day or so, and let me tell you, I'd never felt more alive. Spending time with you. Gazing into infinity. Feeling the energy of your swirling galaxy fill me up with meaning and celestial promise.

My productivity had gone to shit, but I'd come to terms with the fact that my life had changed forever. I'd shed my old ways. What is it all worth in the end anyway—the toiling away in corporate America; the celebration of things so inconsequential as birthdays and national holidays? It all seemed so foolish to me, this inflated sense of self-importance. I'd discovered the truth, that we'd all return to the sky eventually. After we left our bodies, we'd become dust. Starlight.

Luckily, I didn't have to wait for death. I had you.

I didn't know I'd been let go from my job until I showed up the day after I was fired, and Mary from HR called security to escort me from the building. Messages from friends accumulated in my voicemail inbox asking where I'd been, and would I like to meet at the court down the street to play some two-on-two this weekend? I stopped paying my bills, because I realized money was a social construct.

I put all of my energy into planning dates. Seeing you. Touching you. Holding you close. Getting lost in the primordial revolution that had brought me into the light.

"I can't," you said, and the stars in your eyes flickered and dimmed. It was the first time I'd seen the brilliance within you diminish, and I couldn't understand why. I'd done everything right. I made coq au vin, curated a romantic playlist, bought a new suit, spent my savings on a diamond.

I couldn't breathe. I was free falling through space with nowhere to land. Though I could still see your eyes, that swirling promise of infinity, there was now an invisible barricade between us, pushing me away. Grounding me in this bullshit earthly existence.

"But why?" I asked.

"It's only been two months." You looked down at the napkin in your lap. "I do care for you, but..."

Your hesitation was frustrating. Didn't you feel the connection between us? It was your gravitational pull that had snagged me after all.

"Look at me."

You did, but I could tell by your expression that I had raised my voice.

Your brows knit together, and your shoulders rose ever so slightly. I made sure my next sentence was made of silk. "You are all I've ever needed."

Your body tensed, and the atmosphere in the dining room changed. Discomfort bloomed in the air, and you looked like a wild animal. Hunted. Desperate for shelter.

"I'm just a little overwhelmed." You dabbed the corners of your mouth with your napkin and scooted your chair back. "Dinner was beautiful, but I'm rather tired. Can we meet in the morning for a coffee before work?"

I snapped the ring box closed and set it on the table between us. You didn't take it. But I convinced myself it wasn't over. I'd see you again. I'd convince you of the cosmic connection between us.

At the door, you paused and looked up at me, and I fell right in. I needed one last sip of stardust. I grabbed your neck and pulled you close. Your reaction was immediate. You began pushing, clawing, crying, and all of your wild actions made it that much harder for me to stargaze. Couldn't you see that I simply needed some intimacy to help me sleep that night?

I'm not entirely sure what happened next. My memory is inky black. Perhaps you tripped. Perhaps I hit you. Perhaps destiny intervened and struck you down.

I remember the sound of your skull hitting tile. The otherworldly crack. Quick as a snap of the fingers. Heavy and final.

Your blood fanned out beneath you, dyeing your hair crimson. You twitched a few times, little electric pulses that reminded me of how the stars in your eyes would flare when you were happy.

Your eyes. Oh God, your eye!

My knees hit the floor, and I scrambled over to you. I knew in that instant that if you left this earthly realm, your galaxy would be snuffed out, too. I would never see it again, not until my own death. But then, had that ascension ever truly been a promise?

The stars were still there, blinking, but slowly, like a bulb about to extinguish. I couldn't let them go out.

I ran back to the dinner table and grabbed a soup spoon still coated in lobster bisque. I made my sacrifice first, using the scooping motions I'd developed at my first job as a teenager at a local ice cream parlor. Gore dripped down my hand as my eye socket gave way. I screamed until my throat was raw, but when my eyeball plopped onto the floor, I no longer felt pain, only purpose.

I rushed to your body, hoping that I wasn't too late. The galaxy stopped spinning, but I could see the divine luminescence still pulsed, slowly and erratically. I didn't have much time. I scooped and pried. The organ was slick between my fingers when it finally popped out, and I knew I couldn't let it escape. Couldn't let it fall. It had but one destination.

Fitting your eye into my socket wasn't easy given the difference in our facial structures, but I managed it without breaking anything. I figure it'll take some time for your galaxy to recognize a new host. To bloom once again into its magnificence, its unending splendor.

So now I stand here in the bathroom, waiting for the light to come back in your eye, so I can stargaze once more.

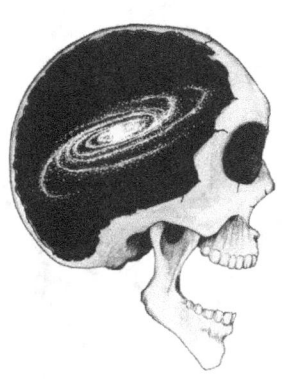

INFINITE FOCUS

DINO PARENTI

Chile, 2021

Three thousand feet above the Chilean Andes, the lava dome of Mt. Hudson threatened menace, even sheathed by snow. A glimmering, gestating cyst awaiting the tiniest poke to explode it, and an effervescent finger whisked the anxieties in my belly.

Thirty-years later, and I'm still ambivalent about the volcano that killed Mother.

Because she *chose* to stay.

The pilot dropped the helicopter for a closer look, and after hugging the western face for a few minutes, he garbled into my headset to check my right. There it rose at the end of a promontory with all the gravity of the mythical: the Bianchi-Santos Observatory.

It had only operated for six months before the '91 eruption closed it indefinitely. At the time, it housed the most advanced telescope in the world: Deep-Space Infrared 1, or DESI for short. The first telescope to employ AI technology, designed to seek-and-study independently. And Mother—the Santos of Bianchi-Santos—had been her creator.

Fifteen minutes later we hovered over a small village hubbed by a Catholic church. The pilot asked if I was sure I wanted to land there.

"As sure as you want to get paid," I replied.

No sooner did my feet hit dirt that the pilot hauled ass out of there. I made a mental note to complain to the travel service as soon as I got back.

Through a tree line still astir by blade wash, my guide emerged. We'd emailed on several occasions while preparing for the trip, and he wore the same red St. Louis Cardinals cap in the one picture he shared of himself standing before the church.

He considered me through a flat smile, ivory cross jutting from his chest like a cracked rib. "*Soy* Ignacio," he said, keeping his distance.

"I'm Olivia Santos. Nice to meet in person, at last."

His head tilted as if to smell the air. "We go. Get dark…*soon.*"

We started down the main cobblestone street. The town droned with morning ritual, people ferrying food, water, and wares along narrow byways. Kids gamboled with stray dogs and kicked around frayed soccer balls. The mustiness of livestock clutched to breezes like lukewarm salutations.

I snapped some shots with my phone, hoping they wouldn't mind my intrusion, but no one seemed fazed.

Out of nowhere, a small, hunched old man appeared, nattering behind us. His eyes were filmed over white, but he stomped about as if his vision still functioned perfectly. Around his neck hung a cross twice the size of Ignacio's. I assumed him the church's head priest, raining holy hell upon Ignacio, no doubt about *me.*

"*Vamos,*" Ignacio said, waving off the gesticulating priest.

We started up the foothills, the priest following awhile in our wake, stabbing fingers at the mountain, beseeching in tears to heed his warnings. How I imagined Mother's colleagues did as they begged her to leave the erupting mountain.

Portland, 2018

What first stood out about the letter was the postmark: Tokyo.

I knew nobody from there.

Then I read the name, printed small and lightly as if by pencil.

Akio Hashimoto, PhD.

Even being November, with all the windows open in my little bungalow, the air constricted like an Atlanta August. Because I remembered him. Remembered what he'd said at the press conference upon escaping the eruption Mother hadn't.

"Dr. Santos had ample opportunity to get away, but insisted on staying with the array."

For nearly thirty-years I'd speculate what was so strong, so compelling that Mother chose certain death rather than flee. She studied her ass off to become an astronomer, but how she still loved her mysteries, the unexplained, sometimes even the irrational—the latter growing as she aged. I often wondered how much my father leaving abruptly after I was born had to do with that. How much *I* did. Mother never said it aloud, but I always sensed she never wanted children. That I'd been unplanned and unasked-for. The sense of chore-needing-done bristled in all our interactions. A methodical, tight-lipped exasperation.

I opened Dr. Hashimoto's letter.

Chile, 2021

We trekked nearly two hours, the sun dipping behind the volcano's lava dome, plummeting the temperature a fast twenty-degrees.

Ignacio and I spoke little throughout, especially after I'd asked why the priest had been so angry. Through his pell-mell English, I gathered that after the '91 eruption destroyed their village, no one was allowed to ascend Mt. Hudson, especially to the observatory.

"God's punishment for man's overreach?" I ventured. In hindsight, it came out haughtier than I'd intended.

"No, no," said Ignacio. *"Es embrujado."*

Haunted.

"Sometimes, the *telescopio*…it still move." He twirled a slow finger to pantomime a rotating observatory.

Sensing my disbelief and inevitable chuckles, he explained that the three astronomers who'd made it down that day were incoherent, shocked, delirious. That they'd seen something beyond the eruption. Something in their telescope.

The trail narrowed to a rift flanked by cairns of scorched stones. Ignacio pointed through them.

"You walk. *Una hora más.*"

From his satchel he drew a set of bolt-cutters.

"What's that for?" I asked.

"You need. At *observatorio*. I no go."

He pitched the bolt-cutters at my feet before turning back down the trail. As I watched his red cap fade into the fog, I thought it miraculous that we'd ever bested the instinct of self-preservation long enough to leave the caves.

Atlanta, 1991

Charlie.

He didn't cower or retaliate like other male chimpanzees when provoked. What he did instead was hold out to Otto—his nemesis—some paper and a large crayon.

He made a peace offering.

Otto, older, grayer, and scarred, twisted his head at the odd tendering from the younger Charlie before two-hand smashing them to the ground. But it diffused the impending conflict. Otto screeched frustration, but in the end, shambled off.

Charlie looked straight at me then through the glass, grinned, and resumed scribbling on posterboard. How I wish mother had seen that; validation that my choice to study what still shambled on Earth was just as compelling as what may dwell beyond it.

Dr. Rosson, my mentor, grumbled under his breath. He was working on a paper about the drive for war in chimpanzees, but Charlie, only there a month, wasn't game.

"Looks like we have ourselves a peacenik," he said.

I gazed at Charlie, returning his smile. "He's perfect."

The doctor just twirled his hand. His way of saying *he's all yours*.

My first day at Emory University's Primate Research Center for my doctorate in primatology, and I'd found my thesis subject on self-awareness in primates.

Chile, 2021

I hiked another hour before I rounded a thicket of aspens, and there it stood. The Bianchi-Santos Observatory, something of a cathedral rising at the end of a narrow granite shelf. Stone panels of beige and pewter cladded the exterior of the complex, while the metal faceted dome absorbed the ambient tones of earth and sky.

A shiver lanced through me. I told myself it was the cold.

I crossed the field toward the cyclone fence encircling the complex, razor-wire siphoning sunlight through the fog, winking steel teeth. Wafts of pine and soot dueled for my attention. A pair of condors glided overhead, hunting for fresh death.

The reason for Ignacio's bolt-cutters clarified as soon as I neared the gates. They'd been locked by a multitude of mismatching chains and padlocks, some older and rustier than others. An overkill to corral some horrid abomination from an old Hammer flick.

It took twenty minutes to cut enough shanks and untangle enough chains to finally get through.

Up close, much of the surrounding rock and concrete walls still bore the char of thirty-year-old lava flow. A concrete platform adjacent to the main structure had been sheared off, leaving only a tangle of rebar. Amazingly, the molten fire mostly waked around the observatory itself, sparing it serious damage.

After the gate ordeal, I was prepared for resistance upon reaching the main door into the observatory, but it opened easily with the hiss of something sizzling on a skillet, and I stepped into the main dome.

Almost immediately I felt the sensation of someone or something else with me. A ubiquitous sense of breathing, like the final decays of echoes, and I steeled myself for someone to appear, my skin tingling in that awful, dentist-drill-contact anticipation.

But I was alone. A fly caught under a large soup bowl—but what a soup bowl! In lieu of triangular space-framing, the dome's structure was supported by a network of complex steel rib vaults one was more apt to see in a basilica than any scientific edifice. But the crowning achievement was DESI, the Bianchi-Santos Telescope itself, set atop a round pedestal in the center. A fire-engine red housing capped by a six-meter-diameter dish of octagonal ceramic glass, designed to glimpse deeper into the cosmos than anything before.

Mother's *real* baby.

Through the dome's open shutters—somehow, I'd thought them closed during our flyby earlier, but I was obviously mistaken—a vermillion fiber of light etched the north face of Mt. Hudson beyond.

It was while staring at this unexpected beauty that I grasped the source of the *breathing*: the wind, skimming down the mountain, cycling throughout the dome, combing through the rib trusses in the vein of pins plucking the individual prongs inside a music box.

No doubt some of my own breathing was being bounced back at me as well, the structure had been so precisely built.

A set of steel stairs ran along the circular pedestal, and these I took up to the control station, decades of blown-in detritus crunching under my feet.

Before the monitor banks, I passed several long workstations covered with dust-caked scanners and plotters. I perused the endless accordion of weather-soiled dot-matrix printouts spilling from their feed trays. Uninterrupted coordinates. Right Ascension in hours, minutes, and seconds. Declination in degrees, minutes, and seconds.

All faded but identical, repeating numbers. All the same point in space.

I approached the control station. DESI's brain. Once again that breathing orbited the dome. Only it was starting to sound more defined, more deliberate. As if trying to piece together a language.

Something marred the monitor screens. From afar it looked like dirt or something crusted, but on closer inspection it all clarified, and my core iced over.

Writing. Words dragged as if by finger across each screen, all bearing the same three words:

I CANNOT SEE

Still another moment before I realized they could've been written in blood, long-since dried.

Atlanta, 1991

My bonding with Charlie was immediate. Within three days, we were inseparable, as if he too yearned to prove his elevated sentience to the world.

He wasn't just receptive to touch, but whenever I spoke, he would abruptly stop playing or eating, and lock eyes with me. I could almost see the struggle in the toggling of his pupils to keep up, like beads on an abacus sliding madly to solve differential calculus problems.

The other chimpanzees ceased interacting with him altogether, as if rebuffing a freak.

Even my usually stuffy, too-lost-in-his-own-mind lab mentor, Dr. Rosson, divulged awe at mine and Charlie's fast simpatico.

"If you're not careful, he'll be accepting a Nobel at the same time you do," he once said after watching Charlie use two different markers to imply cast shadows with basic geometric shapes, after I'd demonstrated just once.

What Dr. Rosson didn't see, because he'd left, was Charlie starting to scribble variations on the same oblong, triangular shape. Dozens of them.

Some evoked Christmas trees with bent ornaments topping them. Some, warped wire hangers.

He did this for weeks, never with Dr. Rosson around, his expression both tense and lost, as if he was trying to comprehend the strange force guiding his hands.

Mostly, I remembered this period because it started a month before the '91 eruption.

Portland, 2018

Dr. Hashimoto's letter began with the usual pleasantries before going into a brief description of his relationship with Mother. *Professional* and *edgy* were used more than once, but the following paragraph was more jumpy, evasive. A ramble, really, of how Mother was determined to save the array as Mt. Hudson erupted—that the telescope had found things no one could imagine—but that she refused to share the data, not to mention leave DESI.

What did Mother learn that she felt obliged to keep from her colleagues? Two had died within a year after, one American and one Italian. No official cause of death was given. The third—Dr. Hashimoto—returned to Japan. He never answered any of my letters or phone calls.

Until today, twenty-seven-years later.

The letter's last two lines, however, were what truly gave me pause. The first was an insistence that I call him ASAP. Something important about Mother he didn't want to divulge in print.

The other was as cryptic as it was foreboding: *The telescope...DESI...is stubborn. She's befuddled.*

Chile, 2021

I backed away from the monitors. In truth, I think I made it down the stairs backwards as well, for to turn away from the screens felt like inviting something to stalk me.

Once down, I explored rooms. Some were empty. Some contained overturned furniture. In one room, painted sky-blue, a cheap household telescope had been set up by a window, pointed westward. I'd thought it rather quaint. A Matchbox sedan on the backseat of a Maserati.

In effect, DESI's baby.

I continued along the observatory's curvature, passing a small kitchenette, and next to it, a room with bunkbeds, each one impeccably made, as if someone was expecting guests.

Choosing a low bunk by the window, I unslung my backpack and began to empty it when a sound from the hallway, soft and creaky, froze me in place.

A footstep?

No. More like the groaning of someone settling into a chair.

"Hello?" I called out.

Stupid. Despite a vague sensation of some other presence or presences, rationally I knew I was alone. Grabbing the bolt-cutters anyway, I quietly ventured out.

The corridor to either side was empty—too long in either direction for someone to have fled unseen. A reflection caught my eye. The door directly across from me. The brass nameplate on it read SANTOS. Mother's office.

Noticing the hasp and padlock above the knob went hand-in-hand with my bewilderment as to how the nameplate could've possibly winked light in a dark hallway.

Portland, 2018

Despite my knowing that Dr. Hashimoto was in his eighties, his voice sounded even older over the phone. Ancient almost, as if drawn from the black depths of catacombs.

As soon as he picked up, he was already talking. No trite, opening salutations or small-talk. He went straight into a matter-of-fact but continuous narrative, mainly about the telescope ignoring all their commands—how it kept recalibrating its lens to the same point in the sky. He paused long enough in places to catch his breath, allowing my perplexed, useless interjections of *uh-huhs* or *yeses* before resuming.

The first time I was left truly dumbstruck during one of his pauses was after he said Mother had warned them all, "raving like a zealot" to never enter her office.

The second was when he explained how Doctors Bianchi and Lowe really died upon returning home after the eruption. That they weren't *natural causes*, as their respective obituaries stated, but suicides. And that wasn't the worst of it.

"Before killing themselves, they bored out their eardrums and eyes."

What he said afterward was vague and mumbled, as if exhausted from replaying the decades-long scenarios in his head. That often he'd catch Mother muttering to herself near the end, much of it about DESI's burgeoning peculiarities. How DESI had started focusing on the astronomers as much as the skies. Expressed odd curiosities about the interactions of her human caretakers, even going so far as to partition and dedicate huge swaths of memory towards amassing such irrelevant data.

Mostly though, Mother babble-spoke glowingly about *me*. How proud she was that her daughter also sought to communicate with non-human beings.

A trait she did her best to dissuade in me.

Dr. Hashimoto then abruptly returned the subject to himself. How DESI had thought *him* an anomaly. How he'd fought off impulses to end his own life, partly, he conjectured, from having a loving family. Mostly though, according to DESI, it was because he'd been the only one not to have peered into the telescope like the others had.

How I should stay away from that accursed place. Move on and live my life.

After hanging up, all I could think about was how Mother *never* spoke about me to others, glowingly or otherwise. Certainly not when I was around to bask in it.

Atlanta, 1991

It got to a point with Charlie, despite testing off-the-charts on all the mirror self-recognition and rubber-hand illusion tests, that he'd gaze at me with something like pity whenever I'd ask cold, clinical questions or jotted down data. It was the same look Mother leveled whenever I spoke about wanting to explore sentience in animals.

"Sentience," Mother would often counter, "exacts a price. Which is why animals are smart enough to keep that consciousness shit to a minimum. You'd be wasting your time, and my money."

She chuckled off the comment, but her humor was always an incisive, barbed thing. If she was ever surprised that I withdrew even further from her after that, then she harbored more nerve than I'd given her credit for. I'm sure she never accepted her complicity in our seemingly life-long rift, chalking it up to me being a messed-up kid. A bad seed she subconsciously—or perhaps deliberately?—sabotaged in utero via simple resentment of my existence.

So she built an artificial-intelligence machine to love instead.

Well, two could play that avoidance game. She had DESI, I had Charlie.

Yet I was worried that Charlie was developing his own kind of resentments and umbrages, retreating to his peculiar wedge-shaped doodles in lieu of slinging low-blow remarks.

Chile, 2021

The bolt-cutters made quick work of the lock, and I eased open the door to Mother's office. What I saw caused the cutters to fall from my hand.

Pinned to every square-inch of wall, in all sizes printed or hand-drawn, a facsimile of the same triangular shape Charlie kept drawing thirty-years earlier.

In-and-around the shape, in thick magic-marker, the same message scrolled in blood on the monitors: I CANNOT SEE.

"Oh Mother…"

The words seeped out of me as a kind of surrender. How one would react to a loved one choosing to cease all life-saving medical efforts.

I stepped in and approached one of the wall charts—a computer printout versus one carved hastily by hand. Upon a quick read of the surrounding information, I immediately examined another, and then another. They all depicted the same data: right ascension and declination matching the repeated printouts at DESI's command station. A star named Wolf 359, 7.9 lightyears away, in the constellation Leo.

A constellation whose outline evoked a warped wire hanger.

Was this DESI's *stubbornness*? What Dr. Hashimoto claimed, despite all their efforts to reboot the system, the A.I. kept retargeting on?

Yet what had *befuddled* her?

Trying to wrap my mind around what it all meant—the telemetries, the bloody words on the monitors, Charlie and Mother's shared drawings—I noticed blinking on a desk.

Mother's desk.

On it sat the same picture I had at home: she and I before The Grand Canyon when I was ten. Next to it, a replica of the same lovely moleskin notebook she'd given me upon my acceptance at Emory's PhD program.

The blinking was the light on an old phone answering machine next to the notebook. My skin hummed with dread, and soon a pair of icy tears were tracking down my cheeks. Because I knew. I knew in advance what the awaiting message was. I'd heard it countless times before.

Portland, 2018

Two days after my conversation with Dr. Hashimoto, my phone rang, startling me awake from an afternoon nap.

UNKNOWN read the screen. Normally I would've silenced it and let it go to voicemail, but Dr. Hashimoto's recent phone call had me jumpy, confused, hungry for answers. Was it him again, calling from a different phone? Perhaps he had more to say but decided on a land-line instead?

Without further pondering, I answered.

Dead air. No response to my voice. At least not initially. Then, a quiet breathing, followed by a low snort or sob. Then the voice.

"I cannot see. That's all she says. I cannot see. Over and over. I believe... she's scared. DESI...is scared. She cannot see. And I won't...leave her."

The click of a dead line.

I yelled *hello* into the phone nonetheless.

Mother. Older and wearier, in a slurry tone. But it was her.

But...she couldn't still be alive?

Well...no body was ever recovered...

I stared at the phone until the screen faded. 3:21 PM read the time, and my hands started shaking. Mt. Hudson had erupted at 6:20 PM Chilean time.

3:20 PST.

"Stop reading into shit," I said aloud to an empty cottage.

Yet Mother remained behind to...comfort a telescope? Because it was *afraid?"*

Bullshit. The woman was bereft of all maternal instinct.

I reiterated that until ten minutes later and another UNKNOWN call.

The same message. Mother's message.

This same call would continue for the next eighteen-months, sometimes weeks between calls, sometimes hours. Even after I'd changed my number, the calls kept coming until finally I saw no other recourse in stopping it but to go to Chile.

Chile, 2021

I pushed the playback button on the answering machine.

"I cannot see. That's all she says. I cannot see. Over and over. I believe... she's scared. DESI...is scared. She cannot see. And I won't...leave her."

Except it played faster than all the previous times.

No—it played at Mother's regular speed and cadence. How it had surely been recorded in 1991. Whoever—or whatever—had played it back to me over the phone for a year-and-a-half had deliberately slowed it down to imply aging.

To imply *presence*.

I backed away from the desk—an instinctual act, as if it were toxic, irradiated. My gaze wandered to the windows. Judging by the light, it seemed as though hours had passed instead of minutes. Moments later, a deep clanging sound echoed through the walls, followed by a steady mechanical rumble.

Outside the windows, the trees shifted as one to the left.

Impossible as it was, the observatory was rotating.

Before running to the main dome to investigate, something compelled me to take Mother's journal.

Atlanta, 1991

With every cognitive and self-awareness test Charlie smashed, the more he withdrew from me, huddling in corners with his drawings, side-eyeing me with what I swear was contempt smoldering beneath his simian brow.

Contempt for my helping unearth the precious minerals of his brain best left buried. Metals he was incapable of smelting, forming, employing. Often, he'd stare at his hands with their limited range as one would a betraying friend.

It wasn't confidence or curiosity I thought I was fostering and thus manifesting in Charlie's expressions, but fear. Fear of outrunning your intelligence and finding yourself marooned alone with nothing but alien thoughts for company.

Did Mother fear that for me the way I did her? Was it why we both made sport of withdrawing from one another?

Chile, 2021

Back in the dome, the observatory was indeed rotating, the shutter splitting to its widest opening. Beyond, a stippling of stars coalescing into the chalky smear of the Milky Way.

Awe and fear touched gloves and started swinging; the facility *shouldn't* be operable.

I knew from research that the complex's power source was geothermal, and upon lapping the array, I spotted a maintenance door tucked under the stairs running up DESI's concrete plinth.

Access beneath her.

I went straight there.

Inside, dozens of conduits ran down from DESI's central axel and into the slab below. No doubt her power supply lines, connecting the array to its geothermal sources.

Except they'd been severed partway up. Crudely, as if by chainsaw, then bent back toward the floor as if to nullify spontaneous regeneration.

DESI should be dead, but no sooner than I re-entered the dome that she began tilting up.

Finding myself as frightened and bewildered as ever in life, I flipped through Mother's journal, frantic for an explanation. After some initial pages of indecipherable rambles and crude, Charlie-level sketches of the constellation Leo, certain legible phrases began breaching through.

Twin worlds. Orbiting Wolf 359. Non-habitable zone…

More rumbles as the structure adjusted right-and-left. The floor undulated mildly, the observatory's spring shock-absorbers working as designed. Nevertheless, the sensation wasn't unlike a wave passing over as one dove under it before it broke.

5th dimensional beings. Non-corporeal. Sense of time quantized. Spherical, not linear.

DESI continued to tilt and adjust, her movements producing whirs and whisps that almost took on the character of voices.

Communication possible. Minute gravitational waves during eruptions. Ensuing harmonic-resonant frequencies allow for transmissions...

DESI clanged to a stop at her maximum tilt. I followed her length to her primary mirror, and whatever atom of sky her eye was fixed on.

Dr. Hashimoto, driven mad. Cut DESI's power, but she continued working! Afterwards, he bit off his thumbs...

Jesus... He never mentioned *that* during our call.

The stench of ozone, sudden and sharp, and all the command station monitors booted on at once. Numbers and images cascaded in a blur.

Bit off my left thumb. Used it to scrawl DESI's cries over screens—anything to blot out their blinding light...

Images scrolling so fast they became continuous white light, the screens first smoking, then bulging simultaneously before melting into black, unctuous tears behind showers of sparks.

DESI...conducting her own human trials along with Wolf 359. Testing our curiosity, our emotions, our limits...

An instant later, the first jolt of earthquake rocked the floor, followed by a continuous, mounting rumble.

I peered up through the aperture. The summit of Mt. Hudson glowed.

DESI can't comprehend our rift. Mine and Olivia's...

Mt. Hudson preparing to blow once again.

DESI knew this. And she was preparing to listen.

I ran.

Atlanta, 1991

Charlie killed himself this afternoon.

He was up on the highest play platform, perhaps twenty-five feet above the floor. I sat on a chair below, writing in the journal Mother had given me, when I heard a screech. I looked up in time to see Charlie sweep all his drawings off the platform before he started pounding his face full-force with both hands.

I screamed at him to stop, but he was already moving—galloping full speed off the edge, diving head-first onto the concrete below.

When I reached him, he was clearly dead, his head stoved in. I assumed the blood streaming from his mouth was caused by the impact, but then I noticed his right hand. Several fingers had been bitten off. When I bent to him, my eyes blurred with tears, I saw the fingers still in his own mouth.

Only later would I learn that on that very August day, literally to the minute, Mt. Hudson had erupted above Mother.

Chile, 2021

The mountaintop beyond the observatory pulsed crimson. Pillars of smoke rose from the lava dome. The air already singed with fire.

Awed by the sight, I wanted to stand there and watch a thing so indescribably terrifying. What Mother likely felt. But a flash caught my eye to the left.

The lens of the small household telescope in the sky-blue room I'd seen earlier. Except something had changed. It no longer pointed up to the westward sky, but downward to the east.

I tried telling myself the shaking earth could've shifted it, but *not* to an opposite window.

Its trajectory pointed just to my right below the catwalk. To a round, steel platform rising several feet off the ground, scorched and shifted off its support struts by the '91 eruption.

As I approached this tangle, the mountain blew its top, the ensuing slip-quake shifting the world to the right and sending me cartwheeling over the catwalk rail.

When I came to, I screamed. Pain lanced from everywhere, and as my panic ebbed, I realized my situation: I was piked through with rebar at the torso, my left arm, and right leg.

Fire and smoke pumped from Mt. Hudson. Red lightning veined through the roiling pyroclastic clouds.

Immediately to my right, something abnormal protruded from the flotsam. A human femur. Following it up, I noted the matted remnants of clothing, and within its crusted folds, saw the edge of something yellow, plastic.

Through my agony I stretched a hand and pulled it free.

A scorched keycard. Yet the name on it was still legible.

ERIN SANTOS.

Mother…

Next to her, the remains of another, just out of reach. Yet the shaking had shed enough debris to reveal the faded St. Louis Cardinals hat, the ivory crucifix against the harp of ribs.

Ignacio…

Even before painfully fishing out my phone, I knew what the images would reveal. A charred, long-abandoned city. Its dead frozen in place. Statues whittled of ash.

Was this what DESI wanted? To bring me here so she could better understand her creator? Understand the maddening incongruities of human love? To see if I would actually come? A kind of reverse Turing Test?

Or was this what Mother always wanted but could never express: to experience these breakthroughs with me?

I pictured her then, standing resolutely on this very platform as massive, scalding death tumbled toward her. I wondered, did she pity DESI for her sentience in the end? Or did DESI pity hers, offering her a reassuring choice: stay, and all your questions will be answered.

Your sentience will be rewarded.

My own options for escape negated, I waited for Mother and DESI to unveil what they had to teach.

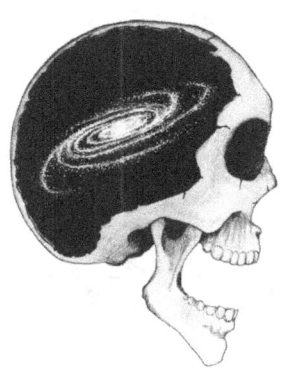

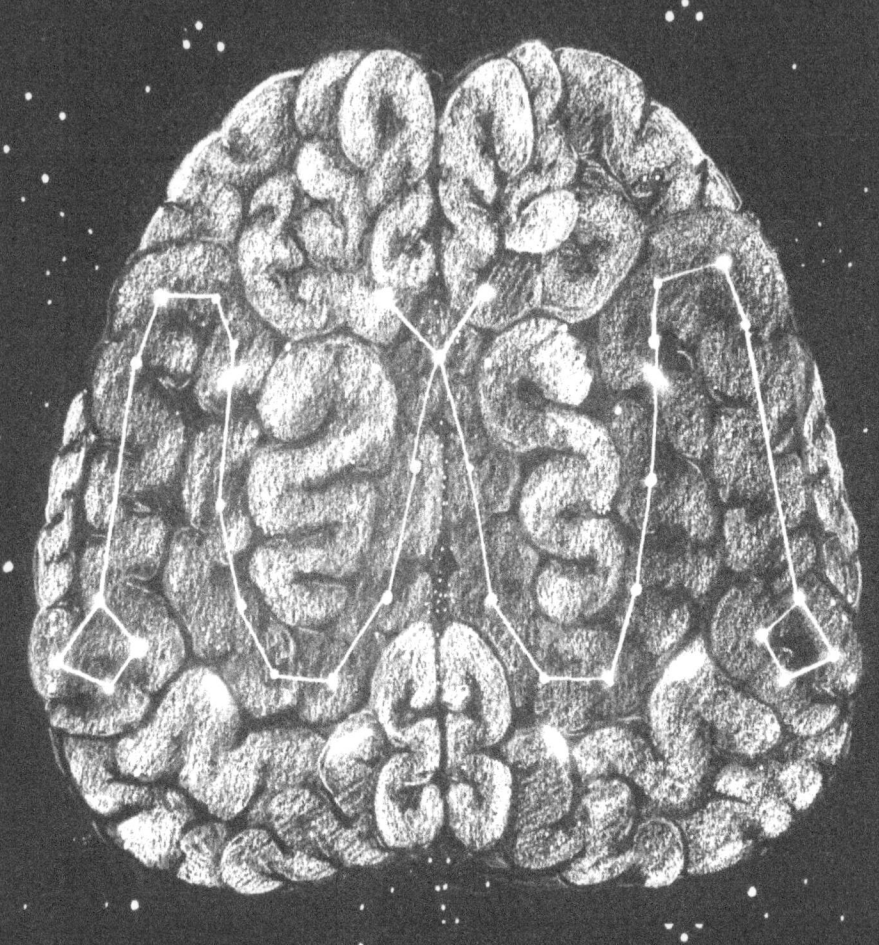

LIGHT ECHOES

PAULINE BARMBY

When I used to tell people I was an astronomer (not an astrologer, the other one, the one with the math), they'd sometimes ask if I got bored. "Don't all stars look the same?"

"Nope," I'd say. "Every star is just a bit different. My exploding stars each go boom in their own way."

I don't say that anymore.

My phone buzzed with an alert as my husband and I settled onto our sagging couch. Supernovae are incredibly inconsiderate. Besides the radiation and planet-rending destruction, they also don't care that it's Friday night and you want to turn off your brain. I scrolled through the accompanying email.

Transient alert

UT: 2025-05-01T02:01:25

RA: 14:02:24

Dec: +63:12:05

Apparent g magnitude: 15.3

Previous upper limit: 22.7

Host galaxy: SDSSJ140237+631258

I squirmed out from under the fraying red blanket and headed to the dining room table. My laptop sat next to a pile of Josh's notes for the neuroscience book he was writing.

"Not again," he grumbled.

"Sorry, love. The universe is cold and uncaring." I logged into our research team's website, pulled up the quick-look image, and clicked to activate the Target of Opportunity observation for spectroscopic follow-up.

"Couldn't you be uncaring back, just for once?"

"I could, but we need the largest sample we can get. If we don't get this paper done, there's no next grant to pay Miranda when she comes back from parental leave."

As a kid watching the stars from my backyard, I'd never imagined that being an astronomer would involve so much worrying about people and money.

"Okay, fine, grad student babies need to eat." Josh sighed.

Tip tip tip, tap tap tap. I smacked the return key with a satisfying two-finger maneuver. "All done."

I scurried over to snuggle under the blanket again. We went back to watching the show Josh had chosen and I tried not to think about grants or exploding stars for the rest of the night.

The next morning, coffee and bagel beside my laptop, I logged in to check the results of last night's observations. The spectrum slowly drew itself on the screen. I squinted and resolved to clean off the fingerprints. Someday.

Silicon absorption, no hydrogen: textbook type Ia supernova, about 0.7 days old, redshift 0.32. Utterly useless for our project, although there'd been no way to know that without the spectrum. I returned to mindless breakfast scrolling, the sesame seeds crunching in my teeth.

Something nagged me about the spectrum and I clicked back to the data analysis window. It still looked like a standard type Ia. The last one of these we'd found had happened a couple of weeks ago; I located the data for that one and plotted its spectrum next to last night's. They were identical.

"What the hell?"

Sure, we divide supernovae into categories, but there's always some variation. No two have exactly the same spectra. Was there a mistake in my data-handling code somewhere?

I made a strangled grunting noise as Josh shambled out of the bedroom, his dark hair doing its usual and adorable morning imitation of a supernova remnant. He yawned.

"What's the problem?"

"Just checking last night's data. I think there's a problem in my code somewhere."

Josh groaned. "Oh no, usually when you say those words it's not long before you're off in another world. It's Saturday, Nate."

"Shouldn't be more than a couple of hours."

"Famous last words." His words were clipped, his jaw tight.

"You know I have to get this project—"

"I know, the project. I just wish everything else didn't always take second place." He gathered his notes from the table and left the room.

Hours later I looked up, Josh was nowhere to be seen, and I wasn't any closer to finding bugs in the data-processing code. The spectra glared at me from the screen. Dammit, this shouldn't be that difficult. I *had* to get it figured out. And what if I couldn't? The coffee and bagel squirmed uncomfortably in my stomach.

The work week had me swamped with teaching. I was trying to decipher an email about some new college grading policy when another supernova alert pinged. My software auto-generated a ToO request; I quickly glanced over the formatted text and sent the request on its way. It was still nighttime in Hawai'i, so they might be able to turn the observations around pretty fast. I went back to the email.

Incoming data.

Wow, those queue observers were good. I brought up the quick-look spectrum and…another type Ia that looked awfully familiar. I plotted it with the last two and, yup, identical. How could the exact same supernova be going off in galaxies located in opposite directions on the sky? This made zero sense.

The heaviness in my stomach felt like an accreting neutron star. My tenure and Miranda's thesis depended on this project. How had I screwed it up so badly?

I wasn't going to get any thinking done in this state, so I shoved myself out of my chair and ambled down the hall to the department admin office. Our receptionist Jennie was on parental leave and had planned to bring her baby in for a visit. The little guy looked super-cute in the pictures she'd sent.

I could hear Jennie's laugh as I turned into the doorway. She stood with her back to the door, examining her four-year-old's drawings that were plastered around her desk. Her infant bounced and giggled in her arms as her hips swayed in the side-to-side baby dance. His dark, curly hair peeked out over her shoulder and he laughed as Jennie tickled him.

"Hi, Jennie," I said.

"Nate! Good to see you!" She turned around and held the baby toward me. "Meet Anil."

This wasn't the child I'd seen in Jennie's pictures. Now that I thought about it, he was a dead ringer for Miranda's baby, who was about the same age.

"What are you doing with Zac? Is Miranda visiting too?"

Jennie's brow wrinkled. "What do you mean? They're the same age, Nate, but they're not the same kid."

Was this some kind of joke? Miranda loved pranks and this was exactly the sort of thing she'd try to pull.

"No, really, where's Anil? I was looking forward to meeting him."

Jennie was utterly serious and the kind of person who always looked after everyone. "Are you feeling okay? You look kind of pale. Well, paler than usual."

I mumbled something about working long days and nights and made a quick exit from the office.

The drivers in this city weren't particularly attentive to cyclists on the best of days, and I wasn't paying as much attention to the road as I should have. I nearly got hit twice. After the second close call, the adrenaline kept me from thinking about anything other than making it home. I walked in the door a soggy mess.

Josh looked up from his laptop. "How was your day?"

I slumped into a chair. My head pounded and the road dust in my mouth had a sour taste of dread.

"Batshit. Nearly got run over twice. A couple more spectra came out looking identical. And then Miranda's and Jennie's babies were the same…" I trailed off.

His brow furrowed with concern. "You're not making any sense."

"You're right, it doesn't make sense. Something crazy is going on. Or maybe I'm the something crazy."

Josh came around to stand behind me. He leaned down for a hug and recoiled at my drenched shirt and dripping hair. "Wow, you're burning up. Are you sure you don't have heatstroke? Come on, let's get you into the shower."

He dragged me off to the bathroom, set the shower temperature for lukewarm, and shoved me in with instructions not to come out until I felt better. As the water cascaded over my head, the tension receded and my ability to think returned.

And then I realized something. For the last part of my ride, all the cars had been identical, every one a black, four-door sedan with a single occupant. I let out a shriek before the shower water turned ice cold.

A few minutes ago I'd been burning up, and now I was shivering. Josh sat next to me on the couch and wrapped the red blanket around my shoulders. A wave of nausea passed through me and I held my head in my hands. He put his hand on my knee and tried to make sense of what I'd told him.

"Okay, identical data from your program, that's one thing. Could easily be an error on your part, or maybe the observatory's right? The identical babies… well, babies kind of do all look alike. The identical cars…I don't know…"

I took a long gulp from the glass of water he'd pressed into my hand.

"I know I sound like a broken record, but you're working too hard, hon. You won't do anyone any good if you burn out," he said.

Josh put his arm around my back and rubbed my shoulder. I leaned into him.

"Okay, you're right. I'll take the night off, try to relax," I said.

"And…start cutting back on your hours?"

"That's not how I get my grant renewed."

He pulled away. "Grants are no good if you're too exhausted to work on the project."

"I can't be too tired! That's not how it works!"

"Why the hell not?" he asked. "You're not a machine, Nate. Professors aren't worker bees, despite what the college administrators think."

"I can't just stop. Just like you can't stop working on your book. People are counting on me."

"I count on you too, you know," Josh said. "And lately I don't get the sense that's very important to you." He stood and walked away.

The next few days passed in a blur of late-term busyness. Cloudy weather at the monitoring telescope sites meant no supernova alerts and no new data, identical or otherwise.

Thursday afternoon I headed to the last lecture of my *Introduction to Astronomy* course. This year's class had the usual contingents of desperately uninterested athletes, know-it-all business majors, and star-struck-but-made-to-study-something-practical pharmacy and nursing students. For once I got to the classroom early enough to set up the technology in something less than a panic. Head down, I pointed and clicked to get all of the programs talking to each other. The light from the skinny windows at the back of the room was periodically blocked by the forms of entering students, and their familiar voices chatted as they found their regular seats. The online students appeared in their usual arrangement of black boxes on the video call screen.

The clock ticked over to the hour. I clicked the last button to finish the setup and raised my head to scan the room.

A hundred identical faces looked back.

I woke on a narrow bed in a dark and windowless room. The dark and quiet reminded me of an observatory dorm, but I hadn't been on an observing run… had I? The air carried a faint whiff of disinfectant and long-present dust. I sat up. Loose clothing scratched against my skin. Hospital scrubs?

"Hello?"

No answer. I stood up.

"Is anyone there? Where am I?"

The door opened and light flooded in. A form I'd know anywhere—Josh's broad shoulders, topped by his square head with slightly protruding ears—was silhouetted against the blinding background.

"Hey."

"Josh?"

He rushed over and caught me in his arms. I buried my face in his chest and held on, breathing in his familiar scent.

"Where am I?"

He hesitated. "Psych ward, University Hospital. You were in class, then you started screaming and collapsed."

It all came rushing back. "The faces…they all looked the same," I said.

Someone in a white coat entered the room and switched on the light. I drew back to look into Josh's face. What I saw was a child's drawing, like the ones around Jennie's desk: oval outline, dots for eyes, straight line for a mouth. I caught a glimpse of the white-coated person in the doorway. Their eyes were triangles, their teeth jagged mountains.

I howled and fell back onto the bed, hands over my face. The light switched off and they left again. I curled into a ball. *What was happening to me?*

Minutes passed, or maybe hours. I heard Josh's low voice outside. He was speaking with someone else; they seemed to be arguing, although I couldn't quite make out the words. Josh's voice grew rougher, more insistent. The conversation stopped.

The door opened, and this time I was fast enough to bury my head in a pillow. Josh sat down beside me.

"We're getting you out of here, Nate. We're going home."

A blindfold was gently tied around my eyes. Josh pulled on my arm and I let him stand me up and lead me down a hallway. A door creaked open and a light rain blew into my face. We walked across what must have been a parking lot and he bundled me into the car. The engine purred and the car began to move.

"Thanks for coming to get me. What's…what's happening?" I asked.

"I don't know for sure," Josh said. "I think it's your job."

Guilt stabbed into me. "I know you think I'm working too hard."

"No, not that," he said. "You know your colleague Anisha, at the state U? Her husband told me that something similar happened to her. And to John Melton at the tech college."

"We all did our PhDs on supernova light curves," I said.

The patter of rain on the car's roof had never sounded so loud. I imagined I could hear Josh scratching his head over the rainy swish of the traffic.

"Hear me out. I know this sounds crazy—"

"Nothing sounds crazy anymore," I interrupted.

"Anisha's husband is a psychologist. He and I talked about this. What if looking at those data somehow did something to your brains?"

My jaw dropped. That was ridiculous. Then I thought again about the identical faces in my class and shivered. "But we were looking at natural phenomena. A light curve can't reprogram your brain."

"Are you sure?" he asked.

"Of course, I'm sure," I snapped. "That's ridiculous."

"So you explain it to me then," he snapped back, swerving us into a left turn.

"I'm an astronomer; how would I know?"

"The brain is incredibly complicated. If there's one thing I've learned from talking to neuroscientists, it's that there's a lot we don't know. Reprogramming a brain with visual stimuli isn't that far-fetched."

"But you're not even a scientist, you just write books about them. You don't know what you're talking about."

Josh was silent for a few moments and I knew I'd pushed too far.

"Suppose you're right," I said. "What do we do?"

The car went over the familiar bump at the end of our driveway. *Home.* Josh's voice shifted as he turned toward me.

"There were these experiments where people learned to see upside down with prisms taped to their glasses. Took about a week for their brains to adjust. I wonder if we can help your brain reprogram itself the same way. What if we interrupted all visual stimuli? Kept you in the dark for a week or so."

I tried to sound braver than I felt. "A week in the dark? For an astronomer? No problem."

A week in the dark is a lot longer than it sounds. I took to talking to myself, then humming, then singing. Most of the time I was able to hold back the screaming. I was lying on the narrow cot, staring at the ceiling, when the door creaked open and squeaked closed. Josh's footsteps crossed the room and his weight creased the edge of the bed next to my feet. His hand ran up and down my leg.

"The week is up. Are you ready to try the lights? We can always turn them right off again."

Was I? I didn't want to live in the dark forever. I took a deep breath and let it out.

"Okay." I sat up and screwed my eyes shut.

A tiny click. My eyelids burned like I was looking down the axis of a solar telescope. I cried out and clapped my hands over my face.

"Easy. It's all right. I'm here." Josh's voice was low, soothing.

The burning sensation eased and I let my hands drop.

"I want to see your face. Let me look at you," I said.

He took my face in his hands. I let my eyes open slowly, like a telescope dome shutter but without the accompanying clanks and motor sounds.

There it was, his kind face with the dark eyes and the little scar between his brows and the scruffy beard. No triangles or squares or Picasso anything.

"Oh my God," I sighed, letting my head fall to his shoulder, and I wept. Drops trickled down the back of my neck, and I realized he was crying too.

"You're back, I have you back." He sniffled.

We held each other in the dim light for quite a while.

"What time is it?"

Josh looked at his watch. "About 10 PM."

I glanced at the door. "Can we go outside? I think I'm ready."

"Are you sure?"

"It might not get easier. Let's just rip the band-aid off."

"All right. Maybe close your eyes on the way, okay? And let me know if you feel anything weird." He took my hand, squeezed it.

Josh led me up the stairs and through our front door. Head bowed, I slowly opened my eyes. There was just enough moonlight to see my reassuringly ordinary feet. Raising my gaze, I saw Josh's relieved face.

I looked to the sky, and the stars shot back identical daggers.

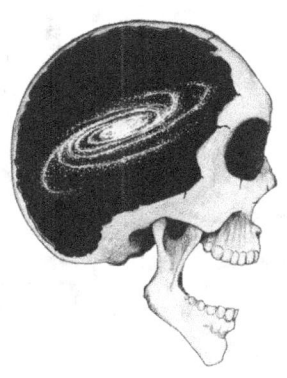

THE
RAVENOUS EMPYREAN

ZACHARY ROSENBERG

Andrew Levi realized something was strange when the night sky consumed that plane.

As was typical for Saturday nights, Andrew was outside his house at the bottom of the valley to be swallowed by the sky. He peered through his telescope at the radiance of the celestial ocean towering above the earth. This time of night, there were few houses with any lights along the steep hills bordering the valley, granting Andrew the perfect view of the silent heavens. The stars seemed so bright that even the gibbous moon could not drown them out.

Andrew removed his eyes from the telescope, gazing at the constellation Cygnus in all its magnificence, the stars positively blazing, when his view was ruined by the distant, whining roar of a jumbo jet. The flickering lights announced the passage of a late flight, spoiling Andrew's view of the constellations.

Then the jet was simply gone. The soft groan of the engine went silent— only the tender sigh of wind against Andrew's hair was now audible. The jet's lights vanished like they never existed. Yet the stars blazed brighter, so furious with their luminosity that Andrew wondered if something was wrong with his vision.

Cygnus remained fixed in place as it always was, but the stars were larger now. With no sign of the jet, Andrew briefly wondered if he had imagined its passage. But the sky above was not the distant firmament he beheld every evening. It seemed closer than he remembered. The waning gibbous moon was a vast silver eye, beginning a predatory wink. Just west of it, manmade lights flickered. Andrew seized a pair of binoculars from his side and used them to scan the sky, mystified curiosity briefly overcoming any trepidation.

The jumbo jet was there, the engine groaning desperately to the night, barely perceptible from this distance. The lights flared again, artificial mementos of man's progress that paled to the natural fury of the stars.

Like a roach dragged into the den of the spider, the plane was yanked back into the ink between stars without so much as a final ripple. And in that moment, Andrew realized that sky seemed even closer.

All through the valley, lights appeared within the windows of houses. People stepped from their doors, fearful and tentative. A community was united through a bond of sudden fear and confusion. The neighbors' murmuring carried across the night breeze, human beings dotting the upper hills of the valleys with binoculars and flattened hands so their eyes might see.

Perhaps man's ascension to the dominant species had been set in motion when the first humans gazed into the vastness of the night and pondered their place. That tableau was now reenacted around Andrew, the terror of the unknown binding them as one. Andrew tried to fight the feeling and locate a rational explanation for this. Nothing in all the human experience was so predictable and fixed as the night sky.

No matter what happened in the world, no matter how governments rose and fell, the night sky was a constant. The sky he stared at every night was the same sky that men and women had gazed upon across tens of thousands of years. It was a sky that encompassed imaginations and fears, whose stars were a beacon, guiding the wayward children of earth through their wanderings and their dreams. The sky represented the infinite stretch of the cosmos, where any random star had burnt longer than humankind had existed.

So why this change now? He might have doubted his sanity if not for all those around him. They surely could not all be sharing the same hallucination, the same madness together. The temperature had dropped, that winking moon gazing with frigid indifference upon the valley.

A voice shouted Andrew's name. Bob Harris jogged over in his nightgown, shivering at the sudden onset of cold. The corners of his garment flapped comically in the wind, his mouth wide open as he fought for something to ask Andrew. Of course, it made sense they would come to Andrew. He was a stargazer by hobby, though hardly a professional astronomer. But he was someone with expertise, which in the face of the unknown was worth its weight in all the riches of the earth.

"What's going on there?" Bob tried to keep the tone casual with a plastered smile. Maybe he even truly expected Andrew to be able to answer this. That Andrew could say this was just a natural phenomenon like a meteor shower, something that happened every few hundred years that they were lucky enough to be witnessing tonight. Bob's face fell when Andrew shook his head, Bob growing even paler in the falling starlight.

"I don't know. I've never heard of this before." Saying it aloud sounded painfully hopeless. Andrew likened himself to a broken telescope—something that should form a clear picture of its target, yet was now incapable of it. "It's like the sky is getting closer."

And there it was, before he even meant to say it. To anyone with the most cursory knowledge of the sky, that would sound utterly ridiculous. It was the explanation a child might conjure. The sky had existed before humankind and even the earth. It would exist long after they had vanished. It had bound humankind together in commonality for all of their existence. Yet what were humans but a species still trapped in infancy?

Who was to say the night sky would follow the rules humans came up with? How could they imagine vast, cosmic infinity could be bound by the shackles of conventional wisdom? The longer he peered at the sky, the more he felt swallowed by its vastness.

It reminded of him of the plane that had been consumed, with all those people inside. Andrew considered telling Bob that, but he thought better of it. He had no true answers and imparting such knowledge would likely only cause panic.

"It might just be something the sky does, Bob." Andrew offered it with as much dignity as he could muster.

The lights were on, all through the lowest depths of the valley to the highest peaks as people came out of their homes to whisper and murmur. Once again, unity took place under the night sky.

Andrew was not the most social of human beings. Interaction was more of a curious study for him than any great form of human joy. The assembly of confused crowds did little to assuage his nerves, particularly with Bob's mouth flapping like a parched fish. Perhaps science was merely an attempt to leash the unknowable, to take it from the penumbras of the obscure and drag it into the light so humans might make sense of it. Fear and enlightenment did not make fine bedfellows. Perhaps the growing unease in Andrew's heart might be lessened if he knew what was happening with the strange descent of the heavens.

Leaving the telescope and Bob behind, the poor man still flapping his lips in confusion, Andrew walked the short distance from his front yard to his home. The stars were so bright that Andrew almost doubted the veracity of the red numbers on the stovetop. It was almost midnight, on the cusp of that brief instant when tomorrow became today.

Andrew made his way to the computer and touched the mouse so the screen flickered to life. To his relief, he still had internet access, so he immediately opened his browser to search. His eyes darted over the screen, taking in the information.

"...Planes vanishing all over..."

"...Satellites disappearing..."

"...Communication cut off..."

"Impossible to see the mountains..."

"The sky is descending. It's coming..."

"The sky is hungry."

He lingered on the last one for a long while.

The sky was hungry.

Andrew knew hunger was a physical sensation only found within living beings. Some plants could be carnivorous, certainly, but the sky was not a singular, living entity, that reacted to stimuli. It was not sapient, nor even a brainless force of consumption like the biggest tardigrade the universe had ever seen.

Shouts came from outside that not even his walls could dull. Andrew shot up from his seat, the words of the sky's hunger echoing over and over in his mind while a pale fear hollowed out his chest. His feet slapped against his wooden floor as he made for the door, back to his telescope. It had grown even brighter outside. The stars seemed closer.

They were in motion. Cygnus danced without ever losing its cohesion. That thin arrangement of stars that resembled a swan did not rest so idly within the sky now. Cygnus moved, as though the black around the stars was an ocean through which the constellation glided. Unhindered by current or resistance, it shifted and swam. And by the stars, Andrew could no longer see the zenith of the valley.

It was gone, as though it had never been. The lights had winked out. There was only the sky, resting upon the hills and the trees, whose upper pinnacles were no longer visible. The sky became a shroud, layered so that no human eye could pierce through.

Constellations swam and waltzed together. Cygnus made Cepheus its partner as Draco wheeled and dipped with Lyra and Vulpecula. Where they moved, so moved the darkness. And where the darkness moved, all that it found was extinguished. It lowered itself. The stars dazzled and flared in the night. Perhaps they were not living things at all, but just appendages. Akin to the tentacles of an octopus: boneless and free in motion on their own, but only existing to find prey and bring it to the maw of the beast.

With the eyes of a horrified populace resting upon it, the sky descended. The houses and the peaks and the trees grew more obscured. There were no human beings up on the hills now. Either they had fled, or they had been swallowed as well. Perhaps this was happening all over the world. Perhaps it was just happening here.

He didn't suppose it mattered. They were all out together and there was little hope of any escape. What a silly notion that was! Who could escape the sky? It was the one constant in human history, the constant that had existed before the first ancestor of humankind had slid its slimy body out of the blue sea. Before the first amoeba twitched in the primordial soup. Before a burning rock had cooled and begun the process of breaking off chunks to create that glaring moon, there had been the sky and an unforgiving, impartial cosmos.

Perhaps it was hungry. Perhaps it did know. Perhaps, just perhaps, it had allowed humanity to grow, as it had allowed countless other worlds to flourish in the meantime. Salting and flavoring this world with dreams and desires the way a skilled chef might sprinkle delicate spices over tenderized flesh.

Perhaps it had unified their dreams, just waiting for the day when they grew so numerous and this world so flavorful that it would finally descend and enjoy its long-delayed banquet. What was four and a half, or even ten billion years? The sky had been there for so long that even such stretches of eternity must seem the equivalent of setting a pot of stew to simmer on the stove, then departing for hours.

The sky was descending, hungry and alive. The constellations spiraled and danced, leading the black curtain lower and lower, like bringing down the denouement to mankind's delusions of kingship beneath the ravenous empyrean. People were screaming, shouting. The shattering of glass rose above the din. Andrew heard sobs, people begging for some release that might be found in knowledge. He came to this conclusion and the fear strangely evaporated. Instead, only a finality of acceptance swelled inside.

Bob was still where Andrew had left him, skin turning sallow in the burgeoning starlight. Bob's eyes were rooted to the dance of constellations. Perhaps there were worse ways to face the end. Andrew made his way to his telescope and pat the cool metal of the tube. He leaned in and gazed through it, probably for the last time.

He looked up for answers, looking between the dancing stars for what he might find. He peered there, into eternity itself, the belly of the beast. But the sky offered no answers. It simply was and would always be. Deep within his soul, Andrew knew this process would repeat itself, might even be repeating itself on any number of worlds throughout the universe.

Humans thought they were special. Perhaps they'd just be a little tastier. Without answers, Andrew withdrew. The houses in the valley above were gone, along with their lights. The stars reigned alone.

Andrew stepped away from his telescope and walked back toward his house and closed the door behind him. Drawing the curtains achieved some measure of relief from the light. Satisfied, he walked to his bed and drew back the covers. With a low sigh, Andrew crawled into bed, keeping his eyes only upon the pillow. He quieted the pounding thrum of his heart, determined to focus only on that pillow.

If he had control of nothing else, let it be what he saw at the end. Let the final sight to grace his eyes be something humans had made. If there was no meaning but that, so be it.

It was growing quieter outside. Doubtlessly the sky and its hunger would touch the bottom of the valley, the empyrean descent not stopping until it had claimed every last morsel. Andrew simply thought of the stars as they had been, as humans had watched them for ages: diamonds in an onyx sea, studying them and not realizing how they had been studied in turn by a cosmos that was not indifferent. Indifference would have been an improvement to hunger.

Andrew kept his eyes down.

And he waited.

IN ABSENCE OF

ZIGGY SCHUTZ

Space is defined as an absence of.
A void, a vacuum.
And yet, it grasps
                    reaches out and steals breath from lungs,
blinds those who dare look at it without respect,
replacing curious eyes with a starscape of scars.

It is the monster in the closet,
          (there was nothing ever there)
Damn that over-active imagination,
          seeing shapes where there is simply
nothing.

Maybe space is the closet itself,
          daring the child to step a little closer,
                    voyage a little further,
and shut the door behind them.

Inky black stretches across the impossible
      and it takes what it wishes.
Crack in the glass? Missing screw?
It finds them with tendrils that block out constellations, pulls apart
the best technology anyone has to offer, effortless.
Advancements, breakthroughs,
         — one giant leap for mankind —
all of it can fall to pieces in an instant,
faced with a thing that has no solid shape, no definable purpose.

Space is an absence of, and so of course it *yearns*.
      It *hungers*.
It envies every little bubble of atmosphere that has been stolen from it.

Can a being that is by its own definition nothing-at-all feel, though?
It must, with how it stalks, how it consumes.
Can space feel fear?
Of course not. Fear is surely some thing, intangible maybe, but very much existent.
But then how else would one define how space stops,
      shivers enough to make the sun flicker,
as it reaches out and brushes against something that so solidly *is?*

Space presses against the mass that is, an attempt to make it not, and the mass
does not budge.
      There is no crack, no weakness to allow an absence to form.

You have spent as long as time has existed, working to make sure you exist too.
You are solid in your faith, in your surety.

Space might be hungry, but you are hungrier.

And as you open your maw,

dripping with stardust and the building blocks of a thousand planets that could
have been,

     but will not be, space splutters,

                                 hesitates.

If it could, it would scream.
But sound cannot carry here, and so it is consumed
     (as it has done to everything else)
Silently. Stretched over eternity and all at once.

And, in the absence of space,
     you smile.

BY THE
HAND OF SORAYYA

INARA ENKO

A stream of visitors drift past twelve-year-old Sorayya, keeping a distance from her as the Milky Way does from the Pleiades. Except for a woman who approaches and places a fifty-riyal banknote in her hands.

"God reward you!" Sorayya says, praying loudly with skyward palms for the woman's health and good fortune. With the 467 riyals she's collected already, that puts her over the 500 minimum she's expected to collect today. And it's still well before the sunset prayer!

When the woman is out of sight, she slips the money into a pocket in the folds of her abaya. She could take the rest of the day off now.

But she's not supposed to leave for a few hours yet. Crowds pass by both before and after each of the prayer times, and those are major opportunities for more donations. She's found a prime spot today with high foot-traffic, and yet not a guard in sight. She'll have to remember it for the future, even though she mustn't frequent it too often. Suhayl says it's important nobody starts to recognize her.

And here's another ten riyals, from a smiling little boy this time. His mother beams at him from a distance, proud that she's taught her son how to do a good deed.

Sorayya smiles back, careful to keep her lips together because she doesn't want to frighten them. The boy in particular looks so innocent, like he wouldn't know it's even possible that someone could receive a beating that knocks out teeth.

That was from the day Suhayl learned one of the guards had spoken to her.

It fills her with shame to remember it. The guard had come to her, but she should have known better than to exchange any words with him. Suhayl had warned them never to talk to the guards. She could have cost Suhayl the house, the ability for him to take care of her and all the other lost children he's taken in. She endangered all of them.

So she lowers her head again, hands open to receive. She should be sensible and stay put. Take advantage of today's good fortune. See how much more she can collect, to stash away for a day when she isn't as lucky, so she doesn't have to show up to Suhayl short-handed. He's always worrying, especially about money.

But if she could do what she wanted?

She'd go to the souq across from the Sanctuary and buy herself a shawarma. A big one, with all the fillings, that the man would wrap in paper and hand her in a plastic bag. And then she'd go to one of those white vending machines and get a red can of Mirinda. She'd slip it into the bag, which she'd slide far enough up her arm that she could hide it under her abaya, and then she'd turn her back on the souq and the Sanctuary for the mountain overlooking the city. Scrambling up the rocky slope, picking out her way among the rocks, she'd find a path that only those who live in the mountains know how to find.

Not to Suhayl's house, of course. She'd choose a path that gives it a wide berth, to reach a rocky ledge much higher up. High enough to obscure the city, so she can gaze at the part of the sky that isn't completely washed out by urban lights.

Even if it will never match the splendour of the sky back home, in the desert where she could see the river of the Haymaker's Way. It's been months since she's seen that sky. She wonders if she's just dreamt it.

But on that secluded outcrop she's discovered, at least she can see the stars. And in their company, she would eat her shawarma, and sip at her sweet chilled soda, and try to remember her grandmother's face and voice.

Seven-hundred and eighty-nine riyals. That is her total after the sunset prayer—and there's still the night prayer to go! She could give 650 to Suhayl, treat herself at the souq, and save the rest for an unlucky day.

But it feels like stealing.

Suhayl uses that money to keep them fed and clothed and for the upkeep of the house. "It's the only way I can keep taking care of you," he's told them many times. And the portion he keeps for himself, he's earned, for all the work he does for them.

So hasn't she earned the right to spend a little on herself, too?

It's not like she does this often. And if she can make it back in the evening at the usual time, how would Suhayl ever know?

Thirty minutes later, Sorayya has been to the souq and made her way up to the ledge. The shawarma is still warm and every bite is glorious: chewy bread, juicy marinated chicken, soft fried potatoes, tangy crunchy pickles, and salad all in a creamy garlic sauce. When was the last time she got to eat something this good? And it was only seven riyals! And two more riyals bought this candy-sweet Mirinda, fizzy and *firawla* flavored. She isn't quite sure what a firawla is, but the drink is bright pink and the can bears a picture of a heart-shaped fruit. All for less than ten riyals! She can imagine that the smiling little boy bought it for her.

When only the empty can and wrapper are left, she stuffs them into the plastic bag. She must get rid of this evidence before she goes back to the house.

Why can't she just stay here? If she had supplies, she could set up camp like back home.

But Suhayl would be frightened if she didn't return. "I'm worried about you, Sorayya," he said the last time he sought her out at night. "Don't you like it here?" He tried to console her with touch, but as always it was *too much,* and she flinched, and he looked at her with wide, sad eyes that made her feel so guilty. "Don't you like it?" with hurt in his voice. "I open my heart and home to you, as if you are my own." And he does; he's not even their father but he still cares for all of them. "What more do you want from me?"

It's no use saying she wants her family back. It's not his fault. So how can she just disappear on him, weighing him with regret that he did everything he could but still failed her?

With a heavy sigh, she takes off her abaya and spreads it flat on the ground. She takes out the money from the pocket, peeling off a few notes to stash away for an unlucky day. One hundred and fifty seems reasonable. She stuffs it into her waistband.

Then she curls up on the abaya, facing the stars. She conjures Jadda, her grandmother, holding her tight and secure. And her warmth, and the way she smelled of bokhur perfume as she explained the stars and their verses and legends.

> *The daughters of Na'esh,*
> *The carriers of the bier.*
> *Whoever says it seven times*
> *Won't consume their parents' fire.*

It was when her Jadda died that Sorayya's father decided they should journey to the Sanctuary to pray for her. And what a sight, after days on the road. Who knew that one building could be so large and sprawling? So vast inside, with its pillars and soaring ceilings? There was so much space that Sorayya could run around while she waited for her father's sisters to finish their lengthy prayers.

But then she couldn't find them.

There were so many people. Thousands of fellow visitors, and those scary hawkish guards by the main shrine. She searched and searched for a whole day, but it was like looking for stars in an alien sky. And she was hungry, with nothing to eat but a small box of dates they gave out as charity. She slept in the Sanctuary itself that night.

The following evening, an older girl came up to her and asked if she was lost. She bought Sorayya a shawarma and a Mirinda at the souq, listened to her story, and brought her to Suhayl's house. There were other kids and everyone made her feel so welcome.

It's not that Sorayya isn't grateful, but all of Suhayl's efforts can't replace the family she's lost. The family that maybe she didn't appreciate enough.

She even told Jadda that time, "I hate star stories! They're too sad. Jawzaa gets killed on her wedding night. The Shi'ra sister can't stop crying for her brother. And those girls carrying the bier will never avenge their father!"

Gentle as always, Jadda mused, "It's true that the women of the stars have tragic fates. But see how they keep their honour in spite of misfortune. There's a lesson in that. And by contrast, the shame of the fugitive Suhayl."

The Suhayl of star-lore is the killer of both Na'esh and Jawzaa, hunted across the sky by the vengeful families of both victims. Of the four stars that bear his name, three mark his path and the fourth one is where he's hiding, far to the south.

"Imagine having to hide like that, all alone. He cannot even greet his sister, who crossed the river after him. And his cowardice and shame will be on display as long as the stars can be seen."

And Sorayya wonders if she's shameful and a coward for hiding like this up here.

The call to the night prayer rings out, jostling Sorayya awake. When did she fall asleep? She scrambles to get her abaya on, abandoning the plastic bag with the evidence of the excursion. Then she rushes to find her way back down the mountainside, a circuitous path so she can feign she'd come directly from the Sanctuary.

Her heartbeat does not calm until she sees the faces of other children Suhayl looks after, going in the same direction.

They arrive at the door more or less at the same time, as normal. After removing their shoes outside, they gather in the central room of the house. A large salon surrounded by seating cushions at each of the walls. The children stand at one end of the room, and Suhayl, fresh from the barber, stands at the other. With his crisp, ironed clothes and well-groomed face, he couldn't seem more out of place.

On the floor between them, on a thin plastic sheet, are two communal plates heaped with rice and straggly shreds of meat. The other children haven't eaten yet. Sorayya looks away from them out of guilt; her own stomach would be gurgling too were it not for the shawarma. She keeps her eyes on the ceiling fan, buzzing as it slices the air.

"Come," Suhayl says, smiling, after a head count. "Show me what you've brought for me."

The children line up and present their cash, one by one. He calls out the amounts, and his mood suggests that everyone has made their minimums.

Sorayya is near the back of the group, unable to look directly at Suhayl either. The room doesn't offer much else to look at. The cracks on the walls are the closest thing to adornment, and an incongruous blue bucket catches drips from the air-conditioning.

When it's her turn, she reaches into her abaya pocket for her money.

Her money?

The pocket is empty. She shakes out her abaya, hoping the roll of banknotes will fall out of her sleeve or a fold somewhere. But it doesn't. So where is it? When was the last time she saw it? On the ledge, when she was counting out—

Oh God, did she really forget to put the rest of it back? Is it still on the ledge? Did it fall out while she was running, trying to get here?

Suhayl says, syrup-sweetly, "Is there a problem?"

All she has is the 150 riyals she'd stashed away. Small mercy she even has that. She contorts herself to retrieve it and hands it over, keeping her head down.

"Only 150?" he says, dripping with disappointment. "Why?"

Should she admit she'd had more? Would it go down worse if he knew she'd lost money, or if he thought she hadn't earned enough? How is either choice better? How is she supposed to choose? She bursts into tears.

"Shh." He pats her head. "It's fine, I understand. You're getting older now. Not so cute, not so able to pull the heartstrings."

A few of the kids laugh. Sorayya wants to disappear.

"Because everyone feels sorry for the little ones, right?" Suhayl looks over fondly at the younger kids. Specifically, a wide-eyed kitten of a boy named Badr, who has brought in 1300 riyals today.

Sorayya bows her head in defeat. "I'm sorry. I promise, I'll try to do better, I promise I promise I—"

"Sorayya." He wipes her tears with his thumbs. It takes everything in her not to shudder. "Ya habibty. Go wash your face and come back to eat. We'll solve this later."

She nods and runs to the bathroom to wash her face. Not from her tears, but from his touch. Why does it turn her stomach? He's being nice. She's lucky. But the last thing she wants to do is eat. It would have been better if he'd actually denied her dinner, as he's done before with kids who didn't make their minimum.

But she dries her hands and face and goes back to the room. And even though her stomach is in knots, and it's hard to swallow the fatty rice cooked in meat drippings, she manages to force down several mouthfuls.

When the meal is done, Suhayl dismisses the children. But as they're leaving, he calls out, "Ya Sorayya! Have tea with me."

There are two cups in front of him, already filled.

"Only her?" says Badr, pouting.

"She's a grown girl now," says Suhayl, "and this tea is not for little children."

What does that mean? Her instinct says to refuse him, but how can she dare? And Badr leaves without asking any other questions, leaving her with nothing else she can do.

She drinks.

The only tea she knows is the Rabea brand with the triangle logo. This does not taste like that.

"You look so tired," Suhayl says when she finishes. He isn't wrong; she's more tired than she can remember. "You can just go to sleep."

So she shambles over to the girls' sleeping room. Mats are scattered over the floor, with a pillow each and blankets to share. She drags herself to a mat at the far end of the room and curls into a tight ball around her pillow. Hugging it the way Jadda used to hold her.

"Those three stars in a row?" Jadda would test her.

"Jawzaa."

"And the red star they're pointing to?"

"The Follower."

"And who is he following?"

"Sorayya!" She grinned. Or *Thurayya* as they say it in classical pronunciation. The Little Abundant One, the star cluster she was named after.

Thurayya was in the sky earlier when Sorayya was on the ledge. The whole constellation, not just the star cluster in the middle, her outstretched arms embracing half the sky. There are stars for her shoulders and elbows and upper arms and forearms, for her tattooed wrist and henna-stained hand on one side, and her amputated hand on the other.

"How come she lost a hand?" Sorayya had asked once.

"She had leprosy," said Jadda simply, melancholy. "The disease had no cure in the old days."

Thurayya doesn't have legs or a torso either. Did the same disease take away that much of her body, leaving just her head and her arms?

Sorayya drifts off to a floating ghost Thurayya filling half the sky, wailing a tragic mawwal, like a funeral singer, mourning that she's wasted away and there's so little left of her. Indistinct faces swarm all around, and Sorayya can't feel her body beneath her neck either, but sympathetic pain shoots up her forearm and throbs, as if she too had a rotting hand that had to be taken off. But then she's plunged back into the dark, leaning against something soft in the back of her father's Landcruiser, the desert stars in all their splendour overhead as they made the journey to the Sanctuary. Jawzaa with her braid and her bow and her footstool, and the two Shi'ra sisters on either side of the heavenly river, and ignominious Suhayl so close to the southern horizon, flashing in and out of visibility between the dunes and rocks.

She wakes up the following afternoon, in an unfamiliar room. There's enough light from the window to see the rust-orange henna capping the fingers of her right hand.

Her left arm ends in a bandaged stump where her hand used to be.

After she's screamed and retched until her throat hurts, Suhayl comes into the room.

"Sorayya, habibty," he says softly. "How are you?"

One look at him and she knows it's him. That he's the one who had this done to her.

"I'm sorry," he says. "I know this must be a shock."

He was supposed to protect her! He said he cared for her like one of his own! That was why she stayed here in the first place. That was why she came back night after night.

"I mean, but I anticipated your problem before last night. And I thought about what to do, and the answer came to me from the stars. Because everyone feels sorry for a child amputee! Who wouldn't give money to help her?"

Money? Was this really just about money?

"You'll see how it's better for you, for all of us. How much you'll earn after this. You'll bring in so much I can even buy you something nice."

Money can't buy what she wants. It can't bring back her hand—or her family. They kept to their desert life and didn't go after money beyond what they needed, even when the government gave them the chance. And why does he need 500 riyals to let her eat two meals and sleep at his house, when she can have a filling meal for less than ten riyals and sleep at the Sanctuary? Why didn't she have questions when she saw how much food actually costs? How was she such a fool to think he cared about any of them? All of the children— they're just money to him.

"But you don't have to go back to work yet. Get your rest. I want you fully recovered."

How does he keep talking as if she's fallen sick—as if this isn't something he did to her?

After he leaves the room, she weeps for everything she's lost. Sobs it all out, like Thurayya in her dream. But then she wipes her face with the edge of her dress.

She will not be like the Shi'ra sister who cries until it ruins her eyes.

She is careful over the recovery days not to show anger or defiance. She can't stomach even pretending to agree with what he did, but she can pretend she's come to accept it. That it's not worth fighting, and she's ready to go along with it.

He sends her back to the Sanctuary in a week.

Patience is hard, especially now that it's harder to make her way up and down the mountain with one hand. But she knows better than to run for it on the first day. No doubt Suhayl has the other children watching her. He's clever enough not to completely trust her.

She smiles to think that he's afraid. He should be.

She scouts the Sanctuary slowly over a week. Following the paths of the visitors, blending in with them, keeping herself in the middle of crowds where the other children are unlikely to see her. Draping her abaya over her head like an old woman, so even if she's in their sightlines they won't know her.

In particular, she scans the guards.

She seeks the guard who spoke to her before. He seemed to have something to say, and at least she knows he has a respectful manner. But even when she locates him, she can't talk to him too soon. A few more days to throw off suspicion, and to be sure of when and where he's stationed.

Finally, on the twelfth day she approaches him.

"I remember you," he says. "You fit the description of a missing girl some people were looking for."

Does she dare hope that was her family?

"But…what happened to your hand?"

She does not hold back. She tells him everything.

The women of the stars may never find justice, but down on Earth, she will make Suhayl face his crimes. And she will not lose any more of herself; she is not Sorayya of the stars.

MOTH TO A FLAME

JEREMY MEGARGEE

Moth gapes at the night sky, her black curls framing a face bordering on cherubic, and she counts the stars on her fingertips. Those bright distant pinpricks soothe her, and she is not herself when detached from starshine. In daylight hours she slinks through the world like an eel provided with only an inch of water, unsettled and incongruent, but under night clouds, moonbeams, and twinkling starlight, a sense of self manages to bloom.

She is always alone. People frighten her, and their big booming talking heads make her feel unsafe. Moth cannot follow their conversations, she cannot match pace with their body language, and she is lost in the rhythm of their honeybee lives. She wishes in the deepest part of herself that she could be among them and of them, but it is not to be. She wasn't born for it, and it hurts to pretend. That lack has created a chasm inside of her, but she knows how to fill it. She finds answers in the constellations, and methods of comfort are passed down to her from the stratosphere.

She licks her lips, fingers brushing across the freckles on her nose and cheeks, constellations that dominate the galaxy of her face, and she thinks of her mouth as a wormhole, those little words that come out traveling from terrible starved distances. She is a taker and a maker, and she whispers sweetly to what she unearths.

Moth knows where to find companions and quiet friends who no longer have the capacity to judge. They're down in the soil, multitudes of forgotten ones, and the stars tell her where to plant her spade. She digs during nocturnal hours, a dirty little mole of a girl, and she pulls at rotten casket lids until her palms are lanced with splinters. There is always the musk of them, that eldritch spice of closed graves, and it excites her to inhale it, because it means a new friend will soon be introduced.

Sometimes her friends are juicy, peeling, plump forms like fruit left too long on the table. They're bloated and gassy, and they belch out pressure from decomposed innards. She is splattered in the black and brown wetness of them, but Moth doesn't mind. Other times they're dry like cordwood, adorable little collections of bone and fabric scraps, and these ones make her feel special. They're wizened, shrunken, leering skull faces with broken teeth, and she cradles them to her chest and calls them fairies of the dirt. She pulls worms out of the dark holes where their eyes and noses used to be. She brushes grit from their brittle brows, and she dances with them, making them rattle for her. There are tea parties and stargazing picnics, and Moth sits in comfortable silence with the dead ones, knowing there is never a need to converse too much, because souls talk too.

She loves all the stars, but one constellation stands out above all others, because it is the one that is the kindest to her. It is the great Fly in the Sky, the Musca constellation, and she always finds it waiting in the southern firmament. It's small, only a few stars, small like her, but it matters. Sometimes she closes her eyes, feeling the wind knifing against her cheeks, and Musca speaks through the crickets and the creek and the hidden living things that exist all around her in this abandoned boneyard.

It buzzes in her head, pleasant warmth, and it tells her the corpses are lonely and lost just like her. No one visits them, no one loves them, and isn't that a shame? Moth knows what it feels like to be unloved. Most of her life has been a delirium, and people don't notice or care.

If a person isn't involved, a person isn't interested. It's easy to slip through the cracks, and she slipped through a long time ago. She never climbed out, she just taught herself to build a nest in the depths of that crack, and Moth acclimated to the never-ending dark.

She has a place, as close to a home as she'll ever have. It's a disused subway tunnel that is accessible through a part of the city that harbors gutted rowhouses and human wraiths that crave nothing but the needle. She takes her favorites there, and they become permanent guests. She wraps them up in bundles and carries them like babes, and if anyone sees her walking in the night, they'd mistake her for a young mother. No one has ever asked to see what she cradles, but if they did, she'd show them. She'd smile and pull back the mildewed blanket with the half-moons, and she'd let the sickly yellow streetlamp glow fall on empty sockets and mossy teeth, and she'd rattle her bundle for the whole world to hear.

But people see what is important to them, and Moth has never been important to anyone, so she is never seen. She moves through her pockets of shadow, and what she carries are her burdens alone. The sole caretaker for lonely stick-thin limbs and gaunt cheeks, and when she comes home through her tunnels and rooms, she relishes her orphanage of bone.

Under crumbled concrete arches that drip water, through twisted webbing of unrepaired rail, and in a place that is deep and forgotten in the world, Moth arrives home. She navigates her rabbit hole, nurturing lit candles that spill over with wax, feeling safe beneath the shadow of an undiscovered ossuary, and twirling like a girl-child that only has the capacity to thrive in a tomb that her own nimble hands erected.

She closes her eyes and inhales, taking in the aroma of her rabbit hole, and to Moth, death smells like cinnamon. Exhumed *friends* line the walls, affixed there with wires and twine, posed like mannequins in various states, empty yearning sockets watching her make her way deeper into sanctuary. The rats share the domicile, and they nibble on the organic bits that still have value, a ceaseless din of chattering crooked teeth, but Moth does not begrudge them. They are misunderstood familiars, and death is not ashamed to feed their bellies, just as it has never failed to give her a sense of purpose.

She is comparable to a rat in some ways, because she is the happiest in her nest. Moth goes there now, her circular bed under the heat vent that blasts out cloying air from an active part of the subway system, and she uncovers her newest acquisition from the boneyard, nestling his wasted form down there in folds of curtain, rug, blanket, and big whorls of discarded wool from the dumpster behind the farmer's market.

She unfurls the layers of cloth that cover her, a butterfly shedding the cocoon she must wear up above, the shapeless husk that lets her be invisible, and when she is all goose-pimpled milky skin and undergarments, she climbs into bed with the cadaver. Moth cuddles in close, and she plants her head against that hollow drooping chest, just sharp ribs and flesh like leather. She likes to imagine that there is warmth still there, and on the nights when her thoughts are wild, she hopes for the beating of a heart that once was.

If she were to be asked what she gets out of it, her answers would seem almost heartbreaking. She is sweet with the corpses, tender and hopeful, and there is even an element of the maternal. She thinks of what it must feel like for a person that has been dead for hundreds and hundreds of years. The kudzu encircling your tombstone, the erosion of time stripping away your name and your birth date, and every single person that ever knew you or could be bothered to tend to your grave died a long time ago too.

That's a different kind of loneliness. The soul-crushing kind that wants to keep you locked in the deepest pit of despair. Moth knows that loneliness. Moth has walked those corridors of absence, and if she can save something from the same fate, she will do it. Even if it's a mummified ragdoll with no life left inside.

There is only one downside to being so far underground, and that is her disconnection from Musca. The sky messages are muffled when she's in her rabbit hole, and it is only that modest pocket of stars that keeps her emerging back into the nightscape. If not for Musca, Moth would dwell with her adopted dead on every day of the calendar. She crawls through labyrinthine tunnels, navigates muck-strewn iron rungs, and finally emerges, struggling with all of her limited strength to shove the manhole to the side and climb free of the depths. There's a bundle on her back, tucked into a beaten knapsack, all bent and folded, and to some it would appear as nothing but twigs and a round protrusion in the inky colors of the night. Moth encounters no one as she walks into the tree line, and so no one sees that it's a cinnamon-scented mummy that bounces on her back.

The wind sounds like wolves tonight, and the howls don't stop. She trudges undeterred even as it pulls at her hair and threatens to unspool her across the precarious rocks that she climbs. Moth has to get clear of the canopy, because she wants to look upon the stars, and she wants to see that wonderful galactic Fly fluttering in the firmament.

She is loved under the starlight of Musca, and laughter blooms in her soul. Her brain doesn't feel untethered and poorly wired when the constellation is visible. There isn't pervasive emotional pain and the sense that she wasn't given a proper chance in life. It is all washed away, and that starlight touches something in her that has never before been touched.

She gains new elevation, and her efforts bring her into a clearing where the branches sway and the grass is so tall it reaches past her shins. There's no light pollution up here, and the city can't taint what's above. There is nothing but a pitch-black portrait filled with small pinpricks of light, candelabras burning in the heavens, and the dark in Moth doesn't feel so dark anymore. It's bearable, and it fades. She can't count on all ten fingers how many times she has stared at Musca on lonesome nights, but this night isn't like the others. There's something new.

There's a luminescent streak in the sky coming directly from the Musca constellation, electric blue in color, turquoise faded and seen from afar, and it tumbles down in a line across the canvas of black. Moth has never seen one before, and it takes her a moment to comprehend that she's witnessing a falling star. Just a little piece of space rock entering the atmosphere, but the glow is beauty to behold, and Moth realizes quickly that there's an opportunity to be seized here.

There are many things in this world that she doesn't understand, but she knows that falling stars are made for wishing, and she must make her wish before the window closes. She doesn't know when she'll get a chance like this again.

Moth closes her eyes, bits of sleep crust caught in her lashes like stardust, and she whispers silently to herself. She twirls and clutches at her chest, and she wishes on that falling star, pouring everything she can into the act of wishing.

When she opens her eyes, the faded blue light isn't so visible anymore, and it seems the magic has departed. Nothing feels different. Trees, wind, and stillness.

There comes a sound, a creaky dry sound, like a hinge that hasn't been oiled in a century, and the scent of cinnamon grows more powerful in Moth's nostrils. A broomstick of an arm reaches out across Moth's shoulder, and fleshless fingers cup the girl's cheek, the bony digits lightly caressing her skin. She smiles, and she leans her face deeper into that welcome embrace.

The corpse gives affection as the night wind sings, and that is enough for Moth.

Wishes do come true.

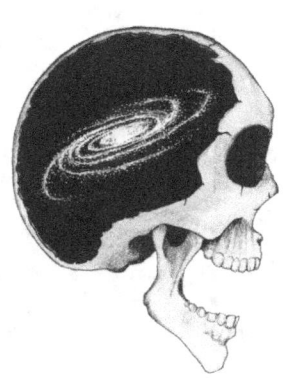

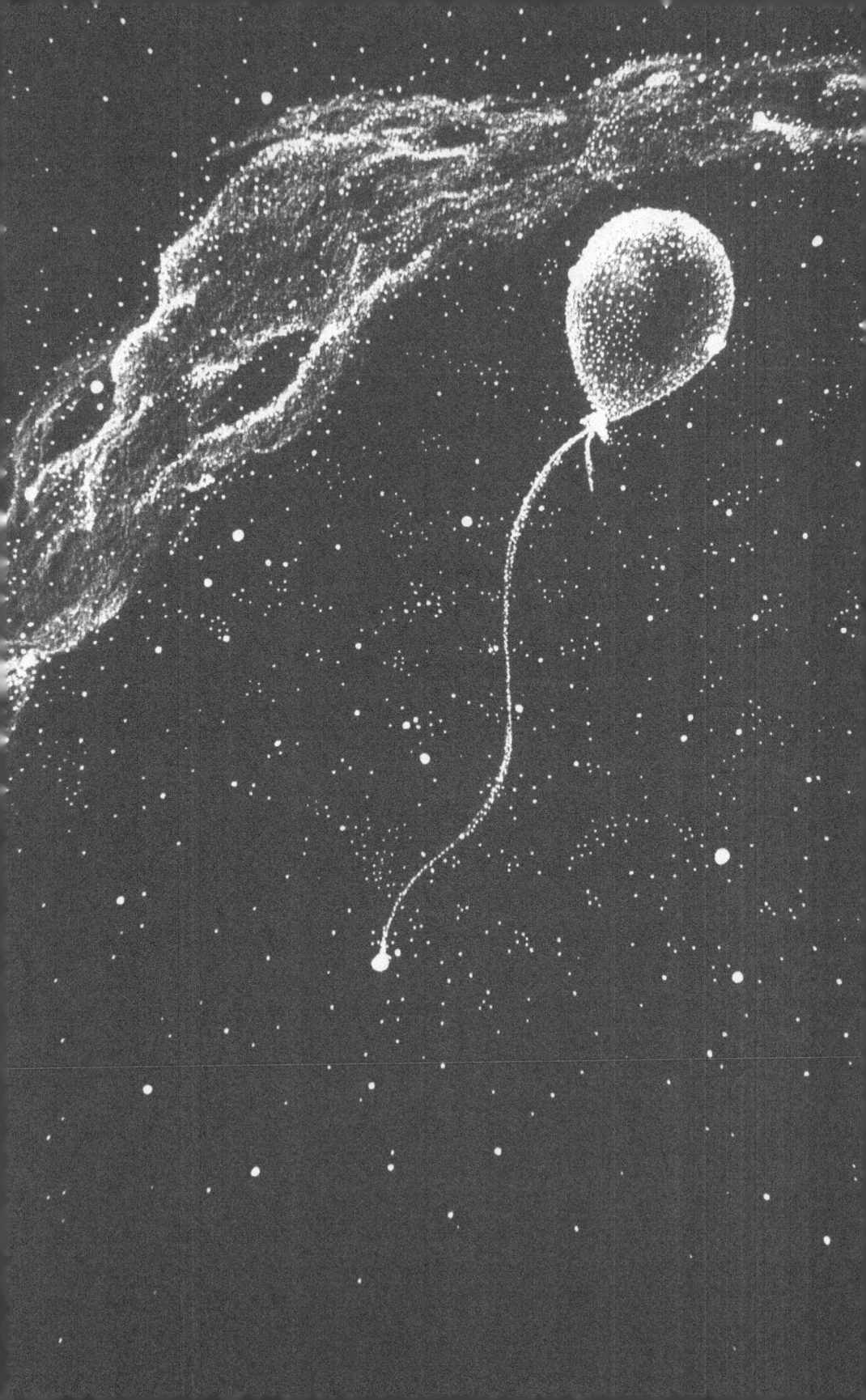

FLOAT

VANN ORCKA

An American getting your name wrong is cute the first time, but after a while, it gets old, right? Especially when you just got done hooking up. We're currently in the post-sex snuggling phase. I'd like to move on to the post-sex small talk, but that's a tall task for a girl like me.

We've been joined at the lips since the foreign exchange students got here two weeks ago. In my head, I keep saying "Jewell-ee-uh," Even though I know it's pronounced "Yool-ee-uh." She's from Germany and I'm a fourth-year German student. I can connect those dots, and yet, I can't. If I'm not careful, I'm gonna say it wrong again and look like a complete dick.

Ich kann ein bisschen Deutsch, but she knows English better than I know German, so that's our language of choice outside of Frau Werner's class. Talking to her is impossible—not because of language barriers or anything like that—because my heart climbs into my throat, and my tongue throbs so big that the words don't come out right.

A paint bucket splatter of stars hangs above us. She clutches my sweater and nuzzles a little closer like a dog making its bed. Her leg coils around mine, she presses into me, and the trampoline squeaks. It's chilly, but she's my blanket. Music pulses from the party inside as the wind lifts my bangs off my forehead.

If I could just say her name, the rest of the words would come flowing out. So, I take a deep breath—her curly hair rising with my chest—and I speak.

"Jewell-ee-uh, can I ask you something… Oh my fucking god. Did I just—?" I cover my face with my hands and my cheeks heat up.

She pulls them away, lifting the curtain to reveal my shame, then kisses me on the forehead. "It's okay. I know Americans are stupid." She pulls back and shows me the crooked smile that always makes my legs numb. "You said you wanted to ask me something?"

"Oh, it feels kind of stupid and cheesy now."

"I like stupid and cheesy!"

"Alright, you asked for it, so here it goes. Aren't the stars just amazing?"

She laughs and grabs my hand. "Absolutely."

I take a deep breath. "Sometimes, I look around at, you know, fucking everything, and it's all just so shitty. I mean, all of this horrible stuff is happening in our day-to-day lives. It's suffocating. And every single person you know and love is going to die. And the earth is dying, too. And we're all just…watching it happen."

Julia squirms. "Uh…"

I'm not sure why, but I laugh. "Sorry, what I mean is…Do you ever look at the stars and feel hope? When I think about how small we are in the scope of the universe, all my problems feel a little bit smaller, too. And that's nice."

"No, I—"

"Maybe one of these megalomaniac billionaires will be on one of their orbital joyrides, jerking off in zero gravity, and they'll decide to use their incomprehensible wealth to fucking do something. They'll look down at earth and think, 'Hey, maybe I should help.' I don't know. Probably not."

"I don't think about stuff like that."

"Jeff Bezos jerking off in space?"

Julia laughs. "No, about how small we are. My cousin told me this story…" Julia pulls her knees into a hug. She chews her lip and looks down at the trampoline, its dark texture swallows the moonlight. "When you think about it long enough—how small you are—does your head get fuzzy, and you feel like you're going to faint?"

"Yeah, kind of."

"Do you stop right when you get too lightheaded?"

"Yeah."

"Well, if you don't stop—you keep going, following that...What's the phrase you told me?"

"Rabbit hole?"

"Yes, rabbit hole. If you keep following that rabbit hole, something bad happens."

I sat up and faced her. "Pfft—what do you mean something bad happens? What is it, some old German fairy tale or something?"

"It's not a fairy tale. Look, you believe whatever you want to believe, it doesn't matter to me." Julia turns away, but it only makes her more adorable.

I inch closer and lean my head on her shoulder twirling the curls of her hair around my finger. "I'm sorry. If I ask you to lay down and look at the stars with me, you're not going to have a panic attack, are you?"

She laughs and punches me in the leg. "No, that still sounds nice."

Our bodies fit together like a puzzle. I look at the stars and all the bullshit of the world fades away. It's just me, the stars, and Julia.

An ant crawls across her hand. She notices it, but instead of crushing it, she just leaves it there.

Julia is her own person with her own past. She grew up in a different country than me, with a different family, in a different town. Seventeen years of memories formed her into who she is, and she's amazing. I will never be able to understand what it's like to be her, just as she will never understand what it's like to be me.

When I look into her eyes, she looks into mine. She sees me. She sees me in a way I will never be able to, no camera or mirror will ever come close. I can't get over the fact that I'm a person in Julia's world and she *actually* likes that I'm in it.

Just over there, where that incessant music pulses, there are about thirty horny teenagers drinking, smoking weed, and grinding on each other—making memories they'll cherish for the rest of their lives, all because Cory Stapleton's parents trusted him to *not* throw a party while they went away for their anniversary.

This is only one house in the neighborhood. Beyond every front door is a different family, and each one of those family members has their own past and their own history and their own eyes through which they see the world. And their realities are different from each other, because the way they see things bend and shape their experiences.

There are about forty neighborhoods in my city, sixty-two cities in my county, and eighty or so counties in Michigan. There are fifty states. America is just one country, and there are so many countries. Think about how many people are on earth!

And earth is just one planet. There are eight planets in our solar system. Over one hundred moons. The sun, of course, and who knows how many comets and asteroids. The stars—there are just so many fucking stars. It's so beautiful and...

My head gets lighter. Julia warned me not to dig into the rabbit hole, but as a result of my history and my eyes and my life, there's a little part of me that always wants to be right. Not to mention the part of me that lights up when I tell someone else they're wrong. It's gross, but I don't fight it. I dig deeper. My breathing ramps up. My chest rises and falls like an asthma attack, reaching for the stars above me.

Our galaxy is just one galaxy. There are hundreds of billions of galaxies in our infinite universe, and the universe is expanding. It can go forever and there will be no end. It's not a circle—it's a line—and it never stops. Ants are ants to me, and I'm an ant to earth, and the earth is an ant to the solar system, and the solar system is an ant to the universe, and the universe is an ant to nothing, because it goes on forever.

I look down and see myself. I'm lying on the trampoline with Julia and we're getting smaller. Julia's resting her head on my chest, but my chest isn't rising and falling. It takes her a second to notice and she sits up.

She screams and shakes me, but I can't feel anything, because I'm above it, watching it happen. She jumps off the trampoline and runs into the house. My body lies abandoned like a doll that fell out of a stroller in a parking lot.

The lights in the house flick on and a dozen kids run out. One kid jumps onto the trampoline—I can't tell who because everyone looks like ants now—and he pushes on my chest like he's doing CPR, but I don't feel anything. Julia screams and sobs into someone's arms, and a well of sadness rises in me, because I want to be the one who holds her when she cries.

The house is just one house in a network of houses connected by these gray lines we call streets. The blue and red lights of an ambulance trace the lines. It snakes along the path like a Hot Wheels car and reaches the house. Two ants get out of the ambulance and run to the backyard.

I can't see what happens next. They're too small. All that's visible are the houses and the main road that connects this neighborhood to the next. A sea of neighborhoods and schools and stores broken up like shattered glass.

The air is heavy. My body wasn't breathing down there, I realize that now. I think I've been up here for a while, because I've become acutely aware of my chest clenching tighter than a vise grip. I'm high enough to see Michigan, a little hand waving goodbye as I float into the stars.

I'm not lightheaded anymore, just the opposite. All the weight in my body is rising toward my brain. My head expands like a balloon, and my body is the string. It follows wherever my head goes, loosely dangling in its wake.

The stars, the sun, and the moon are my neighbors now. I feel big like them, and the earth is the ant. My head is a balloon the size of an asteroid, and my body is the string... and I'm floating.

And then I pop.

HER SISTERS, THE STARS

PATRICK BARB

Every man, woman, and child on board the space ark knew the punishment for witchcraft: Death.

Across generations, dating back to the Mass Exodus, the law remained clear on that point. So, when the Tribunal handed down her sentence, the Witch's face showed no trace of surprise. She took her fate in stride. Later, standing alone and silent in the decontamination chamber, her breath escaping from thin, rations-starved lips to fog up the domed helmet of the old spacesuit they'd locked her in, she waited for her sentence to be carried out.

"I'll remind you, there's no sound out there," the Governor had said to the Witch after the verdict was handed down. "No one will hear you."

After a moment, the suit's internal microclimate processors activated and cleared the fog away from the faceplate, revealing the airlock door in front of her.

Above her, warning lights flashed red, and a pre-recorded countdown, a ghost from several lifetimes ago, spoke in harsh, robotic tones that reverberated off the chamber walls. At zero, the decontamination flush system activated. The Witch stood, silent except for her breathing, as the airlock's wheeled mechanism spun around and around.

Hydraulics gasped as the airlock doors opened...

"My sisters burned like the stars.

"That happened long ago, long before my birth, on a place mentioned in whispers and songs and whispered songs.

"Their skin, hair, even their bones and teeth, once turned to ashes and cinders, were blown away, scattered by the winds.

"Still, I imagine the weight of all they left behind. I imagine it clumped together in a stumbling, gray mass, looking like some shaggy, shedding homunculi. Or a housecat.

"I feel that creature, rubbing its flank against my leg, not begging for, but still expecting my attention. 'Acknowledge us,' it says without saying.

"That purring, that unsound, tickles my brain and the back of the throat—gentle, but insistent. It's the voice of my sisters trying to sing. It's the harmony of all who burned like stars, stars that even after death give light to worlds we'll never see."

All citizen-passengers, whether crew members or not, lined up before the wide viewing windows on the ark's main decks. They stood united, silent witnesses to the Tribunal's righteous justice.

With a single, phlegmy cough, someone broke the reverential silence. At that same instant, the airlock expelled its atmosphere and the Witch, flinging them into the endless, ever-present black of space.

Several citizen-passengers, concerned about breaches of protocol in the sight of holy justice, raised eyebrows in response to the cough and its unintentional synchronization with the punishment.

Still, for others, there was a nagging sense of "That's it?" The latter group's disappointment hung above them like a poisonous cloud in the sweet recycled air of the ark.

The Governor, along with the rest of the Elders, the Protectors of the Ark who all just *happened* to serve as the members of the Tribunal, stood on the ark's command deck, sharing a feeling of vindication.

Not that they let it show. They set their lips in the official fashion, all sharp corners and perpendicular lines. The untethered Witch drifted away from the ark. She floated and flipped, her bulky spacesuit prison somersaulting with a comical grace. She moved farther and farther away from the ark.

Until she didn't.

In discussing the Witch's punishment with the other Elders, the Governor had quoted extensively from the ancient texts which only he could view in full. "If the accused is lost in the cold vastness of space, then she is not a witch. And may God have mercy on her soul. But if the accused remains in proximity to the ark, held close by some unseen, demonic force, then…"

When the Witch stopped short and jerked forward, as though pulled by some invisible, umbilical force, fire danced in the eyes of the Governor and his cohort. They refrained from smiles or snickers of righteous glee. After all, this was a solemn and sacred duty they'd performed.

She was a witch. Their faith had seen them through to the truth.

And the rest of the citizen-passengers? Since none of them could remember a time of witches or even a time when anyone had ever gone outside the ark, they watched in muted acceptance, believing that was simply what happened every time.

"My sisters burned into piles of ashes. And the winds blew, sometimes shrieking and wailing—a toddler's tornado tantrum—and other times as gentle as that same toddler tossing the ashes up in pudgy-fingered handfuls only to let them fall once more to the ground, accompanied by a cherub's giggle, tickling the ear before passing on.

"The wind did not act alone. The rains played a part, washing away my sisters' ashes. Torrents and drops, drizzles and deluges, trickling and flowing down to puddles and ponds, lakes and rivers and oceans, where salt waters sting, bringing tears to the eyes of red-faced, panting youths. Those same younglings pat sunburnt, sensitive cheeks to dry the water in which my sisters' ashes mingled.

"The wind and rains shared yet another partner. I think about my sisters'

ashes buried under shovelfuls of dirt—black loam and gray-brown topsoil, even yellow, pebbled sands. I imagine them covered, while sweat-soaked men licked cancerous lips and muttered their ungodly thoughts to a Mother they believed would hear them."

"The ark's children shall have the option to see justice delivered," the Governor had remarked in his official Proclamation. Despite the execution falling outside their mandatory education time, the children were corralled into the learning chamber with one designated monitor assigned to oversee the ark's youth. As recompense for this disruption of routine, they adjusted the gravity in the chamber, allowing the children to float. And if by floating, they would come to see the Witch's fate and understand its significance, so much the better. Of course, even the Governor, for all his righteous belief, did not think such an event likely to occur.

As expected, when left unsupervised to observe the execution, most children opted to play. Their weightless bodies drifted near the viewing window. They twisted, turned, giggled, and shouted. Their voices echoed, before even louder giggles and shouts from their peers overwhelmed them.

Whenever their faces turned to the window, they looked at the Witch. They pressed sticky fingers against the clear surface and traced outlines of her floating form, alone out there in the endless dark.

But they'd look away. Because what better way to pass the time than to ignore death and live their lives at play?

The weightless children pulled at the air like they were flying. They saw, but they didn't watch.

Except for one.

"Do you think that as the winds caught their ashes, my sisters exulted in one last moment of flight? Dipping and flipping. Swirling and whirling.

"Did no one hear them laughing? Or was their laughter covered up, buried under a cacophony of croaking bullfrogs and buzzing cicadas? Did those strident sounds mark their inevitable resurrection? Did little girls laugh

when they heard the song under molted skins crackling and reborn bodies humming?"

One little girl watched the Witch floating alone in awkward stasis within the infinite ink spill of space.

Crew members and citizen-passengers alike knew the girl as Sally M. And Sally M. knew the Witch by her other name, the name she'd had before they called her "Witch." While the other children giggled and shouted, Sally M. reflected on the words of the Witch.

"It's a flower," she'd said. "Isn't it beautiful?"

Sally M. remembered how her body responded. Her mouth twitched upward at the corners. Her nostrils flared as she breathed in the first new scent she'd encountered in the otherwise antiseptic environment of the ark. Her "yes" trailed behind.

The flower, green and grasping, pushed up from the wet, black substance Sally M. learned to call "soil." Both plant and soil were smuggled from the Earth and passed down through generations from as far back as the Mass Exodus, and maybe earlier. The flower was, indeed, beautiful. The bland, synthesized foodstuffs developed in the ark's laboratories, the gray and brown uniforms worn in the same sexless style by all citizen-passengers, the daily routines the Elders declared necessary and inescapable, these all paled in comparison to that tiny explosion of color appearing like magic from the ancient remnants of the forsaken planet.

The Witch gifted the girl with the chance to see the flower. Later, she entrusted her with its hiding place, tucked away behind a loose wall panel in the Witch's solo living unit. A scrap metal-constructed heat lamp glowed on the flower inside the dark, cramped confines. Sally M. dreamt about the flower, hiding its beauty in the dark, but not alone (because it had the heat lamp's light and warmth for company).

She'd kept the flower secret. Even when pressured by her caretakers to betray her teacher, the Witch, Sally M. wouldn't mention the flower.

After all, along with teaching her about the flower and the Earth on which it had grown, the Witch had also shared with Sally M. the importance and power of a well-kept secret.

"Were the ashes of my sisters, the ones washed away by the rains, burned once more by the sun—that biggest, brightest morning star? Did the devilish sun call my sisters back as vapor? Did it send them up, up, up, to make congress with darker clouds? Did my sisters, in turn, wait until those clouds grew fat and then fall again as still more rain?

"Did they wash through the hairs of teenage girls running wild and free, alone but together, baptized in fire and water and blood?"

"She told her students *we* killed it! That *we* killed the Earth! Can you imagine putting that responsibility on the children?"

From her hiding place under the baby-blue blanket on her bunk, Sally M. watched the Governor shake to hear her caretakers relaying what they'd heard of the Witch's blasphemous teachings. His lips moved, but no sound came. A word caught in his throat. Sally M. pressed the blanket's cotton folds into her mouth to muffle a scream. The Governor scratched his Adam's apple, trying to will the word free.

"Blasphemy!"

It was a word more growled than spoken.

"Witchcraft!" followed.

After the Governor left, the girl's caretakers Sally L. and Arthur L. called her and her brother, Arthur M., into the socialization area of their living quarters. They made Sally M. leave her blanket on the bunk. She stood with a face rubbed raw and red, hair as tangled as the roots and stems of the Witch's hidden flower. Her caretakers embraced her in the accepted fashion, seeing as she was grown from them and it was customary to do so. They reassured her it was good she had told them about the Witch.

She nodded her head because it was the accepted thing to do. Her caretakers were pleased by the response.

But they hadn't understood.

The Witch hadn't included Sally M. among the parties responsible for the Earth's annihilation. She hadn't even said, "We killed the Earth." She told her *they* killed the Earth. The Earth was their Mother and they'd killed her. They'd left her to rot as soon as they could get away on the ark. They'd killed her and told everyone she'd *made* them do it.

After the telling, Sally M. held onto thoughts of death and dying. The Witch showed her a seed pulled from the plant. She'd shown Sally M. how the old plant died and a new, fresh replacement grew from the leavings of its forebear. The girl thought she understood. With her face pressed against the viewing glass, she tried to understand how dark it got out in space.

"For the buried ashes—what happened next? I imagine those sisters, burned up like the stars same as the others, then pressed down deep into the dirt. I imagine other women like me pressing our noses close to the ground, trying to smell past grass, past soil, past the scurrying feet of ladybugs who tickle wispy nose hairs as they flit by for brief visits, before digging down, down, down, to inhale the ashes of my sisters, those who smell of the stars themselves.

"I imagine those women turning their heads so their ears touch the Earth. In my imaginings, in those moments when I dream, I listen with the others. Because my sisters burned like the stars and each star sings its individual song. And I want to hear them all. I want to hear them sing for me. Sing of the Earth, sing of the magic within myself and these shared memories. Sing louder and louder. I sing my promise back, vowing that their songs will not end with me."

The ark's anthem played over the comms. A special touch thought up by the Elders. Nothing in the station's logs spoke of musical accompaniment. But they considered it proper to do so. "In the spirit of things…"

Then, as the minutes ticked by and the Witch did nothing more than float, it dawned on the observers that it would take some time for the suit's oxygen supply to run out. The repetitive blaring and bleating of the anthem sounded less and less of the triumphant ode and more and more like a loping funeral dirge.

Even on the command deck, the Governor forced back a yawn. His upper lip dipped down and his cheeks sunk in, eyes watering. And then, he heard the Witch's song.

They all did.

"My sisters burned like the stars…"

"Stars' songs are songs of waiting since they burn for so long. And when they die, they don't just burn to ashes.

"They expand. They spread their light further, even in death. They shine and sing for us, even years past their demise. I hear my sister's sing-song voices, telling me: 'We called the Earth Mother, and they treated her like one of us. They burned her, trying to make her the star they thought she should be. She still burns now. They left her behind to burn bright like all of us.'"

The Governor pounded at the station's controls. He yelled, and others shouted in response. The shouting and the yelling passed from the command deck, and chaos swept across the station like a virus. As a result, no one had time for the Witch's words.

Except for Sally M., who floated in the children's viewing area and pressed her hand against the glass, feeling wetness behind her eyes and confused thoughts burning inside her head. "They've always believed death could stop us," the Witch had said. "But death is the way our song is spread. They do our work for us in that way."

The Elders wanted to know who to blame. They wanted to know who made them hear the Witch's song. After all, the comms on the Witch's suit were deactivated. And there was no way for them to sync with the station's speakers.

Those in charge continued issuing commands. Some issued commands to no one at all, barking orders at the walls. No one dared call for a moment of silence to gather their thoughts and puzzle out the mystery. Because when they did, the Witch's words remained.

"My sisters all burned into piles of ashes…"

The Governor ordered the few privileged citizen-passengers lucky enough to view the execution from the command deck to leave immediately. He wanted to confer with the Elders in private.

After the doors shut tight and they were all alone, someone suggested they blackout the viewscreens. They argued it would at least be better not to see her.

"Do you think as their ashes were caught…"

The Governor hesitated, almost nodding in agreement. But his breath stopped short between his teeth when he considered the price of betraying norms in the face of such blasphemies.

The ark was all the people had left. They weren't equipped to abandon tradition for mad talk and madder tales.

"Were the ashes of my sisters washed away by rain…"

The words slipped through and back onto the ark, making hairs stand on end. The song's undulating rise and fall, like ocean waves, covered the station. The collective folk memory scratched at the backs of the brains of those who let the words sink in.

"…what happened next…Stars' songs are…even now, she burns…"

On and off, off and on, the Witch's delivery adjusted to the necessary pitch and volume, crafting chorus and verse for the perfect song.

Sally M. floated. She looked down and found herself sitting in a cross-legged position on top of nothing at all. She flexed her tiny toes and waited for the end. She was no longer alone. Even the other children stopped playing their games and laughing their laughs to watch the Witch sing. Outside the viewing area, the adults pounded their fists against the doors. "Don't listen!" they pleaded. Their words traveled to the closed doors in front of their faces and no farther. The monitor pressed at the door controls and shook her head. She could find no logical explanation for how the locking mechanism had triggered and then remained resistant to deactivation.

No one guessed the true source of yet another technological anomaly aboard the ark. They all looked the wrong way while Sally M. whispered the words the Witch had taught her, the words she used to keep doors closed and secrets safe. They worked for Sally M. as they had for the Witch and all the other witches who'd come before.

Outside, the Witch's singing reached a crescendo. At the same moment, the fire started inside her suit. Again, the Elders would argue over who was to blame for this obvious engineering flaw. A perimeter camera outside the station zoomed in on the faceplate. Yellow flames licked at the Witch's face.

And yet, she kept singing.

Someone claimed she'd snuck in an incendiary device. Never mind that they'd stripped her and shaved her, inspected her over and over, before cramming her inside. The explanation meant that they weren't to blame, so they clung to it, sinking their nails deep into its vaporous flesh.

When the suit ruptured and the faceplate cracked, most figured that was the end. Flames and Witch snuffed out as one. Instead, a tower of flame blew out into the black emptiness, and then kept burning.

The Witch's song continued.

Fire split the suit open like an overripe cocoon. The Witch's char-blackened skeleton tumbled out. Black bones in black space. Her skull moved, jaws going open and shut. Open and shut. Getting out her last words. Even as the still-burning flames pulsed and grew, absorbing the last of the Witch in its embrace, an afterimage of bones remained for those who hadn't already looked away.

Sally M. watched the fire that had once been a Witch, a Witch who had once been someone else with another name.

For a fire to burn in the vacuum of space was an impossible thing.

A magical thing.

Then, Sally M. stopped to consider the stars. She recalled the Witch's lessons about how stars burn bright in space for years and years, even after they've died.

When the biggest, most powerful stars burn out, they collapse, pulling everything else around them inside their absence. They pull in everything they once kept warm, everything they once illuminated, everything they once loved and comforted, even when they could not touch them.

And then, all that's left is a black hole.

"My sisters burned until they collapsed. And in their collapse, a new world waited…"

The Witch's song had ended, and it was Sally M.'s turn to sing.

HOROSCOPE OF A TOXIC UNION

JUSTIN MORITZ

If the celestial bodies dictate you and I,
your sun is condescension, your moon withholding,
never rising to the occasion.
But I am no astrologer on a mountainside.
When you hold me close, I ignore our cosmic incompatibility.

I am the tide to your moon,
bound to your relentless gravity.
I flood the villages where I lived before you
till it is just you and I,
making love amongst the water-logged, swollen corpses.

To love you is to stare at the burning sun, unblinking.
Persisting despite the pain of scorched, yet devoted irises,
Sclera sizzling like bloodshot egg-whites frying on concrete.
To you, a blink might as well be a flinch,
a smack the only suitable punishment for refusing to blind myself for your affection.

I pass seers in the grocery store,

their divine sight unfooled by concealer and high collars.

They do not speak, but their eyes seem to warn me:

If his fists are meteors pounding against your Earth,

then one day, you will meet Armageddon.

I peel back my sleeve to seek answers in a constellation of cigarette burns,

but amongst the scabbed flesh, there is no North Star to guide me.

I kneel on bruised knees before the full moon,

scrying for a divine solution in a bowl of tears,

only to be reminded that there is but one way to kill men who turn into wolves.

I await you as dutifully as a planet orbiting its sun,

rising to the sound of you drunkenly struggling with your house keys.

When the first thing out of your mouth isn't *I missed you* but verbal bombardment,

I know that I am doing the universe a favor

by welcoming you home with a shotgun blast instead of a kiss.

If the cosmos couldn't tell me how to fix men like you,

Then perhaps the buckshot in your belly could.

Silver pellets in place of stars, shredded intestines in exchange for the night sky.

Your lifeblood already staining the linoleum,

Death has left no room for interpretation: it is not my fate to suffer men's cruelty.

I become a comet pinballing across the universe.

Returning to the same night skies century after century

if only to announce to the astronomers below,

Never will there be a time when

I burn up in their atmospheres.

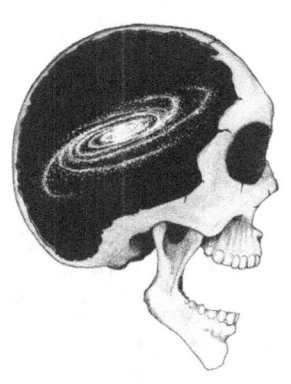

THE ONE WHO RIDES THE COMET

MATTHEW CONDELLO

An unseasonably crisp wind slithered through Caleb's open window, speckled his pale skin with goosebumps and tousled his chestnut curls. The curtains danced in the chill night air. It brought with it the smell of the farmland stretched out around him and something else. A sharp metallic smell tinged his tongue. His eyes swallowed up the stars, deep brown irises swam in the iridescent blue light of the object in the sky.

The comet was here.

It was all anyone had been talking about. Comet Sagan was going to be closer and brighter than any comet had come in hundreds of years, and Caleb didn't want to miss it. As the light of the astral visitor washed over his face he could see now that no one could miss its luminance. It was about the only reason he loved living in the middle of nowhere in their revamped old farmhouse, because at night the world was illuminated with the glow of the galaxy.

His little brother Jack had laughed at him when he said that line out loud a few summers ago. It was Jack's thirteenth birthday, and, stuffed with cake, they lay on their backs soaking in the starry night. Jack had loved to make up new constellations.

"You're so melodramatic, Cal." Jack poked him in the ribs.

Caleb reached over and ruffled Jack's dirty blonde mop. "Melodrama is what you get when you have a gay older brother, and you love it!"

They had a good giggle over that. They had so many good giggles.

Caleb wiped at the tears silently slipping down his cheeks.

Jack should be here. He loved astronomy and science fiction even more than Caleb. Caleb's excitement for the comet felt wrong. Since Jack had disappeared, any bit of happiness, joy, or simply living felt unfair. It was hard enough being a gay guy in a small and narrow-minded town, but doing it without the one person he felt loved him no matter what, the one person who didn't want to change him, well it made him doubt the reason for everything. Their parents had raised them with logical minds. Still, his mind and his heart wrestled with an impossibly heavy void. Even though his brain knew the science, he struggled with understanding how the world could go on spinning. Why couldn't we be like stars, burning so bright that even after we died the universe could witness our light for eons?

Caleb counted backward from ten, taking slow controlled breaths, trying to fight off the anxiety monster sniffing at his defenses. Any thought of Jack being gone was like throwing the gates wide open.

As he exhaled, he bathed himself in the light of the comet. It was unlike anything he'd ever seen. Scientists had assured everyone that it posed no danger to the earth, still, sitting here staring at its brilliant enormity, he couldn't stifle the butterflies inside. He was reminded of how some ancient cultures saw these and thought they were omens of disaster, but Caleb knew better. They were nothing but rocks and ice wandering the sky.

The comet flickered in an orb of rainbow light. He rubbed his eyes and took another look. It flickered again and then flashed in a brilliant glow.

What the hell was that?

If he only had Jack's telescope, he could get a closer look. Two Christmases ago, Jack had begged incessantly for a fancy telescope and got one. Not quite what he wanted, but a telescope, nonetheless. It was old, tarnished brass with a long slender body and 3 wooden legs, like something you'd see as a prop in a movie. It had belonged to their grandfather. Caleb had a vague memory of it sitting in front of a circular window in his grandfather's attic surrounded by clutter.

Night after night, they'd run around their yard chronicling the galaxy. Sometimes they'd try to see into the windows of their neighbors across the cornfield. They were teenagers after all. Those were his favorite times with his brother; together with Jack's telescope, they'd journey across space, talking about how someday they'd leave this place.

And then it all was ripped away.

Since then, Caleb was not allowed to step foot in Jack's room. His parents had closed the door and locked it, only they had the key. He made the mistake once of asking if he could get the telescope out of the room shortly after Jack had gone missing. His mother made a choking sound accompanied by an impossible contortion of her face muscles. His father rose from his brown leather easy chair and approached him. There was an empty darkness around his father's eyes and the glimmering of tears like stars burning in the black, those tears a paltry reminder that Jack had been here, had meant something, had burned bright and then disappeared into the nothingness of the night.

"Dad, please. I just want the telescope. I don't even have to go in if you don't want me in there. I'll let you grab it."

Caleb touched his face, now remembering how hard his father had struck him that day. In seventeen years on this blue speck, his father had never laid a hand on him until that moment. His father's hand had collided with his jaw, and that Big Bang created a universe anew. A universe in which his family only existed in theory.

Since then, scant words had passed between him and his parents. Not like things were heaven before, but this was different, deeper. They would leave him home alone countless nights, going who-knows-where. Caleb couldn't remember the last time they'd included him in any of their excursions. The day-to-day seemed perfunctory. Everything had changed since the final search party turned up not a shred.

Caleb often wondered if they wished he had disappeared instead, but he didn't have the to courage to ask.

Fuck it. I'm gonna ask Dad to let me in the room.

Caleb made his way downstairs and found his parents sitting in the living room seemingly uninterested in the once-in-a-lifetime event unfolding outside their front door. His father sat in his favorite rocker holding a book that looked like it could double as a paperweight, while his mother sat cross-legged on the floor seemingly staring into the black screen of the television. Neither turned to look at him.

"Dad, umm…" his heart raced. *Get it together dude.* "Dad, I wanna use Jack's telescope to look at the comet. This may never happen again in my life, and Jack would have loved this. Please…"

His father's head turned slowly; a wide unnatural smile etched across his face. "Sure Cal, you can use the telescope."

Caleb had braced himself for rejection, or worse another smack to the face, but this he hadn't been prepared for. His father's voice was like hearing a foreign language after all this time, so it took him a moment to process what had been said.

"Wait, you're gonna let me use the telescope?"

Caleb followed as his father silently climbed the stairs.

As the key turned in the lock, Caleb's hands shook.

"Here you go. Have fun and try not to break anything." His father pushed the door open and walked away without a single glance back.

Caleb's heart skipped as he stepped into a time capsule. Everything about his brother's existence was frozen in this place. Luke Skywalker fought across the sheets and bedspread, while a poster with the bold message "TRUST NO ONE" hung from the midnight blue wall. On his desk sat a model of the Enterprise D next to an undisturbed copy of "Contact" by Carl Sagan, the last gift Caleb had given him.

And there it was, the telescope. It was incredible that this inanimate antique had brought them so much joy and had brought Caleb such peace of mind. A gay boy in the country can be made to feel alone, lost, and so much worse. But when he looked out on the universe expanding emptily around them, glowing with the building blocks of time and space, he couldn't escape the simple truth; all of us, our lives, our loves, our minds, are but brief, brilliant miracles wrapped in stardust. This was another thing he had once said out loud. Jack had cringed, but that's how Caleb wanted to see the world and those in it, he wanted everyone to understand that about themselves. Then maybe, just maybe, they might appreciate the person in front of them a tiny bit more.

A loud knock downstairs jolted him back to reality.

Who the hell could that be?

He couldn't remember the last time they had a visitor. Caleb quietly crept to the bedroom doorway. The sound of more than a few voices floated through house. A group of people in his home was as rare as a comet. The creaking stairs underneath plodding feet caused a shiver through his body.

Why are they coming upstairs?

He slowly backed away from the door as it was flung open, nearly hitting him in the face. He stumbled backward, knocking over the telescope. His father and a group of four men with shaved heads, all clad in white sweatsuits and tennis shoes, towered in the doorway.

"Dad, what the hell is go—"

He didn't finish the sentence before they were upon him. Gripping and grabbing at his arms while one of them tried to put a pungent-smelling cloth over his mouth. Caleb summoned a strength he didn't know he had and struggled from their grip, dropping to the floor and scrambling on hands and knees out of the room. Racing toward the stairs, they closed in on him, inches away. He flung himself down the steps, colliding at the bottom with his mother and three other women dressed the same as the men. Their hands slithered around him, trying to get some sort of hold, but he broke free of their prodding and darted into the kitchen.

His eyes frantically searched for something to defend himself with. A long butcher knife sat next to the porcelain sink. He grabbed it and swung around with the blade, facing the people now standing huddled at the entrance to the kitchen. His parents were at the front of the group.

"Caleb, we need you to put the knife down and come with us. Now." His mother reached her hand out for him to take it, but Caleb wrapped his hands around the hilt of the knife.

"What the hell is this, Mom?" He struggled to stop his voice from shaking with the rest of his body.

"There's no time to explain," she said. "We just need you to come with us. Please don't make this harder than it has to be."

His parents each took a step toward him.

"I'm not moving until you tell me what's going on."

His father glanced at his mother and give a small nod. "We are going to get your brother back."

Caleb shook his head. "Jack is gone, Mom. He's gone. What are you talking about?"

She took another step toward him. Caleb thrust the knife out as a warning, making her flinch.

"The comet is hiding the truth, Caleb. There's so much more out there than we ever knew. The One Who Rides the Comet has come at last, and he's going to return your brother to us."

Caleb's legs turned to jelly, and he wavered for a moment. His mother's eyes were wild and crazed along with her words.

What the fuck was she talking about?

"Why did these men attack me?"

"We're sorry. We thought it was the only way. We knew you wouldn't come with us willingly."

"So, you were going to drug your own son and what…kidnap me?"

A man in the back of the group with a dark shaved head and ice blue eyes spoke up. "Enough with this! We are running out of time. We need to get him to the altar."

He rushed toward Caleb. Instinct took over. Caleb had never harmed another soul in his life, but his hand moved with a supernatural swiftness, plunging the knife into the neck of the man.

All hell broke loose. Blood splattered and soaked the white sweatsuit as the man gurgled and choked. Screams erupted from the group, and they all lurched forward together springing upon Caleb. He swung wildly with the knife. The blade fleetingly found flesh, but then there were too many of them. He couldn't fight them all. Someone grabbed his hand with the knife and bit down. He let out a howl as the blade fell from his grasp and they pinned him to the floor.

"Mom, Dad, please…please don't do this." His face was wet and cold with tears.

His mother leaned over and kissed him on the forehead. "Shh, shh, it will all be over soon."

Pain ripped through his head, and then there was darkness.

It was the cold against his back and the taste of blood in his mouth that woke him. His eyes opened slowly. The comet raged with an angry brilliance, lighting the clearing. Caleb tried to sit up but found resistance. He wiggled, realizing that his hands and feet were tied down.

"Ah, he's awake. Let's do this before it's too late. "

The group circled his naked body which was lying on some sort of large rock. The cornfield surrounded them.

His breath came in short, quick gulps. "Please, let me go. You can do whatever this is. I won't tell anyone, but please just let me go."

His father spoke. "We can't Caleb. We can't let you go. We need to get Jack back."

"Dad, Jack is gone. He's dead!' Caleb screamed.

"You're right Cal. Jack is dead, but he's not gone. We can get him back. We need him back."

"How?"

"The One Who Rides the Comet requires a trade."

"Fuck your trade. You've said more to me tonight than you have in the past two years since Jack went missing. What have you been doing all that time? Joining this insane cult 'cause you think it'll bring my dead brother back?

You think this will wash away the fact that *you* were the reason he walked out that door. You two are the reason he's gone."

His father hit him with a closed fist, rattling his head against the rock. "Now we begin."

The cult joined hands and raised them to the stars, chanting words Caleb couldn't understand. His father stepped forward and hovered over him. He pulled out a tool that looked like a large potato peeler.

"The One Who Rides the Comet requires us to eat of the flesh of our sacrifice to give the transferal power. First, we shall have the flesh of his arms, so that Jack can be strong, and we can feel his embrace once again. Then, we shall taste the meat of his legs, so that Jack may stand proud before us. Flesh from his chest will give Jack a strong heart. Finally, we shall consume the flesh from the face, so that Jack can smile at us once more."

Searing hot pain paralyzed Caleb, and he unleashed a horrible howl as his father dragged the tool over his arm, peeling away a hunk of skin. The razor teeth of the peeler chewed through the flesh of his thigh down to his ankle. From there, his father scraped away the flesh from his right cheek, their eyes never meeting. A trickling warmth enveloped him as blood began to pool in the wounds.

Through scarlet tinted tears, Caleb saw his father tear the skin into pieces, one by one feeding it to the circle. Each cultist received it as a communion wafer.

"Next, we must drink of his blood, so that life will flow into Jack once more."

The group swarmed his body and lapped the flowing blood like kittens drinking milk.

Weakness spread through Caleb's body, and the night's chill crawled into his veins.

"Now we call upon The One who Rides the Comet to keep the promise, to fulfill the prophecy, to accept our offering. One life for another. One son for another. Bring us Jack and take our sacrifice. Show us the mysteries of the Cosmos. We submit to thee."

The universe went silent. The breeze that had caressed this cursed night vanished, and the cornstalks stood tall and unmoving. As if the vacuum of space had swallowed them whole. Everything trapped in excruciating anticipation. Eternities of emotions seeped into Caleb, crawling deep through wounds his parents had inflicted, seen and unseen. Rejection, neglect, loss, grief, rage, all consumed him, burning as hot and numerous as those distant stars as they pulsed through his veins, making their way to the center of his galaxy. A heart that had long ago collapsed from the weight of despair and the deprivation of love. Now nothing remained of it but an abyss so deep that even the most powerful telescope couldn't find it. It all passed into this black hole and surged into the falling stars of his tears, scorching the earth of his face.

And still not a sound.

Caleb struggled to speak. "See. I told you."

A flash shattered the sky.

A shooting star streamed across the heavens and came plummeting down, shaking the earth. The shockwave, as it crashed in the corn just yards away, rattled their bones.

Gasps and screams rippled through the group. Caleb could sense frantic, anticipation in each breath they took. And then he heard the rustle. Something approached through the corn.

He craned his neck trying to see what they all were looking at.

A small figure appeared from the corn; he was pale, lean, sickly-looking.

It was Jack.

His parents ran to Jack, swarming him with hugs and kisses.

"Jack...how..." Caleb tried to say more but his voice failed him. The pain and blood loss took their toll.

Caleb locked eyes with Jack, searching for any sign of his brother left in that frail scarecrow standing before him.

The air around them vibrated and blurred. Two quick motions from Jack, and his parents' throats were ripped apart. Their bodies hit the ground in a sickening thud. His hands had elongated like branches on a tree and were tipped with razor-sharp talons. Jack's eyes were like looking into a black hole.

The other members of the cult scrambled into the corn in a panic, and Jack moved in a blur after them. Seizing a small woman before she could make it into the corn, Jack's body pulsated a cold blue light. The woman disappeared, leaving behind a crumpled, blood-stained, white sweatsuit. Jack vanished into the corn after the others, and Caleb cringed at their blood-curdling screams as each one was dispatched.

And then Jack was next to Caleb.

He leaned over, rubbing his head with normal, human hands.

He ran them over Caleb's body, while he shimmered with a warm orange glow. The pain and exhaustion melted away. The deep trenches in his flesh had healed. The grip of the ropes on his arms and legs loosened, and Caleb slowly sat up.

"Who are you?" Caleb asked.

"You don't know your own brother, Cal?"

"You're not my brother. My brother couldn't have done whatever just happened here." His eyes landed on his parents' blood-drenched corpses.

Caleb tumbled off the rock altar.

Naked and exposed.

Frightened and freezing.

The empty sweatsuit caught his eye, and he slid the too-small pants over his chunky thighs.

"Cal, don't run. I don't ever want to hurt you."

"Tell me what's going on then."

"I've seen things, Cal. Amazing things. I've seen the stars and the universe we always used to dream about. I've seen galaxies upon galaxies. I've watched worlds die and new life begin."

"How do I know you're really Jack?"

Jack's head tilted like a curious dog as he let out a long sigh. "Remember when we were kids, we used to play Star Trek together. You always wanted to be Janeway. She was your favorite. I always wanted to be Data. I was the first person you came out to, and you kept saying, 'please don't hate me.' And I just shrugged my shoulders and said as long as you're always there when I need you, I wouldn't care if you were—"

"A Klingon." Caleb's tears came fast and free now. His chest heaved and pulsed. Grief, terror, exhaustion all came to a head. "Jack. I've missed you so much, you can't possibly know. But what is all this? You killed our parents; you killed those people."

"I needed them to perform the ritual. It's the only way I could be allowed to return, but I couldn't keep them alive. Our parents were weak. Unconcerned with the world beyond the tip of their nose. Oblivious to the wonder around them. Why do you act sad? You hated them."

"No. No, I didn't hate them. I just wanted them…I just wanted them to love me. They made me feel like I was flawed, broken." Cal moved in a circle around the altar, trying to keep his brother at a distance. His foot bumped something hard and metal on the ground. He wasn't sure what he'd touched but the weight of it felt like it could be useful as a weapon. He quickly slid it into his pocket.

"The others were collateral damage. Broken minds, broken hearts given over to a cult. This is power Caleb. This is evolution. This is The One Who Rides the Comet. And he's waiting for us."

"Waiting for *us*?"

"I want you to come with me Cal, to see all that I've seen. To become something more. To be improved. Just take my hand and we can get away from this world of pain, ugliness, and loneliness."

The temptation of the offer was nearly impossible for Caleb to resist. As surreal as this all was, his brother was standing here offering him the universe. How could he say no? But something gave him pause.

"I don't need to be improved, Jack. You didn't need to be improved. I was happy with the way things were."

Jack twitched and let out a grunt. "Cal. Don't be stupid. This is what we wanted. I came back for you. I bargained with a God to save you."

Taking a step toward the corn, staring into his brother's black eyes, Caleb shook his head. "I didn't need to be saved, Jack. I just needed my baby brother back. I'm sorry. I can't."

Caleb was moving before he realized it, sprinting through the corn unsure which direction he was headed. The stalks scraped against his bare chest. The tight sweatpants strained against his legs. The snapping of stalks told him Jack was coming. Caleb reached into his pocket preparing himself for a fight. In a rush of wind, his brother's body collided with him like a freight train. The world tumbled and turned as they rolled in a heap into the dirt. Jack was on top of him holding him down with immense strength.

"Cal, I'm going to give you one last chance, but if you say no, I can't let you live. You've seen and know too much."

The skin peeler was out of his pocket and in Caleb's hand, and he swiped at Jack's face, catching the edge of his cheek and tearing away a flap of skin. A black liquid splattered from the wound even as it began to heal itself.

"You're a fool, Cal. I'm sorry it has to end this way." Jack's mouth contorted and twisted in a flurry of fangs. A large, forked tongue flicked at Cal's face like a snake about to strike.

"I'm sorry, too." Caleb slammed the long end of the skin peeler into Jack's eye sending him sprawling backward with an ear-piercing wail. Caleb sprang to his feet and ran. A joyful yelp erupted from him as he emerged from the corn in front of his house.

In this chaos, his internal compass had led him home.

He burst through the front door and he flew up the stairs, not chancing a glance at the cult member he had stabbed in the kitchen. Jack entered the house in pursuit.

Caleb slipped into Jack's room. Frantically, he scrambled for a weapon and his hands landed on the telescope. He held it tight as he crept into the closet pulling the door partially closed.

Caleb's ragged wheezing disturbed the suffocating silence. He carefully peeked through the crack in the door.

Shit, I can't see anything.

In an explosion of wood and metal, the door was ripped from its hinges, and his brother stood in front of him. His face twisted and deformed, hands long twiggy claws, his one eye destroyed. More of a monster than his baby brother.

Caleb used all his strength and lashed out. The beat-up brass telescope connected with a loud crunch as it smashed into Jack's head. Shards of glass from the broken lenses scattered around the room. The creature's body hit the floor as if drawn by a magnet. Caleb stood over him knowing what he had to do, but unable to move. His brother rolled over and opened his undamaged eye. The comet's light cast the whole room in blue and violet.

"It's already over, Cal. You can't win." His voice sounded like hundreds of voices all speaking at once. "The One who Rides the Comet will come for me. And he'll come for you."

Caleb shrugged his shoulders as he raised the telescope above his head. "I already lost when I lost my baby brother. Nothing else could hurt me."

With every ounce of strength, anger, and sadness he had, Caleb swung the telescope down.

Over and over and over again.

Black liquid sprayed from this brother's face and head. A spasming claw gripped Caleb's side, but he kept swinging. The skull splintered and cracked. The flailing and convulsing of the body stopped, and Caleb crumpled to the ground. His sobs echoed like thunder through the quiet of the night.

Blood pooled around him, and dull pain grew into a roar. One of the talons had caught him in the side. Beneath his skin, something black squirmed and spread within. Caleb pulled himself up by the windowsill and leaned out into the night air.

Clutching his side, he made his way downstairs and out the front door.

An unnatural chill spread through every inch of him. Falling to his knees as unbearable exhaustion devoured him, Caleb rolled on his back and struggled for breath.

The sky above burned with a thousand stars; the swirls of the Milky Way could just be made out. The comet blazed like a spotlight. A gentle breeze caressed Caleb's face, and on it, he thought he heard his brother's laugh.

As life slowly left him, his eyes filled with tears that kaleidoscoped the heavens above. A brilliant ball of light descended toward the earth from the comet.

He turned his head away from the blinding glow and a memory stared back.

"Will we make it out of here someday, Cal?"

Caleb reached for his brother's hand.

"We will, Jack. I promise, someday we will."

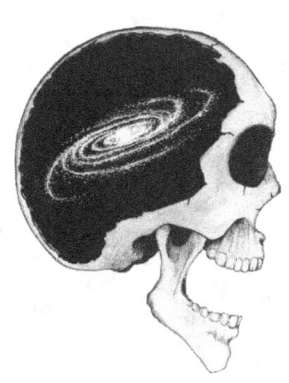

ASTRONOMICAL CHOICES

M. RICHARD ELEY

Kim's head rested against the airplane's window frame. The vibration caused her view of the stars to jiggle. Since the cabin lights were dimmed, she couldn't stop watching the sky. Everything so clear, so crisp. One of the brightest stars seemed to flash. Red, green, red, green. Like a Christmas light. She wondered what its name was.

A raspy voice whispered in her ear. "That's *Ra's Al-ghūl*."

She jerked around, her hand instinctively clutching for her daughter, sleeping in the middle seat.

On the other side of Tonya sat a lanky man, wearing a white linen suit. He turned a page on his in-flight magazine, seeming oblivious to her stare. She didn't remember him being there before. She peeked through the seat gap behind her. A row of three white-haired ladies, sound asleep, each slumped on the others.

She shook her head. Must have been dreaming. Tonya stirred, and Kim relaxed her hand.

In the same raspy voice as before, the man spoke, though it didn't sound close this time. "Nowadays, folks call it *Al-gaal*." He laid the magazine in his lap.

Kim tried to process the situation. All she managed to come up with was "What?"

The man continued facing straight ahead, but he smiled a toothy grin. "*Ra's Al-ghūl*. The bright star you were admiring. *Algol*." He nodded at her, then lifted his sharp chin at the airplane window. "The demon star."

She glanced at the window for an instant, then snapped back around.

The man chuckled. "You have nothing to fear from me. Actually, I am the only one who can save you both."

Kim scrutinized him, sizing him up against every other crazy man she had ever met. He held a calm assurance about him, was well groomed, his reddish skin deeply tanned. He gazed at her while she completed her assessment.

"Thank you, but we don't need anything." She turned away, facing the window.

"Thousands of years ago, some believed a demon serpent occasionally dined on that star. Explaining why it dims and brightens, you see."

Kim continued to stare into the sky, one hand resting on her daughter's leg. She made no reply.

"But that's a silly concept, wouldn't you say?"

She looked over at him. "Sir…just leave us alone, okay?"

"You may call me Druthers."

"If you don't leave us alone, *Druthers*, I'm gonna call—"

"You have a rare opportunity today, my dear. Certainly, the rarest of your life, I would think. Will you dare waste it, Kimberly?"

The mention of her name stopped her reach for the call button. "How do you know my—"

"Oh, I know a great many things." He gave the same quiet chuckle. "For instance, inside our starboard engine—I believe you can just see it from your window…"

She glanced at her daughter, then out at the wing. "What about it?"

"Fascinating machines, jet engines. That one is a Rolls-Royce Trent 7000. Remarkably efficient, impressively reliable."

"Uh-huh. Right." She leaned back in her seat. "You some salesman or something?"

"Salesman? Well, yes, that is true, I suppose I am." He smiled. "A *salesman*. I like that."

"Well, we don't need anything. Thanks anyway."

"But you haven't heard my, ummm..." He tapped his knee, then held up a long, bony finger. "My pitch!"

Kim sighed, settled back and closed her eyes. "Whatever."

"Now, as I was saying, Trent engines are very durable. However, in this case, just as our plane took off, a ten-millimeter nut fell off an airport security van speedily circling the airfield."

"Uh-huh." She sighed. "Wow."

"Yes, and that nut bounced across the runway, hit a rubber seam, and shot thirty feet up into the air. Can you believe it? Thirty feet!"

"Yeah, amazing. So, I'm just gonna listen to some music, and if you—"

"And that nut, no bigger than the tip of your finger—" He stuck out a pinky. "—ended up smack dab in front of the starboard engine on this plane. Sucked it right in." He made a slurping sound and jerked his finger sideways.

Kim squinted at him. "What, during takeoff?"

"Yes, indeed. And that little nut miraculously made it through the first set of compressor blades without touching a thing. Can you believe it?"

"Uh, sure. That's great."

"Unfortunately, though, when it reached the secondary turbine, it hit two blades. Still, such a wonderful product, the Trent 7000, that those titanium blades didn't even break. They shredded that little nut like a carrot in a blender. Amazing."

"Okay dude, I'm over your lectures. You need a—"

"Ah, I apologize. These modern devices fascinate me greatly. I tend to wax on about them." He held up both hands in surrender. "Let me summarize." He pointed toward the wing. "In two-hundred, eighty-seven seconds, that engine will explode."

"What? What are you talking about?" The realization that she might be sitting beside a terrorist shot ice up her spine.

"The turbine blades damaged by the impact will shatter. In a chain reaction of failures, the engine will tear itself apart."

"Please, mister, don't hurt us. My daughter is only four years old."

Druthers shook his head and again raised his hands. "You misunderstand. None of this is my doing, I assure you. I am but a mere bystander in these things."

It dawned on Kim right then: this man wasn't a terrorist — he was a lunatic. Mentally ill. Trying to scare her for a cheap laugh, or maybe con her out of some money. She relaxed a bit before sticking her finger in his face.

"Hey, asshole: *piss off.* Or I swear I'll have you arrested. Get me?" She jabbed her nail dangerously close to his right eye.

Without blinking, he nodded. "You are not so easily convinced. Perhaps that is commendable."

Kim gave him one last jab before lowering her hand. "Yeah. Remember that."

"I suppose I'll need to show you." His hand moved so fast she couldn't pull away. When his fingers closed on her wrist, everything went dark.

Not completely dark, though. Stars. A blinking white strobe. Silver moonlight glinted across the plane's wing as they gently banked over the ocean.

Kim pulled back from the window as a bright light flared inside the jet engine, like an orange flashbulb. Angry red flames shot out the exhaust, sucked back in, then shot out again. Kim screamed as the engine exploded. Loose turbine blades sparkled as they ripped apart the thin aluminum engine cover. The wing twisted, then tore away.

A violent roll clockwise slammed Kim against her lap belt. Luggage and belongings whirled throughout the cabin. Her daughter cried "Mommy!" and Kim reached for her, but the tumbling yanked them apart.

"Tonya, hold on! Tonya!"

"I'm scared, Mommy!"

Kim's hand finally landed on Tonya's, and they both held on tight in the chaos.

The plane groaned and shuddered. With a horrible screech, it split apart a few rows in front of them. Seats whipped away into the roaring darkness. The fuselage gave up its remaining strength and disintegrated into a cloud of debris. As they were thrown away from one another, into the ice-cold night sky, Kim's last vision was wide-eyed terror on her four-year-old's screaming face.

Kim jolted upright, straining against the lap belt, flailing for her daughter. Her fingertips jammed into the seat-tray in front of her. Pain shot through her hands, snapping her into the present.

"Calm down, everything is fine." Druthers withdrew his arm. "For now."

Tonya, curled in the seat, snored peacefully.

"A terrible vision, to be sure," Druthers said. "But, alas, one to shortly become reality. Unless..."

Kim panted, trying to relax her pounding heart. She blinked away tears and wiped her face.

Druthers reached into his jacket pocket, produced a handkerchief, and offered it to her.

Kim didn't move, just stared at him.

He shrugged and repocketed the swatch. "So, you have seen my, ah, *sales pitch*, I suppose we could call it. Now we must discuss the terms."

"Who are you?" Kim shook her head. "How did you do that?"

Druthers smiled. "One of my many talents. Though it was merely a vision, in approximately—"

He checked his wristwatch and tapped its face. To Kim, it seemed to have countless layers of dials. As if a hole in space had opened through Druthers' arm, extending into infinite watches, all ticking separately.

A sudden pain, deep in her head, made her turn away.

"Ah, yes." Druthers tugged his sleeve over the watch. "Two-hundred, eleven seconds before your premonition becomes reality. Would you like to save yourself, this plane, and all these fine people?" He spread his hands wide, gesturing around them. "Three hundred and seven lives? That's worth anything—wouldn't you concur?"

Kim massaged her throbbing temples. "Worth what? Who the fuck are you?"

"You said it yourself. I'm a salesman."

The whole thing was too much. She reached up and pushed the call button. It clicked. No light, no chime. Nothing.

Druthers nodded. "Out of order, I expect. More accurately speaking, I am a collector, of sorts."

Kim called out, "Hello? Could someone help me please? Flight attendant?"

With a slight lean into the aisle, Druthers swiveled his head front to back. "Everyone seems to be otherwise engaged. I expect we have the place to ourselves for the moment."

Kim released her lap belt and stood. As far as she could see, every seat appeared empty.

"Yes, a bit of privacy was necessitated. Now, shall we continue our transaction? Perhaps you'd like to experience the thirty-thousand-foot plummet, screaming all the way, until you smash into the frigid Atlantic water?" He reached for her wrist.

She pulled away, pressed hard against the wall.

"Perhaps Tonya should, yes?" His hand dropped a few inches.

"No!" Kim reached out with one hand, then quickly drew it back. She collapsed into her seat. "Please, leave us alone. Please."

"Well now, if I honor your request, everyone on board will die in less than three minutes. Is that what you want?" He tipped his head and raised his brows.

Kim whispered her answer. "No."

"Ah, how delightful. As I said, I am a collector. In exchange for what you provide, I will convince that sad, damaged turbine to last all the way to New York. After that, I suppose, it will no longer be your concern. You will be safe and sound and on your way to Brooklyn, arriving in time for your sister's wedding. How nice."

"I don't have much money." Kim lifted the necklace she wore and held out the stone. "This was my mother's diamond, is it enough?"

Druthers raised his palms toward her. "And a lovely woman she was.

Sadly, I cannot accept such baubles. I require something more…" He rubbed his fingers together. "Intimate."

Kim nodded. She began unbuttoning her blouse. "Can we do it away from my daughter?"

Druthers snorted and shook his head. "My dear, nothing so mortal as coitus. Though…" He leaned a few inches closer and smirked. "You would enjoy it." He took a deep breath and then sighed. "But now is not the time for such dawdles."

She threw her hands up. "What then, dammit? What do you want?"

Druthers pointed at the sleeping Tonya. "Her soul."

Kim's mouth opened and closed twice. No sound came out.

"You must gift me Tonya's soul. As only a mother can. Freely, without reservation."

"You're, you're the—"

"I am well aware of who I am, and who you are, and who *everyone* else is. But what's most pertinent to your situation is whether or not you agree to my terms."

Kim pulled her daughter against the side of the seat. "How can you even ask? You're deranged."

"Deranged?" Druthers laughed and slapped his knee. "You know, in six-thousand years, after countless interactions with mortals, I do believe you are the first to call me that."

"You are, if you think I'd give you my daughter."

"No, no, no." With a quick sideways head shake, Druthers clarified. "I never asked for your daughter. I only want her amaranthine soul."

Kim blinked a few times. "Amaran...what?"

"A simple trade. Her eternal soul—" Druthers nodded at the girl. "—and in exchange, you both live out normal, boring, long lives. And Tonya should live for, oh..."

He looked at the floor, mumbled for a few seconds, then smiled. "Another ninety-two years, if you accept my proposition. And she'll have four children of her own, and ten grandchildren. One of which will discover a process to grow apples which produce an anti-cancer drug." He nodded. "Bad for my business, I suppose, but an admirable feat."

"But..."

"But nothing." Druthers tapped on his magazine, his shiny fingernail thumping on the cover photo of a jet plane. "Think about these other people. Their very lives depend on your decision. If you don't agree, all are doomed. You, your daughter, everybody." He shrugged. "Doesn't matter to me. But what about their descendants? One may discover faster-than-light travel, or perhaps an immortality drug."

Kim lifted her head above the seats to see up and down the rows. "There's no one here but us."

Druthers lazily waved a hand in the air. "Everyone's still here, don't worry. We're just taking a little break from them. A touch of privacy. As soon as we conclude our business, they'll return."

"Take me instead." Kim nodded. "Take my soul. I give you mine."

Druthers studied her for a full second, then shook his head. "No need to bargain for that." He licked his lips. "We'll see each other again. In due time."

Kim swallowed hard at the implication. "But my daughter's life, I, I can't—"

"I'm no murderer, silly woman. Tonya can live out a full life, same as you. Or you can deprive her of it, end her life before it starts." He pulled an old-fashioned straight razor from his breast pocket, flicked it open, and held it out. "You might as well slit the poor child's throat right now, while she sleeps. Save her from the coming terror." He pushed the blade nearer to Kim's hand.

The plane seemed to constrict around Kim, all she could focus on was the gleaming blade. Snippets of her premonition played in fast order: The explosion, plane tearing apart, Tonya screaming.

"Or..." Druthers' voice brought her back. "Grant me what I ask, and go on with your happy lives for many more years." He circled a finger in the air. "Along with all these other lovely folks, who most likely don't want to die a horrible, fiery death today." He shrugged. "Your choice."

"I can't, I mean, it's not..." She watched Tonya dozing.

The turbojet's drone warbled for a second, then returned to normal.

"Might hurry a bit, if I were you." Druthers pocketed the razor, leaned back, then stretched his head side to side. "You know, these coach seats aren't very comfortable. You should fly business or first-class next time." He peered out the window. "If there's a next time, that is."

Kim wiped her eyes and let out a long breath. "All right."

Druthers snapped upright and twisted toward her. "Excuse me? What was that?"

"I said *okay*, you freaking monster. Okay!"

His face lit with pleasure. "Excellent! A wise choice."

"So, do I need to sign in blood or something?"

A deep chuckle came from Druthers. "I do believe you've been watching too many late-night horror movies. No, Kimberly, your word is your bond. Only one other thing is needed to complete the transaction."

"What?" Her tone became angry. "Just get it over with, dammit."

"Of course."

His hand lightly encircled Tonya's wrist. She twitched and mumbled. After a second, he released her, leaving a star-shaped red birthmark adorning Tonya's skin. "There we are. All done."

Kim stared at the mark. A small curl of smoke rose above it and dissipated.

A loud *DING* made Kim jerk, and her head thumped into the window frame. She was gazing out at the stars again. Must have dozed off, she thought. She leaned back and shook her head to clear it. Next to Tonya, a woman in a tight white business suit, wearing earbuds, rhythmically rocked her head side to side.

It had been one seriously crazy dream. She should cut back on the pre-flight cocktails and Dramamine.

"This is your Captain speaking. Just letting you folks know we'll be touching down in New York in about fifteen minutes. We hope you had a great flight, and thanks for flying SkyBlue airlines."

Murmurs and shuffling filled the plane as passengers collected their belongings.

"That was fun, Mommy," Tonya said. "Can I see outside?"

Kim lifted her close to the portal.

The child held her face against the plastic, looking in all directions. "I can see *everything*!" She put her hands on either side of the window and pushed herself back. "Can we fly again, Mommy? Please?"

Kim didn't answer. She just stared at the red, star-shaped mark on Tonya's wrist.

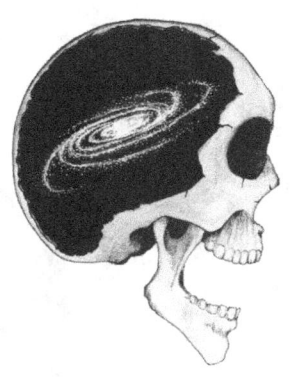

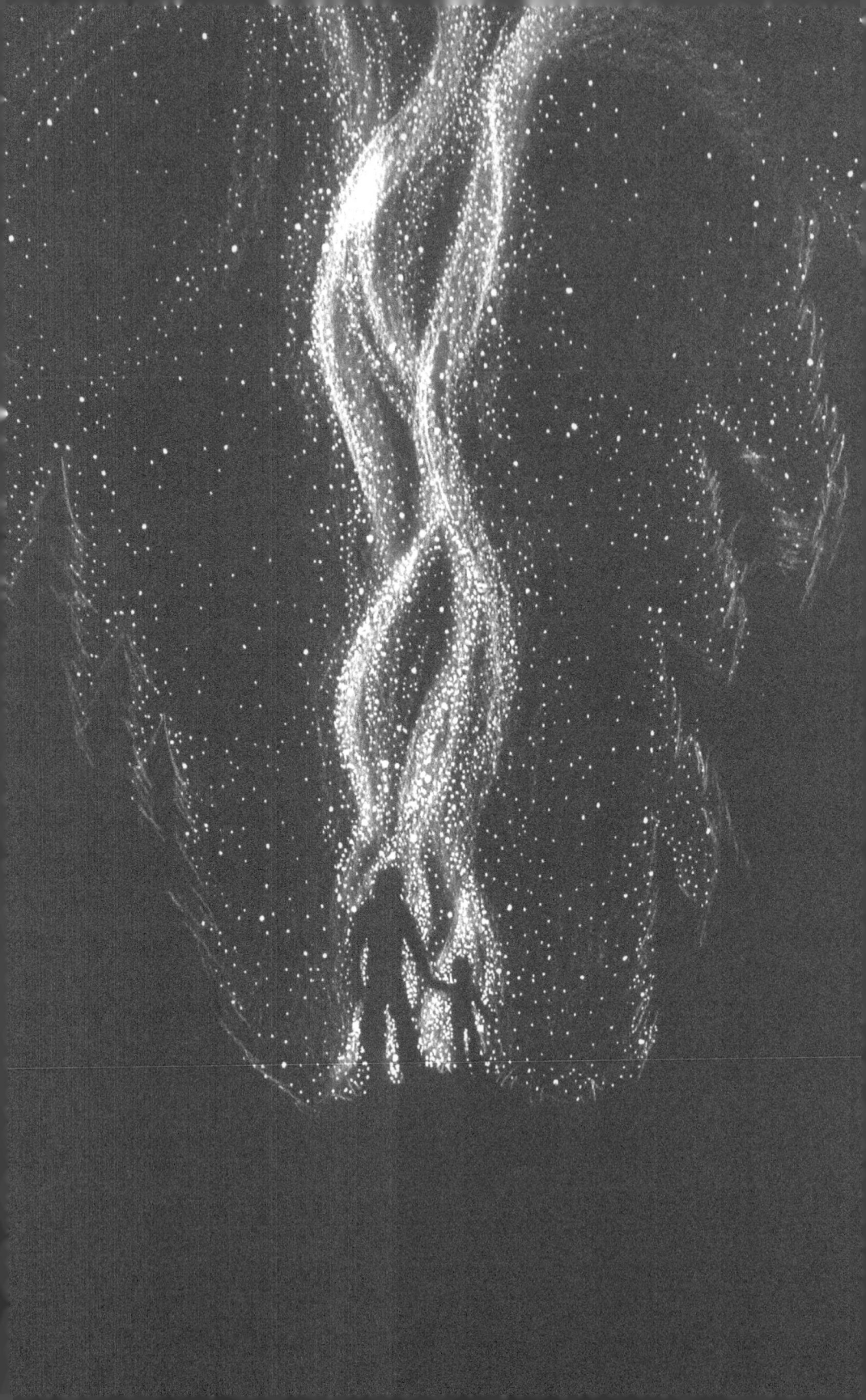

INTO THE
GREAT WIDE OPEN

MADISON MCSWEENEY

When they'd scoured the fields and ditches, finding not so much as a footstep, they pulled on their boots and searched the woods. They walked up and down the perimeter fence, breathed sighs of relief when they came across old reams of barbed wire and did not find a toddler tangled in the strands. When dusk fell, they pulled out flashlights.

The father of the missing child was little help. Joe staggered through the brush in a daze, not sifting through anything, not paying attention. When he tripped and landed in a bush of prickles, knee jamming into a protruding root, one of the searchers put an end to the charade.

"Go home, son. Get some sleep."

Joe didn't recognize the man; it could have been any one of his father's friends. No will to protest, he turned and started navigating back to the tree line. In the corner of his eye, he caught his father watching his retreat.

The clearing was squashed flat, trampled by dozens of boots, and Joe nearly slipped on the guts of a gourd someone had stomped on. Across the field, the kitchen light was warm and yellow, like coming in at Christmas with an armful of firewood. Like apple cider after a day at the pumpkin patch. The moments raced in his head, things he'd done and thought of doing. Another sob bubbled up in his throat.

Sally had taken a sedative and would be asleep by now. Knowing his mother, she'd be pacing the kitchen, dialing the rotary phone as if someone in her address book might have seen her grandson.

Joe didn't know how he got to the garden without collapsing, or how he lowered himself onto the peeling wooden bench without toppling over. All he knew was that he couldn't stand the idea of going inside yet. Instead, he sat and watched the stars come out, one by one, and wondered if they had anything to say for themselves.

"I shouldn't say this…"

"Might as well," Allan said, hands white around the steering wheel. "You're thinking it." Ahead of him, the road blended seamlessly into the inky black of the woods, headlights barely penetrating.

"It's just…did it strike you that the boy didn't seem to be searching very hard?"

"He certainly didn't seem to have any sense of urgency, no."

Marvin flicked his lighter, trying in vain to get a spark to catch. In his other hand, the cigarette shook in his fingers. "Like I said, I feel bad saying it. Kid's barely old enough to have a kid, and now this happens. I can't imagine how that must…but the thing is, I can. F'my boy went missing, I'd be dragging the lake and turning every stone myself until I found him. Joe seemed to be sorta…going through the motions."

Al took the turn onto the main road, too fast. "What are you saying, Marv?"

The lighter cracked to life, the cigarette lit. "I dunno," Marvin said. "Just talking nonsense, I guess."

"So, do you always let your toddler play in the yard by himself?"

Joe suspected the cop would notice any errant twitch, thought he might be timing the rate of his blinks. *Grady,* the badge said, reflecting light from the ceiling lamp. Joe had gone to high school with him, several years behind; bought dope from Officer Grady's younger brother, once upon a time. The pen was taut as a divining rod between Grady's fingers, specks of ink already ejaculated onto the yellow notepad.

He'd asked the same question to Sally, and believed her when she'd said, "No, of course not!"

Now he had Joe alone, his mother's laundry room doubling as an interrogation cell.

(That was a tic, Grady noticed. Everything in the house was "his mother's this" and "his father's that." It was even "his father's garage," despite the fact that Joe and Sally lived in the apartment above that garage.)

"The kitchen door was open," Joe lied, his voice devoid of all emotion, save fatigue. "He was there one minute and then he was gone."

The pen smacked the page three times, like a gavel. "See, I don't know what you mean by that," the cop said. "Do you remember seeing him slip out?"

"If I'd seen him slip out, don't you think I would've grabbed him?" Joe said.

"Exactly how long was little Joey unattended for?"

"I don't know."

Grady was tapping the pen again, letting it swing this way and that before slamming into the pad. "I heard you left the search party early last night."

"Someone told me to get some sleep," Joe said.

"Who?"

"I don't know. Some guy."

"You always do what people tell you, Joe?"

When he didn't answer, Grady laughed. "What am I saying? Teenage father, living with his wife in his parents' garage, in-laws over all the time—I bet you're the most henpecked guy in town." He paused. "You ever get sick of that, Joe?"

Tap, tap, tap.

Close the window, why don't you?

What're you doing out at this hour? It's three in the morning!
You never talk to me when you're upset. You just go outside and get sullen.
Sorry, Sally.
"Does it ever make you wanna just, snap?"

Day two was much worse, Joe discovered. At least the first night, they'd had panic. Today, it had been waking up and remembering, the suspicious questions from the police, and another fruitless scouring of the woods.

Joe re-joined the search party. At this point, he was only there to keep up appearances—but so was everyone else. Joe saw it in their unhurried navigation, their methodical pace, and most of all, the fact that no one was calling the baby's name. None of the searchers said as much, but it was clear they were looking for a body.

"Mary-Ellen called," Sally announced, fists clenched and quaking like she'd tried to strangle the phone cord. "She offered to put up posters around town. Posters! Like he's a lost dog or something! Have you ever heard a stupider thing? How would he even get to town? He's a baby—"

"We're as likely to find him in town as in the woods," Joe muttered, and felt all their eyes frying into him. His father looked angry, his mother pained; Sally's was the only expression he couldn't read.

"Joe," his mother said. "Can I talk to you?"

He followed her into the kitchen, expecting to be reamed out for his insensitivity. Instead, she pulled out two chairs and spoke to him in a low voice, taking his hand as he sat next to her. "I know it didn't always feel like this, but we love you unconditionally. And we love Sally and we love Joey."

"…Thanks." Joe moved to get up, but she held onto him.

"And if there's anything you need to tell us, we're here."

"I know."

Her eagle eyes didn't leave his face, and he suddenly felt like he was back in the laundry room with the police.

"So. Do you have something to tell us?"

What do you think I did? his brain screamed, but he just said, "No."

Her grip tightened. "I hope you understand, Joe, your father and I have made a lot of sacrifices to support your family. Your brothers were all out of the house out at eighteen, but we made an exception for you, for the sake of our grandchild."

Joe barely absorbed the words. It was like he was hidden somewhere deep inside his body and his mother was talking to a semi-sentient sac of flesh. "Of course I understand."

He would have been happy to stay in that buried place, painless, far away from the consequences of whatever they thought he'd done, but he was brought back to the surface by his mother's fingers digging into his hand. Nails like syringes plunging into his flesh, drawing him out like blood from a vein.

"And you do know that we wouldn't be supporting you indefinitely if your son wasn't in the picture."

No free rent for child murderers.

"Of course," Joe said, the only thing he could think of.

In his dream, Sally was pregnant for the first time again, and Joe was breaking the news to his parents. His dream-self briefly registered that this had happened already; then he forgot he was dreaming and was experiencing everything anew, the yelling and weeping, the how-could-you-be-so-stupid and you've-ruined-your-life.

Joe was out the door and off the porch before he realized he had nowhere to go if he left home. If staying at home was even an option at this point. He thought of his father's cold sneer, almost reveling in the fact that Joe had screwed up his life, kissed goodbye all his indistinct teenage dreams. *Childhood's over. You'll have to man up and take your lumps, now.*

Joe knew what that meant, and the fear of it made his knees weak. Fists in his pockets, he lowered himself onto the bench his mother used for weeding. A copse of shrubs sat between the bench and the house, and his parents couldn't see him from the window. Enough privacy to allow Joe to gather his thoughts, but he was close enough that he couldn't be accused of running away. That was the last thing he needed—more evidence of his irresponsibility.

As Joe stared into space from the wooden bench, the stars started to stir. He tried to blink away the optical illusion, but when he opened his eyes, they were only larger. Closer.

As the stars lowered themselves, swimming through the lowest layers of cloud, Joe felt a luminescent sheet thrown over him. The light shone through his clothes, made his skin translucent. Joe tilted his chin to see two sets of rib cages, overflowing with his heaving lungs and beating heart, a network of veins rushing blood to his extremities. A beam of light grazed his cheek, leading his eyes back up toward its source, directing his thoughts away from earth and toward the ether. His feet left the ground.

Then the stars started to speak. Their words were rich but unintelligible. The sound seemed to come from everywhere; it was as if the whole sky was filled with the reverberations of a gigantic bell, struck millions of years ago and still vibrating. Individual voices came out of the ululating wave, speaking simultaneously. Telling him what they'd learned about him as the light grazed his flesh, stripping him to the sinews. Every scrap of doubt, love, anger, generosity, fear, hope, and sadness that made up his soul, the stars examined and found delightful.

He was reminded of dolphins, joyous and intelligent in ways that went beyond human understanding, but with a much more beautiful song.

A voice cut through the din: "What do you think you're doing?"

The vibrations ceased, like the stars, startled, had silenced themselves. Joe hoped his father would leave him alone, just a little while longer until the universe could say its piece.

But the voice boomed again.

"Don't make me come out there and drag you back in!"

The light retreated, and Joe knew the stars were afraid of the old man—perhaps because they knew *Joe* now and knew that *he* was afraid. The last wordless message, before the connection was completely severed, told him that they'd been scared off, that they would never touch him in that way again. The sudden loss made his chest sting.

When his father finally stalked outside, Joe was face-down in the dirt, sobbing. His distress was so palpable that his father's hand, tensed to slap, softened into a caress. "It's okay, it'll all work out. We'll help you." Strong hands pulled Joe up by the armpits, led him back into the house. Collapsing on the couch, Joe squeezed his eyes shut, trying to will himself back into their world as tears streamed down his face.

Hysteria. His mother on the phone to the doctor: "He's had a terrible shock, he won't stop shaking…"

His father sat next to him, rubbing his shoulders, trying to walk back his words. "She can move in here, if her parents won't have her, we'll clear out of the room above the garage, your mother can watch the baby while you're in school…"

So different than his earlier condemnations, the declarations that Joe would have to drop out and join the army.

Joe was fevered for days and barely spoke. The week the fever broke, he married Sally, and six months later, Joe Jr. arrived, a full head of hair with sparkling black eyes, the darling of both sets of grandparents. Joe stuck glow-in-the-dark stars to the corner of the ceiling above his crib. And when he was old enough to crawl, Joe started bringing him into the garden to hear the stars sing.

A drift, as if life was a meandering stream with strange currents, and he was back in his bedroom above the garage, in a reality he wasn't ready to face again. Joe's world was dark and warm, wrapped in the his-and-her stink of a duvet that hadn't been washed in a while. The sound of Sally's soft breathing and the feel of her head on his chest, and beneath him the familiar dent in the mattress.

He realized she was awake when he sensed her muscles tense ready to snap him into pieces if he answered wrong. "You're not the only one who can hear them, you know."

"What?" he asked, groggy.

"The UFOs, or whatever. I can see you from the window when you're in the garden, staring at the sky for hours. And I can hear—not whatever it is you're hearing, but I can hear them nattering at you. It's like radio static."

Joe gulped, not knowing what to say. How ignorant he'd been, thinking Sally of all people hadn't noticed. "I'm sor—"

"I saw what happened," she continued. "I was in your mother's room, looking in her drawer for some sewing scissors, and I could see you from the window. Joey was playing in the dirt, and you were sitting on that bench, not watching him, just looking at the sky. And that was okay, because he was only a few feet away, and you'd have seen it if he tried to go anywhere. I went to tap on the window to wave at you, and suddenly the whole garden flashed white. I thought they'd dropped a bomb on us. Then everything came back and you were alone and Joey was gone."

She hesitated.

"Did you give him to them, Joe?"

"No." Joe was too exhausted to feign horror at the question. "But I think they might have felt entitled to him. Because they helped me, once."

"How?"

He sighed. "It wasn't even intentional. My parents were ready to kill me when I told them you were pregnant. They wanted to ship me off to the army. That night…"

"Was that when you got sick?" she asked. Sally had been told little about the delirium Joe had suffered after his first brush with the heavens, just that he'd passed out and wasn't himself.

"Yeah. But I don't think they actually meant me any harm."

"Can you understand them?"

Joe remembered his last birthday, when he'd gone into one of his funks, and Sally had tried but failed to cheer him up before he went into the garden. *Cheer,* they'd chimed. *Birthday.* The stars didn't fully understand many human concepts, he knew, but they tried their best to say what they thought was the right thing.

"Not in the normal way," he finally said.

"Can they understand you?"

Better than anyone else, in some ways. But he couldn't tell Sally that, even though it wasn't a knock on her at all.

"I think they've been in my mind," he said. "And they try to understand— they're teaching themselves to, I think."

Sally was quiet for a long time, and for too long of a moment, Joe thought she was going to roll out of bed and whip out a tape recorder filled with bizarre ramblings proving that he was looney tunes and had probably murdered their baby and should be locked up. He pictured a swarm of cops bursting through the window, pumping the mattress with bullets, when she finally spoke again:

"Would they give him back if you asked?"

Every stair and floorboard creaked as he crept from the garage apartment into the hallway and down to the first floor. Sally watched him from the doorframe until he was out of view, and then retreated to their window, from where she could see the corner of the garden.

The stars had tried to please him in the past, Joe thought, to the extent that they understood human emotions. If they could enter him tonight, they couldn't help but feel his anguish, know that he wanted nothing more in the world than to have his son back. And wasn't that what they were trying to learn—empathy?

The thought, which had at first felt comforting, made his heart sink as he realized why the stars had not come to him since taking Joey. What good were a few sporadic visits when they could have access to a bundle of pure emotion that would grow and learn along with them forever? He was standing on the stoop when this occurred to him, and it stopped him in his tracks.

The stars were out in full force, stratified layers of light stretching through space and time. A teacher had once told him that many of the stars seen from earth were long dead, the last of their lights hurtling toward them aeons after the source had burned out.

Had he been talking to ghosts this whole time? Was his baby held aloft in a celestial tomb?

"Going somewhere?"

Sally's father stood at the garden's edge. He had a hunting rifle in his hand, not yet pointed at Joe, though Joe could tell the option was on the table.

"Look me in the eye, boy," Allan snarled. "Tell me where my grandson is."

Joe's voice broke. "I think he's dead."

Through his tears, Joe didn't see the barrel raise, though he heard the gun cock. He didn't run. He didn't think he wanted to live anymore, anyway.

Off to the side, a patch of grass lit up as his parents turned their upstairs light on. Had they heard Allan pull in? Were they watching from the window right now? In any case, they wouldn't reach him in time. Allan could pull the trigger before Joe's parents reached the bottom of the staircase.

Joe squeezed his eyes shut. But instead of darkness, he got a blinding flash that seemed to tear the world in two.

When he opened his eyes, he thought a bomb had gone off. Allan was face-down on the ground, wind knocked out of him, rifle lying just out of his reach. Bright red afterimages danced around the garden, like cartoon rabbits taunting the vanquished hunter.

When the flash faded, Joey was cross-legged in the garden, babbling contentedly, eyes blinking at the sky. Joe looked up, amazed. Above, the stars winked at him, their tone almost apologetic:

We just wanted to see.

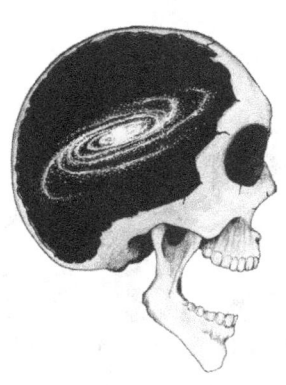

YA-YAI MAKES THE BABY MOBILES SPIN

BERNARD MCGHEE

Everyone eventually forgets about Ya-Yai but that doesn't mean it forgets about you.

Sure, new babies are always being born. But it longs for the ones that get away and grow up. Its soul is warmed when it remembers the hours spent floating over your crib or in the corner, near the ceiling.

How you laughed and cooed as it entertained you with its puppet show of bloody heads. How you squealed with terror and delight when it opened up its stomach and sent its entrails spraying across the room. How you drifted off to sleep listening to it sing the songs of the cold, dark universe. Its name was your first word. You would look to the ceiling and call out "Ya-Yai" over and over again. Ya-Yai knew then that it would love you forever; that your place was living with it and all the others on its planet far away.

At least, that's what was supposed to happen. After about a year of visiting you and making you laugh and spinning your baby crib mobile, the night finally came when the stars and planets lined up just right, opening a pathway. With the right mix of songs and glowing rocks, Ya-Yai can usually coax them out of their slumber. Out of their cribs; out of their rooms; out of their bodies. Back in its home, it can adore them forever along with all the other sleeping babies it has called over the centuries. The parents left behind will call it *SIDS* or *crib death* and never once wonder who was making the mobile spin.

But being open to the universe works both ways, and a parent's instinct to protect can be stronger than expected. Sometimes it's a dream that their child is drowning that wakes them up with an intense feeling of dread. Sometimes they imagine they hear their baby crying. Other times, it's just an unexplainable compulsion go into their baby's room and check on them. They walk into the room and scoop up their child. The journey is interrupted and the moment is lost.

That's how it happened with you. Ya-Yai howled and cried radioactive tears of blood as it watched your mother walk out of the room with you on her shoulder. But no one around could hear or see it anymore. It cried as it floated up into the night, into space and back to its own lonely planet, far beyond the galaxies discovered by humans.

There were other babies after that. There were other mobiles to spin. But it never forgot about you. How it could it? Its name was your first word. How could you two not belong together?

Back home, Ya-Yai runs its taloned, tentacle-like fingers through the hair of one of the babies as it sleeps. It looks out over the vast field of sleeping babies that covers the face of its green dwarf planet for as far as it can see. The beauty is so overwhelming Ya-Yai wants to rip its own eyes out. Instead, it makes a promise to itself that it will find you again. No matter how long it takes.

Ya-Yai doesn't know how long it waits for you. Its little planet's sun is so far away that it appears as little more than a bright star above. Days and years slide by like water in a subterranean river.

It loves all its babies; all the ones who can see it; all the ones who hear its songs and giggle at its tricks as it dances across their bedroom ceilings. It loves them all more than it could ever find the words for. But it can't stop thinking about you. From its cold, dark home, it gazes up at the stars and wonders if you've held on to any of your innocence as you grew older away from it.

Then one day, while Ya-Yai is singing to a baby that's just woken up from a nap, you walk into the room. It's so shocked to see you again it almost drops the rib bones it was clicking together to keep rhythm. You walk right past it and pick up your son from his crib.

The mouth on Ya-Yai's skeletal face hangs open as it watches you change the baby's diaper. It isn't until you've finished and are sitting in the rocking chair to give your son a bottle that Ya-Yai gets the courage to take a few steps closer. It leans in, its face just a few inches from yours. It really is you.

Ya-Yai sees past the bleary eyes, uncombed hair and baby food-stained green nightgown to the beautiful baby who stared up at it and called out its name. Even the tune you're humming to your son with your eyes only half open is from a song Ya-Yai used to sing to you. It's a song your son already knows.

The next few weeks are a gift. Before, when a parent walked in, it was an interruption of its playtime. But even as it sings and dances and performs tricks for your son, it can't wait for the moment when you come into the room. Sometimes you're tired and bedraggled, especially if the baby woke you up at night as it sings along with Ya-Yai. Other times, you're dressed with makeup on, ready to face the day. Either way, you look just as radiant to Ya-Yai. It can hardly believe it found you again.

It wonders if some deep, primal part of you is aware that it's come back. But on the surface, you never seem to notice, even as your son stares over your shoulder at Ya-Yai, captivated as it juggles flaming rocks and jaguar skulls right behind you. Sometimes, it even sings at you. But you never notice. You change your son's diapers, give him his bottles, rock him to sleep and never once wonder who's making the mobile spin.

All the while, planets revolve and moons rotate, soon to line up with the right stars. It won't be long before another bridge between Earth and Ya-Yai's far away planet opens up that's strong enough for it to bring someone back with it. Before—so many times before—Ya-Yai would wait for the night when the pathway opens and sing the baby up out of their crib and into the sky. As long as there were no ill-timed interruptions, that was how it happened. It had thousands of times before.

But one afternoon, while watching you shake a rattle in front of your son as he plays on the floor mat, Ya-Yai realizes the youngest baby doesn't have to be the one who comes back with it. What if there was another chance to bring home the one who once said its name and stole its heart so long ago? Ya-Yai looks up past the sky and the blinding daylight of your planet's star into the endless cosmos beyond. Things are moving into place. It will just take a little longer. Ya-Yai smiles. Your son smiles back. You giggle and ask him what's on the wall that's so interesting.

Days go by. Ya-Yai isn't sure how many. It tries to ignore your lying sun. But one night the sky glows a little bit brighter and it knows the time has come. It takes one long, last look at your son. After this night, it will still see him but it won't be able to play with him again. It kisses him on his forehead then floats down the hall to your bedroom.

You're asleep in bed, lying next to your husband. Ya-Yai doesn't recognize him. It forgets about him and goes around the bed to your side. For a long time, it watches you lay there as your chest rises and falls. You were sleeping just like this the first time it saw you. To Ya-Yai, you don't look all that different from then. It imagines that no time has passed since the tear-filled night when your drowsy mother snatched you up from the crib and out of its life.

It begins singing. It sings one of the songs it used to sing for you years ago, the same song you still hum to yourself without knowing why. It's a song that's mostly wordless and made of sounds human languages rarely use. It's a song about deep, dark emptiness and also a song of starlight shining in colors beyond the imagination of any human mind. It's a song of the universe and when the youngest humans listen long enough, they begin to understand it.

You probably don't hear it at first. Ya-Yai knows what it usually means when there's an interruption before it can get one out of the atmosphere. But even though Ya-Yai becomes almost non-existent to those that grow up, a small part of them always remembers.

When you first hear the song, it comes in the middle of a dream. And even there, the music is faint, like a radio playing from the bottom of a well. You don't recognize the song, but you know that somehow you've heard it before.

It gradually gets louder. You breathe in time with the rhythm. You hear strange words and realize you know what they mean.

The song is louder now and it's not in your dream. It's something you're hearing in your bedroom, right next to your bed. Your eyes snap open and you bolt up to a sitting position. Your head swivels around as you search the dark room, your ears filled with a song of which you can't find the source. Your husband keeps snoring next to you. The singing is so loud now. How can he not hear it?

Then something catches your eye. A pinprick of light in the dark so faint you're not even sure if you're really seeing it. It's something you have to first see in your mind before your eyes are allowed to find it. The light gets brighter, becoming a small, yellow orb. Another one appears next to it. Ya-Yai's eyes stay locked onto yours as it keeps singing. Your heart races and terror erupts within you, but you can't make yourself look away.

Ya-Yai keeps singing and now you see it. Its four scaly arms are all stretched out to you, beckoning you to it as red tears of joy run down its calcified face. You want to scream but when you open your mouth you find yourself singing along with it, using words you forgot you knew and making sounds your forgot you could make.

Ya-Yai wraps its cold arms around you. It's singing softly into your ear now. You sing along in your head but your throat has gone quiet. Something is rising inside you; something that lifts you off the bed. The covers slide off as you float to the ceiling. For a second, you wonder if you should try to grab something and pull yourself back down. Down the hall, your son is crying. You can't see him but he's standing up in his crib, reaching a tiny hand toward you. But after a few seconds, the song is all you can hear and the song says this is how it's supposed to be.

In Ya-Yai's embrace, you pass through the ceiling, out of the roof and into the shimmering night air. For a moment, a cloud fogs your vision. Then you rise past it and see the moon getting bigger and bigger. Then it gets smaller as stars drift by. Stars are all you see now. You close your eyes and when you open them, you're looking at a different set of stars. It's ice cold but you're not freezing. There is no air to breathe but you're not suffocating.

The song still fills your ears but you can no longer tell if it's Ya-Yai singing or you singing. In the distance, a tiny green planet is getting closer. You never knew you could feel so relaxed and at peace. You don't try to fight it as your heavy eyelids close. Ya-Yai sings you off to sleep as your feet touch the rocky, green surface.

Back in your bedroom the baby's crying has finally woken your husband. He sees you lying motionless next to him and gives you a gentle shake. When you don't move, he rolls you over to look at your face. He screams.

They'll settle on calling it *natural causes*. Some will speculate that a postpartum sickness caught up with you. A few will even whisper that your husband might have poisoned you. But they do what they can to help the new widower and never once wonder who's making the mobile spin.

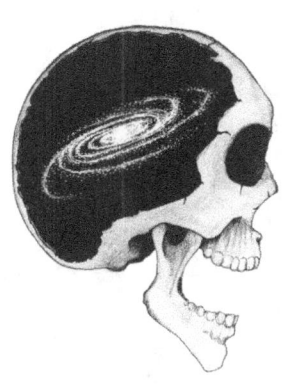

THE CENTER OF EVERYTHING

ELIZABETH DAVIS

"All of this is meaningless"
She told me as she stood on the edge.
"All of this, every single bit. Doesn't even matter
If I leaped." My heart jumped into my throat, blocking words,
I pleaded with eyes that twinkled with tears, as the star light caught
in our atmosphere, caught in our eyes before passing away from us, not at all
the way her gravity caught me,   holding me in Strict rotation.
"It   doesn't   matter,"   she   said "For we all end the
same. Not dust or stars.   We end in the center of it
all, Somewhere out there   it is." She waved, feet
jittering on the rooftop   edge. "The end of us all.
Of everything. Just waiting   for the sun to burn out, for it
to collapse and become a dark   parody. For it to consume us
like Chronos consumed all the gods he birthed, Until it is eaten, as time
is eaten by his own father. The Big Bang made our beginning and
end and nobody will remember us, not even the black hole.
For do you mourn the cells of our body when they die?"
With that she jumped, flying for moment
Before I followed her down.

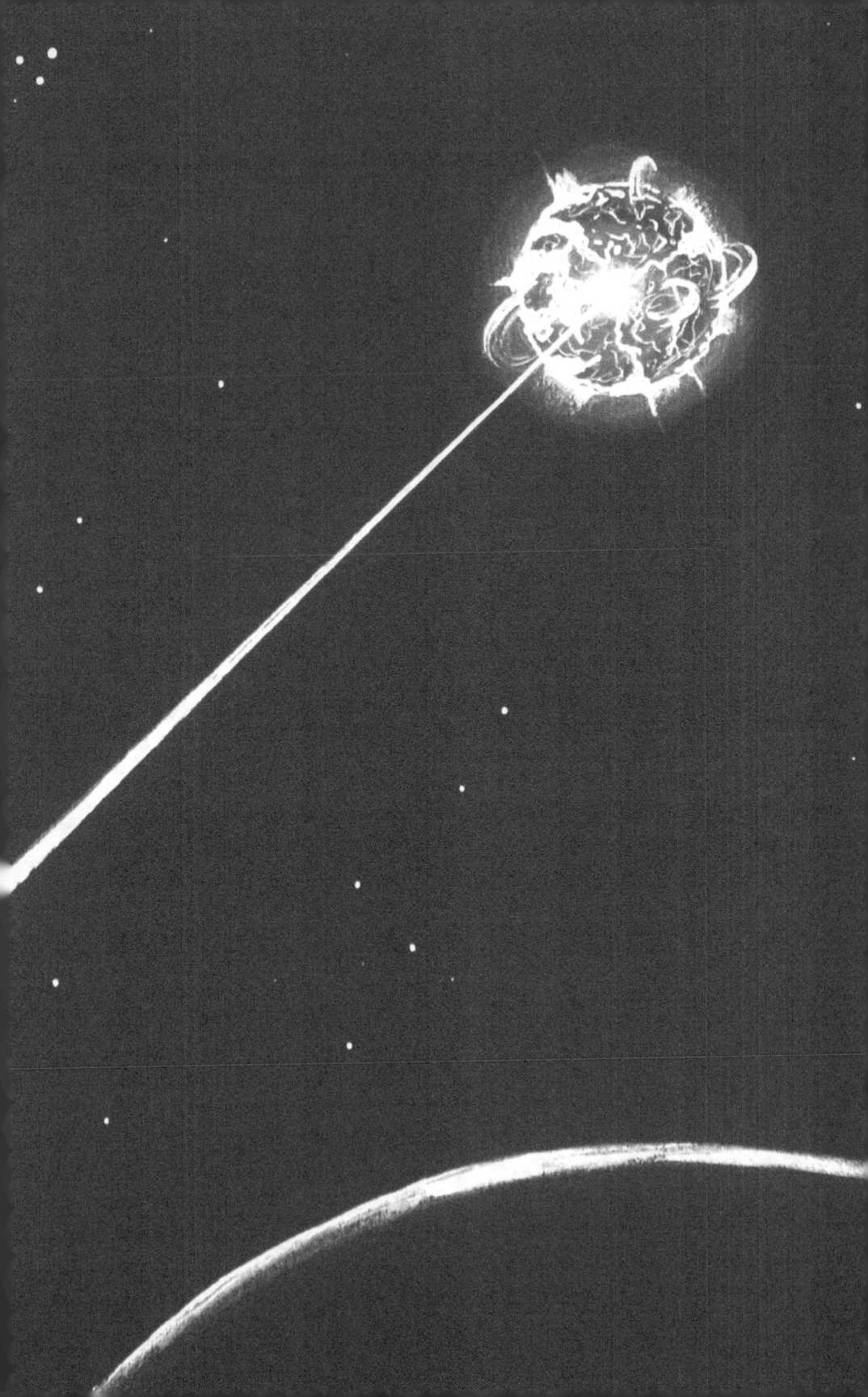

THE RITE OF THE MILK OF THE STARS

LINDSEY RAGSDALE

When Gemma wakes up in the dark, her wife is gone.

She pulls on her robe and pads into their small kitchen, bare feet thumping on the metal floor. Their home is a simple box of metal and glass. Driane calls it a cage. Gemma rolls her eyes, but sometimes feels trapped all the same, in this ten-story structure plummeting through the mesosphere. It's the only home they've ever known.

Driane is standing by the plate glass window, staring out at the unchanging constellations. The stars of Alpha Centauri wink from just over four light years away. The Monolith stays fixed above the Southern Hemisphere, orbiting slowly above dead and silent Earth fifty miles below.

She's in a mood. Gemma knows better than to disturb her. As quietly as possible, Gemma begins breakfast, and when Driane's tense shoulders slump at last, Gemma approaches her with a mug of steaming coffee. "Hey, lovely." She kisses Driane's hair and presses the warm cup into her hands. "Sleep okay?"

"Not really." Driane sips the hot liquid. "Nightmares again." She turns and smiles at Gemma, but it's forced. Driane's gray eyes are lined with a hint of crow's feet. Though Gemma and Driane are genetically engineered, ageless clones of each other, appearing as women in their mid-forties with curly black hair, gray eyes, and stocky builds, Driane crops her hair short while Gemma grows hers long.

Gemma runs a hand through Driane's curls. "Are you watching that Archive footage again?"

Driane shrugs. "So what if I am?"

"I worry about you, Dri. All those records of war and bombs and people killing each other. No wonder you have bad dreams." This is a familiar conversation, and Gemma knows how it's going to end, but she tries anyway. "How about you give the historical records a rest? Or watch something happier?"

Driane wrinkles her nose. "Ignoring the past won't make it disappear."

"Is it worth all your sleepless nights?" Gemma strokes Driane's arm. "Take a break for a few weeks. At least until the Rite—"

"Yes, I know, the *Rite*." Driane grimaces.

Gemma thinks she detects venom in Driane's tone, but that's impossible. Their sole purpose, for both of them, is to carry out the Rite. The women have been created for the sacred work of preserving humanity and awakening Sol. Just fourteen days remain until the Observatory is fully charged. The culmination of decades of waiting and hovering in the dark.

Gemma tenses. "Driane, do you need—"

"I'm fine." Driane laughs, embracing her wife. The tension dissipates, and Gemma closes her eyes in relief. "You're so serious all the time. Don't worry about me." Driane turns to the table. "What's for breakfast?"

They eat in the dim light of the kitchen, nothing but the stars keeping them company.

Gemma climbs the stairs up four stories to the Observatory, located at the Monolith's apex. The structure is powered by a simplified nuclear reactor, deep in its core. Driane's responsible for reactor maintenance and the Stasis Chamber, but the Observatory is Gemma's domain.

The Observatory is fully encased in thick, frost-coated glass, the ceiling bulging upward like an enormous soap bubble. A machine of mirrors and gears, scopes and prisms, occupies the center of the room. It pulsates with a faint, cold light. Photons that have traveled the long distance from the Alpha Centauri system—the stars closest to Earth—have been absorbed by this contraption. Gemma has been nurturing this photonic accumulation. Every day she adjusts spectrometers and apertures, making minute calculations dependent on the Earth's axial tilt and position around dead Sol.

In two weeks, this photonic battery will be full, the Monolith will be at its nearest point to Sol, and Gemma will conduct the Rite. The official name is some long scientific term, but Gemma and Driane call it the Rite of the Milk of the Stars. Gemma found the name in a poetry book in the Archives years ago.

If successful, the Rite will unleash the photonic power of the Alpha Centauri system into Sol, power it's been storing up for the past fifty years, and restart Sol, like a defibrillator uses electricity to restart a heart. It could be the beginning of a new age of humanity and life on Earth.

Gemma begins to work, feeding data into several computers and recalibrating her instruments. She's so absorbed that the hand on her shoulder causes her to yelp and spin around. "Driane, you scared me!"

"Sorry, love," Driane says. She's holding a thermos. "You forgot your tea on the counter."

"Thank you." Gemma takes the thermos and sets it on her workbench. "I guess I was so excited to get up here that I left it behind." She runs both hands through her thick hair. "It's hard to think of anything else but the Rite. These two weeks will fly by, I know it."

Driane nods. "Gemma–" she begins, but falters. She takes a deep breath and tries again. "Gemma, do you think anything will really change?"

"Besides re-charging Sol and giving the Earth and humanity a second chance?" Gemma grins, but she knows Driane's not joking around. Gemma's been the optimist of the pair, ever since they both awakened on the Monolith and eventually fell in love. Driane's the realist. They make a good team. "I'd say that's one hell of a change."

Driane shakes her head, mouth set. "Earlier, when you asked me what was wrong, I brushed you off. I shouldn't have done that. This time, I'm serious.

Can you try, for just a moment, to be serious with me?"

Gemma takes Driane's hand. "Go ahead. I'm listening."

"You know I've been watching a lot of videos and reading about human history, in the Archives. Humans have done a lot of really bad, unforgivable stuff. I was just learning about the Tuskegee Experiment yesterday. Three days ago, the Holocaust. Last week, the Great Leap Forward. Example after example of people in power using their influence in terrible ways. And it culminated in this." Driane points through the glass bubble into the night sky, where they both know Sol lies dark and dormant. "Even you know the consequences of the Helios project, fifty years ago. Humanity thought it could harness the power of the sun. Instead, we killed it. And we murdered the entire planet in the process."

Gemma winces. "*Murdered* is a strong word. Humanity didn't mean to kill anything."

"It doesn't matter," Driane says. "Whatever we meant, look at the results."

"Humanity made a mistake," Gemma says. "A big one. There's no doubt about that. But the Monolith was built to correct that mistake. You and I are protecting the three thousand people in the Stasis Chamber, preserving the Archives and Seed Vault, and conducting the Rite. We have a huge responsibility. It's the reason we were created! You're telling me you don't believe in the work we've been doing our entire lives? How can you say that?" Gemma's eyes glisten.

"We do our work well," Driane says, drawing her wife close. "But is the work worth doing?"

Gemma pushes Driane back. "People learn from their mistakes. And there's a lot of goodness in humanity, too! The Archives aren't just war and death and famine. There's birth, and life, and charity there. Knowledge and invention and imagination. Look at this place. It was born of science and hope. *Humans* built it."

"Does the good outweigh the bad?" Driane whispers. "Do we really deserve a second chance?" She stares at the ground, as if she can see through the hundreds of miles to Earth's dead surface, and wraps her arms around herself.

Gemma takes a deep breath and wipes her eyes with a shaking hand. "I think you should go lie down. I'll come check on you later, okay?" She kisses Driane's temple and guides her to the staircase.

Driane trudges the four flights down, and before the echoes of her steps have ceased, Gemma's thrown herself back into her work.

Two days pass without Gemma and Driane speaking to each other. They've fought several times over the past fifty years, but they always make up, being the only company available. This time is no exception. Gemma gives in first, feeling guilty for pushing Driane away.

Driane's monitoring the colossal instrument panel in the Stasis Chamber, two stories below their living quarters, when Gemma comes into the room. "Hey!" Gemma calls down the row of pods, as not to startle her. Driane raises a hand in greeting and turns back to the panel.

The brightly lit room hums more loudly than the Observatory. There's a constant low gurgling sound from the liquid flow of nutrients and waste removal in and out of the pods. Three thousand pods line the room in rows, each row as a spoke of a wheel, with the instrument panel at the hub. The room has high ceilings and is studded with metal catwalks, as pods vertically line the walls as well. The pods are cool aluminum and opaque, each one containing an adult or child.

Gemma trails her fingertips over the surface of the pods as she passes, murmuring a greeting to each sleeping person lying in wait. Somewhere in this room lie the scientists that created her and Driane, and she's excited to meet them in several days, as the sleepers are scheduled to wake once the Rite is performed.

Driane's pressing buttons in a flurry once Gemma draws near.

"How's it going?" Gemma asks. She holds up a plastic box. "I brought you some brownies. Extra caramel."

Driane turns to Gemma, cheeks flushed. "Aw, Gem. Thank you." She kisses Gemma, long and lingering, and Gemma figures everything's going to be okay.

"Look, I'm sorry I got upset with you," Driane continues, opening the box. "Let's just forget about it." She takes a big bite of a brownie. "These are great. You sure know how to make a gal feel special."

Gemma laughs, and they lean against the instrument panel in companionable silence.

"Everything look good?" Driane asks. "For the Rite?"

"Yes, photon levels are high and all the model scenarios I've run have gone perfectly. We're supposed to do a dry run each of the five days leading up to the Rite."

"The Rite of the Milk of the Stars," Driane muses. "I remember when you read me that poem. It made you cry. In a good way, I think."

Gemma smiles. "Of course it was. Like all the pieces suddenly clicking into place. Almost like destiny." She looks at her wife, seized by a sudden question. "Do you worry things will change once everyone wakes up? It won't be just the two of us anymore."

"You know I doubt a lot of things," says Driane. "But us being together, for the rest of our lives...I've never doubted that. Never."

Gemma puts her arm around Driane and looks out at the waiting pods.

The day of the Rite has arrived. Gemma's eyes fly open and she jumps out of bed. Driane stirs beside her.

Gemma's excited for the Rite, but feels a twinge of sadness, knowing her cozy routine with Driane is about to come to an end. *Every end is another beginning.* Now the two of them will live together on Earth's surface, in a little house with sunlight streaming through the windows every morning. Gemma's seen sunlight so many times in the Archive footage, and she aches to feel the warm rays bathing her skin. A primal instinct no amount of genetic engineering could erase.

Gemma prepares coffee and breakfast, but she can barely eat. She paces as Driane pushes scrambled eggs around her plate in silence, face wan. Gemma notices, but she writes it off as Driane's anxiety about the Rite. Understandable.

Gemma doesn't need Driane's help, it's a one-person job, but she asks Driane to come to the Observatory with her.

"I should probably monitor the reactor," Driane answers, not looking at Gemma. "While you're restarting Sol and all. In case there's a power surge once the Observatory is running at full capacity."

Gemma knows Driane is right, but feels a moment of sadness thinking that they'll be separately watching Sol blaze back to life. She wants to be holding her wife's hand, her past and present by her side as they both look to the future. "You're right. We'll stay in touch over the comm. Then we can go to Stasis together." Gemma claps her hands with joy. "I can't wait to meet everyone!"

Driane puts down her fork with a clatter. "I can't take this anymore. Gemma, those people ruined the planet. How can you be so *happy* to meet them? You're just going to erase everything they've done?" Driane's voice is escalating. "They meddled with Sol and they killed it. And it wasn't just humanity that died. They killed all the plants and animals. As if it was their *right* to do so."

"The Rite will fix all of that," Gemma says, getting out of her seat. Not Driane's moodiness and negativity, not today. "Sol will come back, and so will the Earth. It's a new beginning!"

"Humans don't deserve the luxury of starting over." Driane grips the edge of the table. "They've ruined everything already, and will ruin it again if they get the chance."

"Then what's the point of all this?" Gemma's voice grows louder to match Driane's. "What are we waiting for, alone in the dark? I've spent my entire life looking out these windows, praying for the day we'll get to have Sol back. Don't you want to see that world again? All those people in Stasis are counting on us. We're their only hope."

"What did humans see when they looked at the stars?" Driane says. "Why did they call their beacons Centaurus?" She stabs one finger toward the window where Alpha Centauri twinkles faintly. "They saw death. They saw a beast killing another beast. They chose to paint that in their sky and think of death and violence every time they looked up at their 'hope.' What kind of twisted nature does that?"

"Driane," Gemma pleads. "These people are our family. They created us and gave us each other. We can't turn our backs on them now."

"They're not our family," Driane snarls. "We were created in a laboratory to serve, to go about our happy little tasks here, every day like the last. And we're supposed to be grateful? We're slaves here, Gemma. We'll never be anything but slaves to them."

"Stop it," Gemma snaps, fear gripping her heart. "You're scaring me, Driane."

"Humanity is over," Driane says in a steely tone. "They had so many chances and wasted them all. They don't deserve another."

Silence grows between them. Gemma, desperate, changes tactics. "Why don't you rest?" she says in a softer tone. "Take a sedative and we can talk about this later. I'll take care of everything."

"No," Driane says, eyes blazing. "Gemma, we don't need anyone else. Let's just live out the rest of our lives together here. The reactor will keep going for hundreds of years. We can just live for each other. Don't we deserve that, at least?" Her face is twisted, torn between anger and despair. Gemma's heart goes out to her wife, but there's no question of *if* the Rite will happen. It must. Their whole lives have revolved around this moment.

"Driane, you know I can't do that," Gemma says in a gentle tone. "We must carry out the Rite. We must wake everyone in Stasis. We don't have a choice."

"I have no hope humanity will learn from their mistakes." Driane stammers. She lets out a sigh of relief. "I've been keeping that from you for so long."

Gemma feels, for the first time in fifty years, that she's looking at a stranger.

She makes an executive decision. "Driane," Gemma begins, heart aching, voice trembling. "Let's look out at the stars one more time. We don't have to do anything right now."

Driane nods, shaking, and stands on wobbling legs. She shuffles to the plate glass window and Gemma follows, but not before discreetly palming something from the first aid kit hanging on the wall.

They stand together, one last time, side by side, and Driane takes a deep breath. "Gemma, I hope you know, whatever happens," she whispers, "I love you. You, and this place are all I ever wanted."

"I love you too, Dri." Gemma embraces her wife and unloads the syringe into Driane's neck.

Driane slumps immediately, and Gemma catches her, easing her body to the floor. Driane gives Gemma a shocked look of bewilderment before her eyes close and she goes slack.

"I'm so sorry," Gemma gasps, pulling out the needle. "You'll understand when you wake up." She clasps Driane's limp body to hers, pressing her face into Driane's hair once more, tears leaking from the corners of her eyes.

Gemma arranges a pillow and blanket under her wife's sleeping form and locks their quarters from the outside before she heads off to the Observatory, wiping her tears away as she walks.

It had to be done.

The Rite is underway.

Gemma's made the final calculations and adjustments, aimed the Observatory apparatus toward dark Sol, and all she can do now is wait. The machine hums as accumulated photons glow in a laser-focused beam out the glass bubble, swallowed by the darkness. It's too bright for Gemma to look at. She'll witness the fruits of her labors in eight minutes, once Sol's first light travels back to Earth. Everything is going to plan.

Gemma runs down the stairs to the Stasis Chamber, ready to awaken everyone. She sprints down the pod-lined aisles to the instrument panel at the hub. People from all walks of life lie ready to bring the world back online.

From farmers to engineers, teachers to soldiers. The small spark of humanity that's left, prepared to kindle a new age.

Gemma reaches the instrument panel and blanks for a moment, looking at the constellation of blinking green and amber lights spread out before her. This is Driane's domain, and though Gemma has innate knowledge of Stasis systems (as Driane does of the Observatory) it takes her a moment to orient herself.

Gemma runs through the checklist, bitterly thinking Driane should be in her place, and finally presses the button to begin bringing everyone out of stasis. A faint, low chime sounds, and pumps begin chugging in the walls to drain liquid from the chambers.

There's a grinding sound that rumbles the metal flooring, and a red light ignites, high up on the left side of the panel, under which is printed DRAIN BLOCKAGE. It begins to blink rapidly, and Gemma hits the button that opens the pods in tandem. She doesn't want people to drown in the nutrient fluid. An alarm sounds as pod doors begin to swing open, releasing fluids and tubing. A minor hiccup, but—

The smell hits her. She's never smelled anything like it before, but the animal part of her brain knows what it must be.

Rot. Decay. Putrid flesh. Dead, stinking matter pours out of each pod, spilling all over the floor in pale red chunks, spreading in syrupy pools. Noise from above draws Gemma's attention to a rain of human juice pattering down through metal catwalks, leaving stringy matter hanging from the pod doors and honeycombed catwalk flooring. The soup splashes around her and the odor coats her windpipe and tongue in thick waves. It is cloying and rancid and greasy, and Gemma throws up on herself, collapsing by the panel.

The front doors of each pod have retracted into their bases and slimy, decaying bodies hang in the sodden straps of each cradle, hair lank, skin pale, limbs bloated. The ones with some semblance of human form sport faces bulging and slack, jaws hanging, glazed eyeballs staring at nothing. Eyes that Gemma prayed would gaze upon the newly awoken Earth are blank and would only ever look into darkness. Just as Driane and she had done for the past few decades.

Every single person is dead and rotted away.

Gemma realizes the magnitude of what Driane has done. What she planned for days, or weeks now, from the looks of the corpses. Driane drained the pods of stasis liquid, allowing the bodies to fester, and rigged the alarms not to sound. The drain blockage must've come from bits of putrefied flesh clogging the hoses. Gemma heaves again and presses a sodden hand over her mouth.

She stumbles down the rows, trying not to feel three thousand dead gazes on her back, and staggers out of the abattoir that used to be the Stasis Chamber. She has failed every one of them.

Gemma pulls herself up the metal staircase, just in time to see the first pale rays of light blooming from distant, reborn Sol.

THE DEAR DARLING THINGS

JACOB STEVEN MOHR

A piece of the greater world fell glittering. She watched it plummet slowly, rotating through meager strata of atmosphere and fine half-weightless grit toward her beaming face. Blasting heat from stabilizing thrusters atomized the rock and rubble beneath their jets; then, an eternity later, there was glorious contact. The lander presented a ticklish weight. Four broad titanium alloy feet pushed into her dust, slipped sideways a few meters, then lay still. Above, the heavens roved in endless twinkling arcs, and the world poured down its blue-green splendor.

Then came the first great wonder: the tiny craft disgorged something. A ramp descended tongue-like from the curved belly, releasing down its sloping length a tiny timid mass. An offering—no. It was much more than that. A white biped, like a *yggsthoth* in drastic miniature, though closer in stature to the dark-dwelling *ghrol'lkulu*. It had stiff bulky limbs, a bulbous head, and a gold reflecting curved plate for a face. Fragile steps brought it nearer and nearer to communion. Emotions stirred deep. She had been wrong. Here was the world itself, an emissary piece broken off from the shimmering whole. A curious pseudopod, extended in exploratory greeting.

How thrilling! She struggled to remain tranquil, to quell a shiver of pleasure that might disturb her visitor. And patience met a reward; in time, a second clumsy morsel joined the first. Volcanic hearts screamed with elation. It was happening. It was happening at last. These teasing twin pressures bounded childlike, with skidding steps, exploring. Exploring *her*. She marveled. She had not expected the world to be so young, so unsophisticated. But it was no matter. Contact was pleasure. Contact was bliss.

New sudden energies burned the atmosphere—blazing out from crude antennae within the guts of the landing craft. A greeting? It was not. It was an outgoing message, a sonic broadcast, vibrations intended for the greater whole. She pressed outward eagerly, adjusting to the frequency of the tremors:

"...one giant leap for mankind..."

Mankind. This word did not stir memory, nor did the others. But this was no matter. They were the world's words; the world could keep its secrets a while longer.

The two white pseudopods returned momentarily to the landing craft. Soon there was a thrum of great activity across her surface. A series of smaller devices were deployed and assembled; using these, the bipeds surveyed a greater swath of her panorama. They accepted her gifts, samplings of crumbling secretions from her surface, though they did not appear to notice her invitations toward further exploration. And they made her a present as well. A kind of banner atop a ferrous structure, affixed to her surface, its colors resplendent against her great desolation.

All the while, the buzz of their vibratory signal made her giddy as she absorbed it in secret. She could hear, under the calm of their voices, the starfire burn of pleasure in their blood. It was mixed with fear, with uncertainty—cocktailed into a delectable mixture she could lap at, drink up in great mouthfuls. And all the while her third visitor circled in another yet larger vessel, remaining in constant ecstatic communication with the two below. It was perfect. A moment flash-frozen, as though it might extend forever. And surely it would. Surely bliss like this was fated to remain, and remain and remain...

But—horror! Aching dismay! Heart-wracking agony!

A blur of chittering signals passed between her two pieces of world, and their crude and curious surveying devices began to un-assemble. These pieces were fed back into the lander, followed by the shambling bipeds. The ramp's tongue slid back between its jaws and disappeared. They'd left their gift sticking resolutely into her, the banner unfurled but hanging motionless—they were going to leave her.

They were going to *leave* her.

The vibrations began a solemn rhythmic countdown, and the thrusters hummed. Their heat brought no comfort now. How was this possible? How was this permitted? Did they not realize there was so much more of her? Were they so incurious—or merely heartless, indifferent to her pain? Did they not smell her heart-sickened pheromones, or the cosmic spatter of her tears? No, surely it could not be so. The world would not send itself across so great an expanse for such a communion, only to deny her this last feast of pleasure. It was not possible. And yet...

And yet—what if they did depart? What then? What could she do?

In the past, the world's glamour had seemed quite near at times, but in her hearts she knew it was not truly so. And she could only expand herself so far, come so close. The greater world above had deafly ignored her invitations, demurred from her flirtations and summons, for such a long time. Who could reckon when she might receive an answer like this again? Could she remain as she was for yet another age, coquettishly angling her face to catch the starlight, posturing and preening for a world she now knew cared nothing for her at all?

No—she would not do it. And the decision, once made, was easily acted upon.

The lander's thrusters had blackened the surface which opened beneath it. A long yawning crack—she extended herself through it, the grasping secret parts of herself, wrapping tight around the tiny craft and drawing it deep, and deeper within her. She could feel the hum of the world's displeasure, but she hardened her hearts against it. This was necessary. This was righteous. They would forgive her this trespass, they must. They would understand. She would make them understand. How she had adored them. How she had longed for them.

A creak, then a wrenching tearing noise…*Clumsy, clumsy.* The chassis had come apart in her eager ungentle grip. The pseudopods, the pieces of pieces of her beloved, tumbled loose in the chasm of her.

But there was no terror. No buzz on the airwaves. No siren alarm. No communication passed between these visitors and their companion above, still in constant clocking orbit. She had sealed herself. She had closed up like a mouth, and now she had them. Let more come to retrieve them, more emissary parts of the world-whole. Surely this could be spared. They could parlay, and take communion from each other. In the meantime, her innermost self shifted and flexed. They became part of her, with her. They would know her secrets now. She would teach them. There was time for that.

She pondered the last few words that had sparkled from the lander's apparatus:

"…and I'd like to thank you very much…"

Not meant for her, perhaps. But she would hear those words again, all for her very own. They would thank her. She was certain of it. When at last they understood her love, the ponderous enormity of it.

My dears. My dears, my darlings…

She would wait for that. She could wait forever.

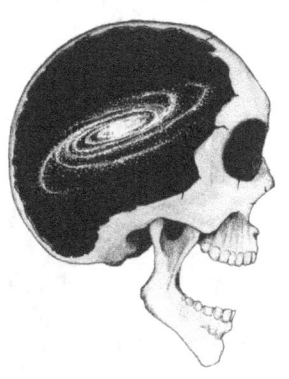

EARTH 10

TONY LOGAN

"May 2nd. Day ninety-five. Commander Gabriella Winchester's log. Kraken appears to be in good health. Her tank is relatively clean, and she has eaten the previous night's food. Darting from side to side. Normal activity for a bobtail squid." The astronaut pushed off the wall gently and floated to the other side of the room. "Second animal set, Mickey and Fievel continue, despite the lack of gravity, running circles in their circular cage. We aren't sure why they do this. But they do it in five-minute bursts. They also have eaten their evening meals and—"

"How's the zoo today, Commander?" Mission pilot Curtis Dunne floated into the lab. He rolled his shoulder while bracing his body with his free hand. A few audible pops echoed.

Gabriella stopped the recording device.

"Whoa, old man. You falling apart already? We still have eighty-six days till we get to go home."

Curtis nodded emphatically. "I know. You give me a countdown every day, Gabby."

Gabriella stared at the racing rats. "I can't help but wonder what it's like to be ignorant of your surroundings like them?"

"I don't follow?"

"We know we're floating in space, surrounded by the black vacuum, being bombarded by cosmic rays. Any major hiccup and this whole place could explode. They don't. They eat, sleep, and carry on, unaware of the greater universe around them. Gotta be nice sometimes."

"Ignorance is bliss, you mean? Nah. I'm happy being on the top of the intelligence scale. Well, top two." He smirked.

Gabriella rolled her eyes. "I'm almost finished recording the lab behaviors. Are the Ruskies up?"

"They're finishing their morning workouts." Curtis stuck his finger in the mouse cage and wiggled it.

"Good, the treadmill will be free soon. Better be careful. Mickey bites."

Curtis withdrew his finger. "Still ready for tonight?"

"Yeah. Max has no idea. Which is great. I'm getting tired of hiding—" Gabriella froze as Cosmonaut Maxim Balandin floated into the adjacent module. He wiped his sweaty black hair with a towel and sipped from a drink pouch. He nodded to Curtis and waved to Gabriella.

His counterpart, Viktor Kozlov, drifted in behind him with a spoon dipped in a peanut butter bag. "Dobroye utro."

"Morning to you too, Vic. The gym all squared away? I want to get my workout in before the Capcom briefing."

"*Da.* Roscosmos has similar call transmitting in two hours," Vic said, his voice gravelly and thick with an accent.

Gabriella would never say it aloud, but Viktor reminded her of a Bond villain. He wasn't rude or mean. Just stoic. They were all in good shape, but his build was intimidating.

Curtis grabbed the side of the capsule and propelled himself into the common area.

With the flick of a few switches, Gabriella concluded her lab reports on the animals and then moved to the gym module. In the last month, a quiet tension grew on the International Space Station. As Russia moved to occupy border countries, tensions between them and the UN ratcheted up.

ISS Gym was a small space attached to the lab with an exercise bike and a treadmill. Not high-tech, but necessary to fight natural muscle and bone loss from being in space for months at a time. The way the leg and waist restraints pinched her smaller frame as she ran always distracted her from enjoying her workouts. She would add it to the multiple minor problems aboard the station. The station was fairly accommodating for being almost thirty years old. A beep sounded, and the machine stopped, ending her run. She gasped in short bursts as she freed herself from the Velcro straps.

A voice called out from another module. "Gabby. Come on! We're live with Capcom in six minutes." Gabrielle rubbed herself down with wipes as she drifted. Her long sweaty brown hair would make Medusa feel self-conscious, but she had learned to let go of superficial appearance customs, especially on a ship with three men. Although, the removal of bean paste from Max's dinner menu selections was a command decision she had to make. Her face scrunched at the memory.

Gabriella stretched her shoulders as she floated into the closet-sized communications mod. The room grew brighter as Curtis turned on the monitors. Every wall of the ISS had items strapped, duct taped, or Velcroed to them, but she squeezed in.

On the monitor, Ground Commander Rodriguez appeared grim. Bad news was coming.

"Good morning, ISS. I must ask if you are alone? Sensitive items need to be discussed."

Gabriella looked at Curtis. Stoic concern had already settled across his face. He pushed off the wall and allowed his head to poke out into the main corridor, returning quickly with an *all clear* signal.

"Go ahead, Commander."

Curtis stayed on the edge of the capsule keeping an eye out. Gabriella switched the monitor to text only and hit the mute button.

She took a deep breath and read. The text confirmed her suspicions about Russia's instability.

After signing off, she stared at Curtis. "It's Vic and Max. They are our friends."

"I understand, but if Russia does go to full-on war with everyone, we have to be ready for *any* scenario." Curtis put his hand on her shoulder.

"Let's just stay vigilant for now."

They glided into the corridor. At the other end, Max sipped from her drink pouch. When Max saw the Americans, he smiled and waved. He held up a drink packet with her color sticker on it. Capcom nutritionists sent her a load of Green Tea packets in error. She hated the aftertaste, but Max liked them, so she let him help himself.

The Roscosmos communications pod flickered down the hall. Viktor was having a briefing. Being the team leader, he received it alone and would debrief Max later.

Gabriella nodded.

It was customary for everyone to report to the common area—the largest room toward the center of the station—a few times a day, especially for evening meal. They would eat, play cards, or read separately, but in close proximity. It helped them bond. Gabriella could sense the tension in the air, but everyone pretended it wasn't there.

Each person had their own food. Hand-picked by the organization's dieticians and adjusted to individual taste.

The crew prepared meals in rotation. Tonight, it would be Curtis, then Max, Then Gabriella, and finally Vic.

Curtis put his pork hamburger with egg in the heater. When he withdrew his hand, he chuckled and pulled a red sticker off his hand. "Oops. My food sticker came off." He stuck it to his chest and sipped his tea through the straw.

Gabriella hadn't seen a sticker come off accidentally. Sure, they had heard tales of astronauts peeling them off and applying them to another's granola bar in a half-handed attempt to get another one, but they normally stay attached.

Unless the stickers were tampered with? She had snuck contraband in her sleep pod, hadn't she? Surely Vic and Max could get stuff onboard. Her heart quickened. Her body fought a shiver as she felt Viktor staring at her. He made her nervous, but he wasn't a killer, right? If she was wrong and accused them, they'd shun her. Her gaze followed the long hall to the emergency return capsule. She bit her lip.

Curtis pulled his food from the warmer. "Yikes." He released it and let it hover in front of him as he shook his hand in the air. "Too hot."

Max was up next. He placed his pouches in the warmer.

Curtis leaned over to Gabriella and whispered into her ear. "You got the Ruskies' stuff?"

She nodded to a bag velcroed to the left of her. "In there."

Vic turned his head toward them. He glided over to the bag and snatched it from the wall. "*What's* in here, Commander?"

Curtis floated over to Vic. He grabbed the Russian's shoulder. Vic braced himself and shoved Curtis into the food warmer, sending food packets floating in all directions.

"Do not be putting your hands on me, Pilot Dunne."

"Calm down, Vic. It's not what you think." Curtis righted himself and held up his hands.

"I think I be the judge of this, Pilot Dunn." He unzipped the bag and turned it inside out. Four mini vodka bottles and a chocolate brownie pack spun in the air in front of them. Confusion flashed across Vic's hardened face.

"I got a friend of mine to smuggle them in a resupply last week. It's Max's birthday today. Well, according to Russian time. It's all relative in space, I guess. We only have a couple of candles and they're too big for the pouch." She smiled.

Max's eyes lit up. "Wow! That's outstanding." He sipped from his drink pouch.

"Can we mix them with our pouches, I wonder?" Gabriella asked.

Victor glared at the Americans. "Russians drink vodka straight."

"Hey it's fine, Vic." Curtis patted Vic's arm. "We're all jumpy. Floating in space in a pressurized tube a couple of hundred miles above Earth will do that." Curtis grabbed his food and drink pouch and sipped. "We have to let what's happening on Earth be—"

Curtis' face scrunched up and his eyes widened. Doubling over, he convulsed in the air. Vomit and foaming saliva expelled from his mouth.

Gabriella launched herself toward him. She pulled him close as his body stopped. "Did you poison him, you fucker?"

"Da. Both of you. Your drink packets."

Max spit liquid from his, then spun wildly and vomited. He kicked while clawing at his throat, eyes bulging as panic flushed his reddened face.

"We switch packets sometimes, Victor. You killed your own man!"

Victor pushed off the wall behind him, rocketing toward Gabriella.

Gabriella launched herself down the long corridor.

Red lights flashed inside the ISS, indicating an emergency message from Homebase. She watched Victor float toward his monitor. While guarding the corridor, she scrambled into her survival bag and pulled her knife. Less than two inches long but razor sharp. She stayed, her gaze peering down the hall. Broken words came through the static-filled monitor.

"Launch...Devastated...Supply...God..."

A viewing window confirmed her fear. Hundreds of pinpricks of white circles appeared and spread across the Earth's surface. Gabriella's body shook. Tears streamed from her eyes as nuclear fire expanded over the surface. She punched the window and screamed until her throat cracked raw. Curling into a ball, she shuddered.

Gabriella thought of her father. When she was young, he would take her to the pier at night and set up his telescope. Spending hours hunting comets or watching meteor showers. He would give her a quarter for every constellation she could name by sight. After high school, when she told him she was going to college for Astronomy and then to work for NASA, it was one of the few times she had seen him cry.

"Gabby, I'm so proud. Your name will be a part of history."

She dug her fists into her aching eyes. Through blurred vision, her father's home, Boston passed by below. It changed from greens and browns to blacks and reds. Her only comfort was he died quickly.

She went over the events in her mind. The EBS wouldn't have had time to tell the world, and even if they did, Dad didn't watch much TV. His phone was on the charger in the kitchen. He'd be asleep in his chair with a Crichton novel in his lap. Moxie chewed a bone at his feet. There'd be a loud bang, Moxie jumped and ran into the bathroom. Dad sat up for a moment but lay backward. The quakes and shocks came next, but shortly after, everything would have been consumed in a million-celsius fire. There are worse ways to go.

Gabriella rubbed her swollen face on her sleeve and watched the corridor for Victor. He would come for her, eventually. A vodka bottle spiraled slowly past her. Plucking it from the air, she got an idea.

The entire station shuddered. Gabriella grabbed onto the sides of the module. Once the turbulence calmed, she snatched her drink pouch and knife. At the far end of the hall, Viktor glided in.

"What's happening, Viktor?" Gabriella called down the hallway.

"The thrusters controlling the degrading orbit have failed."

"I don't believe you."

"It's true. I disabled them."

"The entire station will crash."

"Da." His gaze lingered on her utility knife. "What you going to do with blade, zhenshchina?"

"Whatever I need to." Gabriella held it in front of her.

Viktor scoffed. "This station…" He waved his finger around. "…will crash. I'm taking the escape shuttle to the Earth and landing in Russia."

"Russia's gone, you moron. Everything is gone."

"Untrue. It looks bad from here. Once the fallout lands. I will be safe with my family underground. Promises were made to me."

"That's how you justify killing your crewmates?"

Viktor looked back at Maxim's body strapped in his sleep pod. "That was regrettable, but he wouldn't have had the steel to dispose of you Americans. His sacrifice will be remembered. In the New World. The Russian World."

Gabriella scoffed. "You gonna kill me too?"

Viktor shook his head. "Nyet. You remain onboard."

He turned and swam toward the long hall leading to the shuttle docking.

Gabriella grabbed the edge of the capsule and yanked herself forward.

Viktor torpedoed himself with fast-grasps of the walls. He approached the door lock and typed in the access code. The latching mechanism clicked a few times, then, with a loud clunk, the door popped open.

Gabriella tackled Viktor against the wall. They rolled around like sharks in a fishing net. Viktor's size and strength weren't as advantageous as she had imagined. Gabriella slashed her knife at Vic, opening a wound on his hand. Blood spread out through air in a collection of wobbly bubbles. Viktor braced himself with his legs and grabbed Gabriella's knife hand. His other hand closed on her throat. He squeezed.

Gabriella choked and let the knife spiral away. Viktor grabbed her with both hands now. Her head filled with incredible pressure as she gasped for breath. She snatched her juice pack from floating nearby and sprayed it all over Viktor's face and up his nose. Viktor released his grip and leaned away, coughing and swiping at his face. He coughed. "Tea can't save you,"

"It's not tea, comrade." She lit a match. The spilled vodka hung in the air making a fuse. Viktor's eyes widened as he watched the ignited liquid follow the path to him. His face burst into a fireball. Gabriella grabbed the capsule's door frame and kicked him, somersaulting his body down the hall. Fire engulfed the clothes and the end of the hallway. She slammed the door shut and launched the escape vehicle. Her head smashed into the top of the shuttle as it launched. Before her vision darkened, an explosion rocked the shuttle.

Gabriella awoke floating in the cabin. Pain throbbed from the bump on her head. She rolled her neck and strapped into the pilot chair. Forcing a glance through the windows, debris from the station filled the area. The Earth was still burning. The opposite window filled with a dull blue light. She leaned over and the moon glowed against the black void. It seemed so close, yet she knew it was two hundred and thirty-nine thousand miles away.

"Two hundred thirty-eight thousand, nine hundred miles away." She heard her father's voice in her head. He hated when she rounded up anything in astronomy. He was gone now. Mom was too. And she never got to make it to the moon like she had promised.

Wait. Why not?

There was a standard two-week supply of food in the cabin. Mostly protein bars and a couple of jugs of water with cleaning tablets. She aimed the ship at the moon and turned the thrusters to full. The small ship blasted toward the rocky satellite. Although her ship wasn't technically built to make the trip, Gabriella would make it to the moon or die trying.

A week and a half later, Gabriella could make out geologic patterns on the surface. She would prefer to land on the moon, not die in a crash on the surface, but technically, either would fulfill her promise. Aiming for the smoothest patch of rock, she descended. Slowing the ship's descent used the rest of her fuel, but she wasn't leaving. The craft buckled and shook as she entered the moon's light atmosphere. Her shuttle landed rough and scraped to a complete stop. Gasping for breath against the restrictive harnesses, she could see the blackened planet she once called home.

She read her instruments. The celebration would be short. She had two protein bars left and maybe twelve ounces of water. These things didn't really matter, with only two hours of air left. She smashed the air gage panel. Spending her last moments counting down like a New Year's Death party wasn't ideal, so she sang a few songs she loved. A Bowie favorite seemed appropriate. She knew the air grew thin when the hallucinations began.

She stared at the gray rocky surface of the moon.

"I wasn't the first human on the moon, but I would be the last."

There was a comfort in that.

She smiled as a tear rolled down her cheek. "I did it Dad. I had to improvise. But I did it."

Green and yellow lights encircled the remains of Earth. Voices echoed around her shuttle. A male-sounding one and a female-sounding one.

"What a shame." The female one said.

"Yeah. I thought we had it this time." The male replied.

"They always end up blowing themselves up. I told you they don't need nuclear power."

Gabriella trembled. "Uh, hello. Is someone out there?"

Silence.

Then the female spoke. "I thought you said they were all gone?"

"I checked it. Zero survivors on Earth Ten. Only a few deep-sea animals and some microbes."

"Well, somebody's left. And now they have heard us."

"Hello. I'm Gabriella. Who is out there?"

"Hello Gabriella. Umm. You can call me Alicia." The female voice said.

"Alicia?" the male voice questioned.

"I like that name. Just pick one," Alicia said.

"Okay. I'm Tree. Where are you, Gabriella?" The male voice said.

"Tree? That's not a name?" Alicia snickered.

"Uh, I'm on the moon. Where are you?" Gabriella asked.

"That's it! That's why she didn't register in the Earth program. A-lish-a."

"You didn't allow for anywhere else?" Alicia asked.

"They barely got anywhere with space travel. They hadn't since Earth 4, remember?"

"Are you God, then?" Gabriella asked?

Silence.

"Yes," Tree said in an ominous tone.

"Stop it, *Tree*. Don't fool with the lady. She just watched her planet die. Poor thing," Alica said.

Gabriella coughed.

"Are you okay, dear?" Alicia asked.

"Air's almost out. Going to suffocate soon."

"Tree, give her more air. Hurry!"

"I can't just give her more air. I'd have to write a code for that specific shuttle. It would take longer than she has."

Gabriella slumped in her chair. "Goodbye."

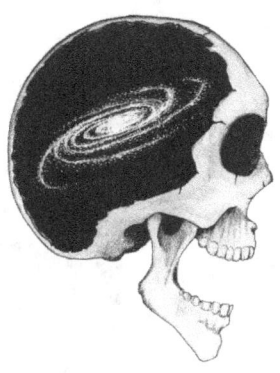

NECRONAUT RETRIEVAL FAILURE

KIM Z. DALE

"Rest in peace among the stars." That was the company's tagline. The advertisements showed a smiling actor being propelled into space. When the airlock seal hissed open, the fictional client relaxed their head against the back of the capsule. They closed their eyes and fell blissfully into death while floating into star-speckled vastness. No pain. No terror. No soul-eating alien lifeforms.

The reality of assisted space suicide differed significantly from those advertisements. First of all, no one was truly allowed to "rest in peace among the stars." Leaving a bunch of dead bodies floating around in space went against the UN's Space Debris Mitigation Guidelines. No one wanted astronauts crashing into a corpse on their way to the ISS. That's where necronaut retrieval came in. My job was to collect, process, and return the remains of people who paid millions of dollars for the privilege of dying in space.

Dying in space can take up to two minutes, but people become unconscious after the first fifteen seconds. Fifteen seconds may not sound like much, but it's an excruciatingly long time for someone asphyxiating in a vacuum while the gases in their body expand and stretch their skin to its limits. Virgil warned me that the faces of retrieved necronauts often froze in expressions of agony and terror.

Virgil, the senior retrieval engineer, was on the very first necronaut mission and has been on every one since. No other retrieval engineers came back more than once. I asked Virgil how he felt about all the time he spent on Purgatory, the necronaut retrieval station.

"Purgatory is my home. The company makes me go back to Earth periodically for physical exams and mandatory time off, but if I had my druthers, I'd always stay up here with them."

"The necronauts?"

"The stars! On Earth I can only dream of them."

"I admit it's different, but you can still see the stars from Earth."

"Only with my eyes!"

Virgil was a bit strange, but I was trying my best to get along with him. He was the only other person on the retrieval station who was still alive.

By the time the necronaut capsules reached the retrieval zone, their passengers were already dead and frozen solid. Upon their arrival, we used the station's large robotic arm to transfer the bodies to the cryomation chamber. Once everyone was inside the machine, I hit the button to make the interior mechanisms vibrate. The vibrations slowly increased in intensity, shattering the frozen corpses into dust. The remains were then vacuum-sealed in pouches the size of throw pillows for easier storage.

At first, everything was the same as in my training simulations. The sensors indicated that the newest set of necronauts were being effectively disintegrated. A gage showed the volume of residual metals—such as dental fillings and medical implants—being separated for recycling. I watched the machine out the window, pleased with how well I was handling my first set of retrievals.

Then, I saw the lights.

Hundreds of tiny lights were seeping out of the cryomation chamber. I worried they were sparks. I thought something had gone wrong with the machine, but sparks usually radiated out from their source. These lights darted back and forth like tiny fireflies. Like they were alive.

"Virgil! Are you seeing this?"

Before he could answer, the swirling cloud of twinkling flecks shot at the window of the station. I jumped away as they thwacked against the glass. Unlike bugs hitting a car windshield, the lights continued to move after impact. They slid across the smooth surface until they formed letters: S-A-V-E U-S.

Save us.

Virgil let out an angry swear, which was almost as startling as the weird lights since I'd never heard him say so much as *darn* before. He hastily closed the shutters as the lights shot away into the darkness.

"Why'd you close the shutters?"

"They've never been able to communicate before. It's a troubling sign," he said, more to himself than to me.

"Who are you talking about? What were those lights?"

"The couriers."

"What type of couriers? They looked like nanotechnology. Are they some sort of experimental project?"

"In a way."

"They flew out into nothing. Where are they going?"

"The couriers return to the stars. It's their job. Just like your job is to feed them."

"Feed who? Or what?"

Virgil reopened the shutters and gazed out the window as he spoke. "You know them as stars, but that's not technically correct. Earth's scientists can't see many details of things that are very far away. They assume every dot of light in the night sky is a giant fireball like the sun. That's true for most of them, but some of what people call stars are something else. Some of those stars are living creatures."

"Wow. So that's what I saw out there? Living stars flying around?"

"No! I already told you. Those are the couriers. They collect sustenance that the Overseers—the living stars—need to survive."

"What do living stars eat?"

"Human souls."

"Human souls?"

"Well, any souls really. It's just that here, in Earth's orbit, we specialize in supplying human ones."

"What do you mean 'supplying' human souls?"

"The souls have to be broken into very tiny pieces for the couriers to be able to carry them to their luminary Overseers. Luckily, the cryomation process breaks down more than the necronauts' bodies."

"Why do the couriers want us to save them?"

"They don't. It seems that for a few moments the souls were able to control their transports in order to send a message. I suspect some residual bits of your predecessors' psyches found a way to communicate with the others."

"My predecessors?"

"Yes, the previous people who served in your role didn't approve of our arrangement, so they had to be sacrificed. It seems that even in death they maintained their opposition to our cause."

"Our cause? I never agreed to be a part of this."

"Then you will become another soul to be consumed."

"Virgil, this is crazy, but even if it's real, you're an old man. I don't want to hurt you, but if it comes down to it—if you try to kill me or something—I'm pretty sure I can take you. I'll tie you up and call back to Earth and…"

"You are probably right. You are strong enough to overpower the old man, but you are not stronger than us."

Virgil—or the body I had known as Virgil—opened his mouth. His jaw unhinged and his lips spread until I was staring into a void the size of a large wall mirror. Inside the maw was as dark as the expanses of space, but its center glowed with a murmuration of tiny, fiery parasites. It was a miniaturized version of the swarm I had seen over the cryomation chamber.

I ran. The station wasn't very big, but I tried to get as far away as I could from my alien-infested coworker. I needed to get to the comm center and notify Earth. I needed to find a weapon. I needed to do something, but all I could think to do was run. I weaved through Purgatory's metal passageways. Virgil's footsteps echoed close behind me, moving with a speed I was sure the old man's body wouldn't have been capable of alone.

My thoughts swirled with all the recent revelations. Alien lifeforms! Soul harvesting! Murder! Unfortunately, my lack of focus caused me to run straight into a dead end—the worst dead end. I had cornered myself in the airlock used to exit the station for repairs. Of course, if I were exiting the station to do repairs, I would put on a space suit first, but I knew my pursuer wasn't going to allow me that preparation.

"You should feel lucky. Most people have to pay a lot of money for the privilege of dying in space."

"You don't need to do this," I said to the thing I once knew as Virgil.

"The Overseers require sustenance. This is how they survive."

"I understand that everything needs to eat, and taking the necronauts makes sense. They wanted to die. Maybe they didn't actually sign up for having their souls eaten by aliens, but at least they were already dead when it happened. I'm sure your Overseer star things didn't intend for you to kill people just to get their souls."

"They do not care about our methods. They only care that they are hungry. And they are very hungry." Then, Virgil or the parasites within him opened the airlock.

Like I said, fifteen seconds may not sound like much, but it's an excruciatingly long time for someone asphyxiating in a vacuum while the gases in their body expand and stretch their skin to its limits. Floating like a grotesque balloon, I pictured Virgil at the controls ready to retrieve my body for processing. What would it feel like to have my soul eaten by a living star?

Lights sparked before my eyes, but I wasn't sure if they were the couriers or a symptom of my forthcoming unconsciousness. As dizziness took over, a thought entered my brain that was not my own. It was a message. I could sense it was instructions. I was being told how to warn others, but the details came in fuzzy like a radio station just out of broadcast range. I tried to focus on the thought. Just when I almost understood, my fifteen seconds were over, and I fell into oblivion.

A PROMISE; A SURPRISE

AI JIANG

He bought me a star, placed it in my palm
in the form of a certificate—*75% off*—
between slender fingers so thin, almost translucent.
The red ink of the verification stamp half faded, bleeding,
melting into the date of purchase half smudged.
He rushed to get it a day before my birthday, I knew,
but he'd tried to cover, change the shape of the numbers,
so it seemed as though he had been planning this for ages.
A promise was what he said it was. *A promise*

for what?

He left for that very star on the certificate months later,
telling me just before he boarded his ship that it was a not a star—
it was a planet. And that it was meant to be a surprise.
A surprise for what? A new energy source, brighter than the sun,
more luminous than the moon, more alluring than the twinkle
in my eye. And he would bring it back, just for me.
But the way he spoke of it, eyes aimless, wandering, glowing,
told me he would bring back the light but leave himself behind.
And the promise? The surprise

for what?

STELLANOVA

C.R. BEIDEMAN

. . . the faith of my own eyes.
—Tycho Brahe

Karakum Desert, 1572:

To escape King and his palace and his subjects, I have built an observatory in the desert. A strange new star hangs in Aristotle's immutable Heavens, and I must read what God has written there. I have been ready for aeons and this is my exit. My camel is outfitted and saddled. I ride solitary but I'm never alone.

Endless sandstorms renew the desert and I am wreathed in myopia. When it settles it will not be the same Karakum, I will have changed as well. Already my camel's eyelashes shimmer with wind-cast grains. The iron key hanging from my neck chimes with the silver bridle. Ungulate strides—a lifting and falling rhythm—hold me in a spell. I endure the wind-cast grains like swarms of gnats in King's marsh where our hounds sniffed morels. There I spoke of fortune's wheel, of riddles in the stars. What does the ghastly *stella nova* portend?

My compass needle flicks in the presence of iron. I must wait for darkness before I may navigate. But as I ponder the mystery, the storm quells, and the silo materializes before me. I could have ridden right by.

I keep the only key. I keep this secret far from King in the heart of the desert where the air is dry and the stars steady. Were I to allow anyone ingress, they would use my instruments and observe my Heavens, and my instruments and my Heavens would be marred. I remove my sand scarf and the key from my sunken neck. The forged lock groans as I turn with both hands. I unload the heavy burden from my camel and carry it on my back. Inside, my hoarded larder remains unspoiled. Wine and water. Sacks of grain. Barrels of salted meats and fish from the Baltic Sea. This shady tower brings relief, but the star is burned foremost upon my mind's eye. Glad to be rid of the spitting camel, I shoulder the door closed. She will return to King without me. I lock the door. Silence carries up the silo and down my ear canal, disintegrating to electricity and settling like silt to a bed of sedimentary memory. Standing here in the dark, I recall with hesitance my bull elk, Elskede—mane the color of winter moonlight, antlers outstretching any wingspan—who roamed the palace's corridors, possessing a different kind of majesty. A gift from King.

An arc of light drips through the shuttered dome. Sand rests in miniature dunes upon the marble floor. My dull eyes adjust to the dimness, distinguishing my possessions: kegs of water and coastal wine, stacks of firewood and sacks of flour, my detailed map of Hven and the plans for my first observatory, Uraniborg. My astrological wheels hang brittle on the concave walls. My crucible and lead bars and gold ones, my stoppered herbal tinctures, my eyes dismiss them all as the pursuits of an overactive mind. Mere remnants of youth.

I remove my itchy silver nose, burnished by sandstorm, and place it on its holder on the ebony mantle. Seeing my nose on display, I think of young Johannes who with gall peeked behind my little mask, and who carries in his impetuous head the fate of astronomy.

I do not tarry. My arthritic fingers crank, and each clanking gear might as well trace a second, a year, a millennium, because at my age and in this desert, time is nothing. Above, the arc of light grows. The brisk tower becomes a heat sink. Standing here illuminated, I study the gilded torch holder bearing my likeness. In bas-relief I see myself as I was—my mustache full, my body round and ready to burst. My expression seems one of waiting to be excused.

I built the silo to eighty of King's feet, and I do not hesitate ascending the spiraling steps. This star has rekindled in me the fevered haste of youth. But as I place my foot upon the first stair, unbidden I see my Elskede lying inebriated and broken at the foot of the palace stairs, his bulging black eyes reflecting torch flame. That was the night my revels ceased. If only I had been able to excuse myself.

Winding makes my head dizzy, and my burden curls my back. The air thins. I must rest. Men measure history by kings, but history is also interregnum, interregnum, interregnum.

I reach the loft where an early moon rises against a peach-colored sky. Its sliver hangs like a sleeping eyelid. The alloy skeleton reaches for the Heavens, shining concentric cylinders narrowing toward the prism. I have brought the glass—polished by Johannes' steady young hands. Placing the first lens, I see myself reflected. I see the exposed cartilage where the insulted sword removed my nose. I see my wine-stained mustache and beard. I see my bald, spotted dome. And I see my twin, who died before baptism. I fear that my life has been a long return—that my skull and his (cremated long ago) are becoming one.

By the time my instrument is prepared, the stars shimmer like wind-cast grains. One of them intrudes upon these immutable Heavens.

The new desert night burns the tip of my missing nose as I point my enhanced eye beyond Mars, who no longer amuses me, and I am painlessly stretched through the astral marsh to Cassiopeia. I focus my instrument and measure the new star. The incomprehensible distance pins me to my three-legged stool. I shiver until dawn when the merciful stars fade from my sight.

All but one.

Upon waking, my eyes expect to see King's palace and my ears to hear church bells, but I am alone in the desert, my camel gone the way she came, and still the terrible *stella nova* lingers in the Heavens. Do I trust you, Aristotle, or my own blaspheming eyes? Is this my observatory or is it my prison?

THE CHILD OF MISERY

SALVADOR AYALA

Great. We're doing the hobby question. Sergio chewed his pasta a bit more thoroughly to buy himself some time. The cacio e pepe was delicious and much fancier than anything he'd ever made at home, but it didn't seem worth the price tag. At least he wasn't paying this time; it was their third date, and Richie had insisted on footing the bill. Their previous date had been a movie, and their first date was a trip to one of those axe-throwing places, so they hadn't had nearly as much time to talk about themselves. Sergio would have preferred to been asked about his research as a grad student working on medieval history; he could talk about that for hours, but he found the idea of discussing himself at length embarrassing. By now, his chewed-up pasta had been reduced to the thinnest of gruel, but he had one more tactic up his sleeve.

He swallowed the mush, wiped the corners of his mouth, and played his card: "You first."

"Man of mystery," Richie replied.

Sergio couldn't tell if he was joking or annoyed.

"I'm a bit of an amateur astronomer. I've got a real nice telescope, and I like to take it out into the wilderness and look at constellations, which makes, by the way, for a very romantic date."

"For half a second there," Sergio quipped, "I thought you were going to say that you're an astrologer and were gonna ask for my birth times and all that."

"Not that kind of gay. Ok, what about you?"

"Well…" Sergio ran out of stratagems. He frantically tried to recall what he ever did for fun, before he let his work consume his life, and finally blurted out, "This is going to sound weird, but I used to love taking trips to…um…are you familiar with Strange New Jersey? It's a website."

"Yes, I know the Strange New Jersey site. I grew up here."

"Right! Well, I didn't. So, I used to drive out to weird places from the site just to say that I did. I've been to that one cursed tree and that giant clown statue. That's my hobby, I guess. That and binging Netflix shows."

"Netflix doesn't count," Richie said, a quick glint of curiosity in his eyes. "But it's funny you mention Strange New Jersey. I've never checked out any of those places. But get this: I grew up a few towns over from the Royal Oaks Observatory."

"Never heard of it."

"No? I don't remember a whole lot, but I think it's supposed to be haunted."

The conversation drifted to other topics. Sergio couldn't stop staring into Richie's hazel eyes, really taking this opportunity to admire his features, to which his dating profile hardly did justice. He admired Richie's thin, coy lips, and the cute dimple that showed up on his right cheek whenever he cracked a joke, and that tiny scar that cut a trench in his perfectly shaped eyebrows. All of these held Sergio in rapt attention, and he soon forgot all about the dreaded hobby question.

Later that night, as Sergio lay in Richie's bed next to him, both of them panting and exhausted, the smell of sweat lingering in the air, Richie turned over to Sergio and whispered, "I just now remembered why the observatory is haunted."

Sergio stared at Richie, noticing the beads of sweat clinging on his brow and the line of muscle that ran from his ear down to his collarbone, still kind of goosepimply either from the air conditioning or from orgasm.

"You were thinking about ghosts while we were fucking?" Sergio snorted.

"Not during! Just now!" Richie caressed Sergio's chest, running his fingers through the fine black hairs. "It's pretty wild. Apparently, some rich guys got trapped there one night, and the building caught fire with them in it."

"Huh." Sergio made a mental note to check out the observatory the next time he got the chance.

A few weeks and another date went by, and he had forgotten all about the ruined observatory until one day Richie texted him a YouTube link titled:

EVERYTHING YOU NEED TO KNOW ABOUT NEW JERSEY'S HAUNTED OBSERVATORY.

Sergio was in the middle of responding to his advisor's patronizing email, asking him when he'd send over the latest version of his current dissertation chapter. Just before that, one of the leading journals of medieval literature had rejected his revised essay, declaring that it was *still* not cutting-edge enough. The miasma of failure hung in the air. Sergio welcomed the distraction. The background of the thumbnail featured a lightning bolt striking what Sergio was sure to be the Griffith Observatory in Los Angeles, and the foreground was taken up by a skinny white guy making an obnoxiously terrified face. Sergio raised an eyebrow and clicked the video. Once he got past an advertisement for car insurance, the narration began:

Hi everyone! Mr. Spooky here. Today we're talking about one of the scariest places in New Jersey. But first! Do you ever think about how safe it is to surf the web? I know I do. That's why I use…

Sergio groaned and skipped ahead a couple of times. Maybe too far ahead.

…wasn't an accident. Or at least that's how the rumor goes. It can't be verified, but many think that Pearson and others were in the middle of a black magic ritual when a vigilante mob blocked the doors and set fire to the observatory. Pearson, along with a prominent lawyer, a dentist, and some other pillars of the community perished inside. It's said that the people of Vela Township blamed Pearson and his cronies for a rash of teenagers who went missing. To this day, something lurks where the observatory once stood. Some

say it's the ghost of Pearson, seeking a final victim. Others say it's something darker and more sinister than a mere ghost. People speak in hushed tones of something called the Child of Misery. Anybody with more details, feel free to add them in the comments! This has been Mr. Spooky, signing off and reminding you to keep seeking the shadows!

Richie sent a follow-up text: "Weird date idea. Hear me out. We go look at the stars at the observatory next Saturday. I'll bring my telescope."

A huge part of Sergio was telling him to say *no*. This was someone he had met about two months ago and barely knew, even if they had great chemistry. And this date idea surely involved trespassing and lurking out in the wilderness in the middle of the night, two things that struck Sergio as especially risky behavior. And yet, another part of him whispered that this seemed like a fun outing. What was he going to do? Go out on another dinner date? Maybe go catch a comedy open mic night or a musical? Perhaps go to one of those pottery places where you paint your own coffee mug? Sergio knew how boring these things could be. The small voice grew a little louder, promising adventure and probably more romance, and promising to help him forget, at least for an evening, that he was broke and hounded by deadlines.

"This is totally my shit. I'm in," Sergio texted back.

That Saturday, Richie and Sergio trespassed on fenced-off property as the sun finished setting on a humid Central Jersey summer night. After the fire, Vela Township had closed the ruins to the public, but fans of dark tourism, or of necking under the stars, still found the right gaps in the fence. Getting up to the charred remnants of the observatory required a brief hike up a slope, and it seemed like every mosquito out for blood was gnawing on Sergio's exposed legs. A few feet ahead of him and wielding an impressively bright flashlight was Richie, who trudged up the grassy path, effortlessly hauling his telescope and its compact tripod strapped to his back.

"I don't know if you know this," Richie said, not even remotely out of breath. "I mean, I know this because I'm a big astronomy nerd, but not far from here is the Holmdel Horn Antenna."

"What's that?" Sergio huffed and puffed his way up the slight incline.

"It's where they first discovered cosmic background radiation. Back in the sixties. It was all the rage. Pearson and his buddies probably wanted to hop on the bandwagon. Maybe that's why they built this."

The dense shrubbery gave way to a clearing where nothing seemed to grow. Richie's flashlight revealed a crumbling, cylindrical skeleton of a building. A stubby dome stuck out from the top of the ruins, moonlight reflecting off parts that had not yet been covered in rust. As they got closer to the building, Sergio caught sight of graffiti scrawled on portions of wall still intact, mostly nonsensical Satanic-sounding gibberish, a few triple sixes here and there, and no shortage of clumsily spraypainted penises. Richie unloaded his telescope and began setting it up, while Sergio circled the building a few times. He couldn't explain why, but he got the sense that the two of them weren't alone.

"Who do you think is haunting this place? You think it's Pearson?" Sergio asked.

Richie didn't answer right away. He fiddled with the telescope's knobs and pointed it at different parts of the night sky. In between his calibrations, Richie stole glances at an ornate, star-shaped pendant he wore around his neck. Sergio thought he saw some movement out of the corner of his eye, but when he turned his flashlight in that direction, there was nothing there.

"I don't think it's a who," Richie said, never taking his eye from the eyepiece. "You know all those teens who went missing? I did some more reading. Pearson and his friends had been trying to summon something by sacrificing those kids."

"Easy there, Alex Jones."

"I'm just repeating what I read. Besides, you really don't think rich weirdos don't get up to no good? Witchcraft or otherwise?"

"Sure, I guess."

"Anyway, rumor goes, the night the observatory burned down, they were close to finishing something called the Child of Misery Ritual. For months, they had been torturing teens. Did you know that this observatory is built over a quartz deposit? They were hoping the quartz would pick up on all the suffering and channel that energy into a being of pure negativity that they could control. They just needed a final sacrifice that would bend the creature to their will, but they died before they could complete it. And now, their monster just wanders around here, attacking unsuspecting people in the dead of night. Of course, it's all bullshit."

"Of course," Sergio said, but Richie's bit of folklore and his flippant tone unnerved him. He thought he heard some gravel crunch, but it was just Richie moving his telescope a few feet farther from the observatory and once again recalibrating it. To Sergio's dismay, the implement was getting a lot more hand action tonight than he had gotten so far.

Once again, he thought he saw motion and turned to his left.

This time, there was definitely something there. The silhouette of something, anyway.

The rough outline of a man shambled clumsily toward Sergio. It flickered in and out of existence, and what little Sergio could perceive of it terrified him. It looked incomplete, one of its arms too short, parts of its skin transparent so that he could see its muscles and bone and intestines peeking through. Its face was a blank mass with cords and bulbous shapes writhing obscenely beneath the flesh. It vanished and then reappeared, each time with its missing patches of skin in a different configuration, revealing other parts of its emaciated anatomy. As it got closer to Sergio, the air grew colder. Sergio's vision dimmed. He grew lethargic and intuited that the faceless apparition was somehow draining him of energy, of joy. He feared what else it would take from him if it got closer. It let out a low growl and reached toward Sergio.

"Richie!" Sergio called out.

No response.

"Richie!"

The ethereal being plodded closer and closer. Sergio couldn't take his eyes off it. It reeked of mildew. Whatever hid beneath its face spasmed as if in pain. Or anticipation.

"Richie! Why aren't you answering, maaaan?!" He turned around to find Richie holding his telescope with both hands, like a baseball bat. The pendant on Richie's neck glowed faintly, and the grotesque creature hissed in defiance and backed away slowly.

"Sorry." Richie smirked. "I was just checking to make sure that the stars are right." Before Sergio could respond, Richie swung the telescope at his head and knocked him out.

Sergio might have remained unconscious had he not rolled over to his side and caught a solid whiff of the putrid rat carcass lying inches from his head. The offensive stench jolted him awake. It took a few seconds for his eyes to adjust to the darkness in the observatory. His wrists and ankles hurt from the zip ties biting into his flesh. He struggled to get to his feet, trying to gain a better sense of his surroundings. In the center of the ruins stood a crumbling pillar holding the cadaver of a gargantuan telescope that had long ago been scavenged for parts. The night sky and its pinprick stars peeked through the holes where years of rain had eaten away at the building's dome. Just around the corner, Richie chanted something in Latin—poorly.

"It's *oohmbraa*, not *uhmbrah*, pendejo." Sergio grunted as he struggled to get to his feet. His head was pounding. A small trickle of blood ran down his right eyebrow. Richie paid him no heed and continued chanting until reaching a startling crescendo. Outside, the half-formed, semi-transparent man-thing let out a mournful howl. Richie came out from behind a pillar holding a knife and a mostly melted candle.

"The pronunciation doesn't matter," he said. "Only the intent."

Sergio eyed him furiously. He focused on Richie's face and the betrayal and the anger, so that the panic coiling around the bottom of his spine wouldn't crawl up and engulf the rest of him. Richie calmly walked over and gave Sergio a gentle shove, which sent him sprawling on the ground.

"Pearson was my grandfather. On my mom's side." Richie's voice was distant and self-satisfied. "For a lot of his friends, the cult was just an excuse to do rich pervert shit. Not for him. When that *thing* went up in Holmdel, when we finally got solid proof that the Big Bang had created this universe, my grandfather went to work on this observatory as its dark reflection. The Big

Bang." Richie scoffed and continued his monologue. "The idea sickened him. A spontaneous, meaningless universe where we're just insignificant specks." He paused and stared at the curved, ceremonial dagger in his hand. "Well, it couldn't go unanswered. He believed that we *do* matter. That the strongest among us can bend the very elements to our will and call upon the stars to do our bidding. All that's needed is the right knowledge and just a little bit of blood. When you really think about it, Enoch Pearson was a true humanist."

"That's not what humanism is."

"Yeesh. It's a good thing you're so damn cute." Richie leaned in and ran his fingers through Sergio's curly hair, "Because your pedantry is a huge turn-off."

"So, what now?" Sergio said through gritted teeth. "You gonna feed me to that thing outside?"

"That? Oh no. It can't come in here. I'm going to gut you," Richie said mockingly and checked his expensive, glowing wristwatch. "In about two minutes or so. I'm going to finish the ritual, and I'm going to control the Child of Misery once and for all."

"You're a real piece of work. Did you even like me?"

"Aw. Come on. Don't take it personally. I kinda had to like you. For the ritual to work, it had to be someone I've fucked. Them's the rules. For what it's worth, I think you were pretty good at it."

Richie leaned in, this time to kiss Sergio on the lips. There was no passion behind the kiss. Only a dark glee at his eventual victory. He stopped and stared into Sergio's eyes one last time, but his cruel, counterfeit tenderness was met with a vicious headbutt. Richie staggered backward and fell on his ass. While Richie struggled to get his bearings, Sergio raised his bound hands up to his mouth and tightened the zip tie even more, numbing his hands. He lifted them high over his head and brought them arcing down and apart. The zip tie snapped, and Sergio was free to defend himself. Richie lunged at him with the blade, but Sergio sidestepped the deadly thrust. He clocked Richie with a mean right hook. The momentum carried him forward, and his bound ankles made balance impossible. Sergio tumbled down. A dazed Richie lunged at his fallen target, but Sergio caught the blade before it could find his throat.

"You're only making this harder on your— " Richie's condescension cut into a surprised yelp as Sergio bit his wrist, drawing blood. Richie loosened his grip on the knife, which allowed Sergio to get ahold of it. Realizing the tables had turned, Richie stepped back while Sergio swung the dagger madly to keep him away. As quickly as he could, he cut his leg restraints and hopped up to his feet. Richie made one last mad dash toward him.

The sacrificial blade found a victim, though not its intended one. In his desperation, Richie charged too recklessly, and Sergio buried the ornate knife deep between the stargazer's ribs. With a look of shocked defeat, Richie crumpled to his knees and coughed up a small jet of red. Sergio withdrew the knife and stepped back, ready to take another jab should he have to defend himself again, but there was no need. Something major had been severed in Richie, and his white American Eagle shirt was soon more crimson than anything else.

"It's still out there," he gurgled sardonically. "You'll never…"

But he didn't finish that sentence either. The light behind his eyes gave out, and he collapsed in front of Sergio.

Outside the observatory, the translucent, mannish thing let out a satisfied moan.

It took several minutes for the adrenaline to finally subside. But even when his heart stopped pounding a hundred miles per hour, Sergio still lacked the mental clarity to come up with a plan. He could call the police and tell them a stripped-down, less weird version of events, forever upending his life—assuming they actually believed he acted in self-defense. Which they might, given Richie's family history. Or he could try to wipe away all traces of his presence at the observatory and go home. With luck, Richie would become just another addendum in Strange New Jersey's catalogue of haunts and tourist traps with nary a mention of Sergio.

He was still trying to make up his mind when the sun started coming up. Its rays cut through the overcast sky and poured through the holes in the observatory's dome. The light warmed Sergio's tired, huddled body slightly, yet a coldness remained inside him. He suspected it might never leave. He wondered about Richie's dying proclamation and walked over to a gap in the wall to get a look at the faceless entity.

The Child of Misery stood motionless. Sergio eyed it with disgust. It cocked its gelatinous head to the side in response. With each second of daylight, its already luminous, insubstantial form grew airier and mistier. Right before it vanished completely, it stretched a withered arm out toward Sergio. He couldn't tell if the gesture was a threat or an appeal.

Sergio didn't know if it was gone forever or just for the day. He didn't know what he was going to do about Richie's corpse. The only thing he knew is that he wanted nothing to do with that abomination born of sorrow and pain and wickedness.

"Child of Misery, huh?" he said aloud. "No thanks. I'm a grad student. I've already got enough misery."

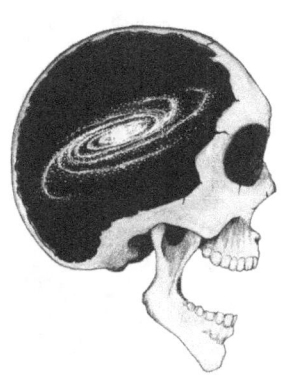

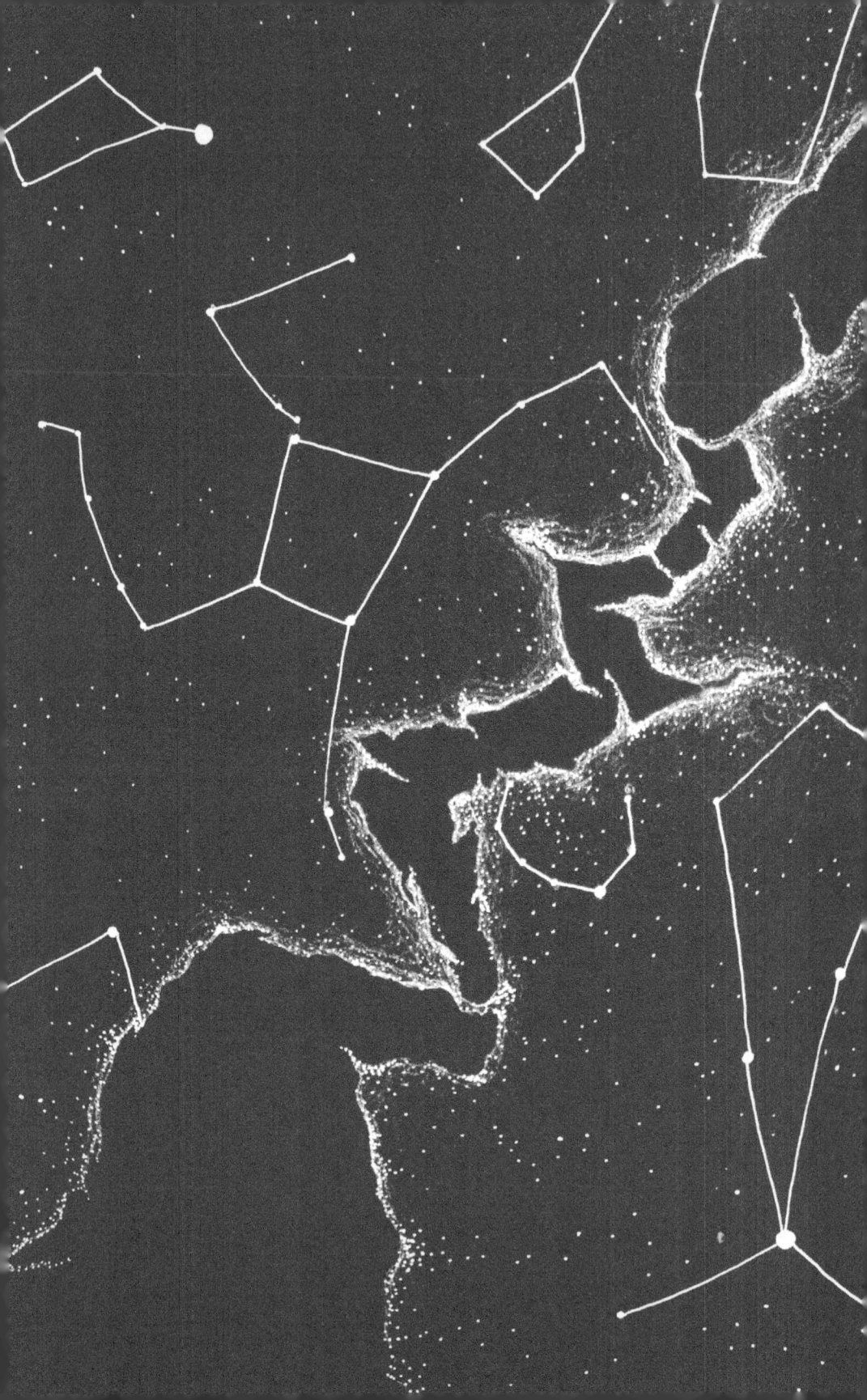

PLEASE DON'T BE A SERIAL KILLER

KATE OTA

Lyra North adjusted her microphone and smiled at the audience as their recliners moved from flat to seated positions.

"Thank you all for visiting the Orlando Planetarium. Have a stellar day."

Chatter, which had never subsided during her presentation, gained full force as the crowd of tourists hauled themselves from the comfortable seats and headed for the bright exit. Their floral shirts and casual shorts were typical for this time of year. Since receiving the heat advisory alert this morning, Lyra knew she'd have a packed house of people avoiding the theme parks.

She didn't mind the noise, except that the kids who'd rather be on roller coasters disturbed patrons who showed genuine interest. One such man, who'd sat enraptured in the front row, had been to the planetarium three days in a row, though he always left without a word. She figured he bought an annual pass, realized he hadn't used it enough for the cost, and was visiting as much as possible the week before it expired. Nothing too out of the ordinary, besides that he was cute. Today, he approached Lyra's lectern.

"What can I do for you?" She offered her best smile, though on the clock it was hard not to plaster on the usual service-sector fake grin.

"That was wild. I'd listen to you talk about stars for hours." He leaned on her lectern. "Ryan Baltum, nice to meet you."

He flashed a sexy smile. Normally, she'd panic at a guy's attention. She'd listened to enough true crime podcasts to know that's how serial killers always started with their victims. And yet there was something different and comforting about him she couldn't put her finger on.

Heat flooded her cheeks. "Lyra North. That was my last show for the weekend. I do the matinée on Monday."

He ran a hand through his thick, blond hair. It went down to his shoulders, like a surfer's, and his brown eyes studied her with sharp intelligence.

"You ever freelance? Gig economy and all? Or are you a professor and this is the side hustle?"

"No, I just finished undergrad and I'm working here to save up for grad school someday. Besides, who'd want to listen to me talk about stars without a planetarium dome?"

He shrugged. "Me. Want to hang out tonight and use the actual stars?"

She couldn't even pay her friends to go stargazing with her. It was like the man of her dreams had materialized before her. "Ye-yes. That would be great. Except—" she bit her lip. "There aren't good places in Orlando. Too much light pollution."

"I know a spot. When do you get off work?"

She hesitated. Reality check: a customer had never come to so many of her shows, and asking when she was off felt a little stalkery. But that genuine smile. He had dimples. "Eight."

"I'll pick you up."

They exchanged numbers, and he left.

Despite needing to clean up and help her coworkers in other parts of the planetarium, Lyra sank into the nearest seat and creeped on Ryan's social media. He was one of several Ryan Baltums, but his profile pictures made him easy to spot. No red flags for misogyny, racism, or other sociopathic tendencies. Not too many followers, but not too few. Only a year of activity, maybe he was a late adopter. A few pictures with other women, but not so many he seemed like a player. He liked *Hitchhiker's Guide to the Galaxy* and had attended a Doctor

Who con—exactly her scene. He had a bachelor's in math from Rutgers, but had lived in Orlando for at least a year. Something must have brought him down to Florida, and she doubted it was an animated mouse.

Finally. A normal guy—not a gym rat, conspiracy theorist, actor trying to get hired at the parks, or retired old man. And he wanted to hear her spew nerdy facts about space.

He might have been too normal. Too perfect. Most people who knew a serial killer would later report never suspecting them of anything.

"Ahem."

Lyra bolted upright in her chair and smiled at her coworker, who lurked in the shadowed doorway.

"Well, my stars, is the employee of the month slacking for once? Listening to another true crime podcast?"

Lyra rolled her eyes. "I was employee of the month eight months ago. And no, I was internet-stalking a cute guy because those podcasts have made me a little paranoid. But I'm getting back to work now."

"Did you know a professor from the university is here? She's showing the director some new celestial object to confirm someone hasn't named it yet."

"No. What kind of object is it?"

Her coworker shrugged. "Didn't catch what it is. They were talking about moving the telescope to point toward the Hercules-Corona-Borealis Great Wall."

"Interesting. Whatever it is, I hope they announce the findings later."

After work, Lyra stood outside Ryan's unscathed, but not obsessively cleaned gray Toyota Corolla. Not an exciting choice—but a serial killer would drive a boring car.

She snuck a glance at the backseat. No axes, no duct tape, no rope. Instead, it held a picnic basket and a telescope. It looked like he'd shrunk the giant backyard telescope from her childhood to be no longer than her forearm.

Ryan grinned at her from the front seat. "Ready?"

"Will we be able to see anything with that? It's so petite."

"Don't worry, it's exactly what we need."

Satisfied in her safety, she climbed in. "Where are we off to?"

"A spot south of Canaveral National Seashore."

Her stomach dropped. "That's an hour away, if traffic cooperates."

"I brought snacks." He lifted a plastic bag from the center console. "Homemade cookies."

She eyed the bag. He could've roofied the cookies. After three days of observing her, maybe he'd decided she had healthy organs worth harvesting. Or maybe he'd chop her up and feed her to the gators.

The chocolatey smell wafted out as he reached into the bag and chose a cookie for himself. Although, it could have been the only non-roofied one, and he was putting on a show.

He must have read the anxiety on her face. "We don't have to if you're not comfortable. I've gone stargazing there before, the view's amazing, but I get it, you don't know me. You can veto." He blushed.

Guilt plucked at her. If she kept assuming every guy was a serial killer, she'd be single for life. "Let me text my roommate and turn on the tracking app on my phone. And text her your picture."

"For sure. It's what I'd want my sister to do." He smiled for her camera, then pulled the car out of the planetarium's parking lot.

They spent the rest of the drive exchanging flirtatious banter. Both loved seafood and hated goat cheese. She even ate a cookie, and after half an hour without wooziness, she determined he wasn't trying to drug her.

The sunset cast the car with golden light, and Lyra enjoyed the view without Orlando's skyline. Red and pinks streaked the sky like bloody fingers dragged across the clouds. Just when her guard slipped lower, she noticed his eyes constantly flicking from the road to the sky.

"Do you see something?" Lyra asked.

"No. Just enjoying the view." He smiled, showing off those dimples again, but Lyra's stomach wouldn't unclench.

About fifteen minutes after dusk, they passed through the gate at the seashore and Ryan waved his annual pass toward the guard.

As they wove through the park, talk radio caught Lyra's ear. "—professor released an unofficial statement this evening about a strange object in the sky. Before anyone panics, we should make sure that giant lens is clean, huh?"

The radio hosts laughed and moved on.

"I wonder if that's the professor who was visiting the planetarium before I left. Guess he found something," Lyra said.

"Cool." A commercial started and Ryan turned the radio off.

"He was looking between Hercules and Corona Borealis. We can stargaze in that direction, even though that's pretty far for a personal telescope."

Ryan nodded. "Sure."

They drove through the national seashore and farther south on a road surrounded by mangroves. Finally, they parked in a lot with only two other cars. A red flag went off in Lyra's head that this place had few witnesses. Perfect for a murder. Or worse, the other drivers were in on it and they'd all murder her together.

They unloaded, and Ryan cradled his telescope like a beloved pet. It melted her heart a little. Lyra carried the food.

"This trail leads to the beach." Ryan pointed with his head, and they walked among the swampy mangroves. "Watch your step."

"I'm a native Floridian; I'm an expert at this game."

The trees and Spanish moss created a canopy so thick she couldn't see the stars, and the weak light of the waxing crescent moon barely reached them. A rickety boardwalk led over brackish water. The salty, rotting-seaweed scent of the ocean and the roar of waves reached through the forest.

Ryan turned on his phone's flashlight. "It's a little too dark. Don't want to fall in."

Lyra eyed a floating log mere feet from the boardwalk. Her anxiety said gator, and she wasn't about to mess around with that. "Yeah, good idea." She refused to add her phone's flashlight to the path; it used too much battery. If this turned into a murder situation, she needed to be able to call for help.

The creeping sensation of being watched made the tiny hairs on Lyra's neck stand straight. Perhaps Ryan didn't need weapons. He pushed his victims into the swamp at the wrong moment and then poof. Gone.

She lifted the basket's lid. If he was a killer, he'd have only brought food for one or a ton of knives and zip ties. In the darkness, she made out a weird phone charger, two glasses, a bottle of red wine, and two containers of square-shaped desserts.

Then again, maybe the second serving was for a co-conspirator—a bribe to keep Ryan's secret and—

"You okay?" Ryan touched her arm.

Lyra jerked out of her spiraling thoughts. "Yeah. I'm fine."

"Getting hungry?"

"Starving. How much farther?"

"Not long." Ryan turned back toward the trail, and his light fell on a thick log over the boardwalk.

"Wait—"

A log—nope. Always a gator in Florida. A gator rose out of the water and released a deep, angry bellow. Its mouth revealed an endless row of teeth, each as long as Lyra's pinky. Icy adrenaline spiked through her; the monster must have been twelve feet long. It heaved its chest onto the boardwalk, which dipped and creaked under the enormous weight.

"Jesus." Ryan stepped in front of Lyra and handed her the telescope while he put his arms out.

The boardwalk gave way as the giant reptile put its entire weight on the structure. Wood and creature splashed back into the murky depths, creating an eight-foot-wide gap between them and the beach.

"We can jump that," Ryan said. "With a running start, at least."

"Are you insane?" What a lame murder attempt. He might as well have asked her to leap into the gator's jaws. "Let's go back to the car."

"We really need to get to the beach."

"I understand that was your plan, but drowning or being eaten is not worth preserving this date's vibe. I'm out."

Lyra spun around and walked toward the lot.

"Lyra, please!" His footsteps slapped against the wooden slats.

She sped up.

"Hey, wait. My telescope!"

She sprinted, and he followed. Now that she was being chased, she was sure he'd been planning to kill her all along. Who else but a psycho murderer would ask her to jump over infested swamp water to get to a beach? Hard pass. Swiping left. She needed out. At the edge of the sandy asphalt, Lyra checked over her shoulder.

She tripped and fell on the telescope and basket.

"No!" Ryan rushed to her side. "Are you okay?"

"Get away!" She swatted his outstretched hand.

"Hey, calm down."

"You chased me."

"You took my telescope. I need that."

Her panic ebbed, heart slowing, and the layer of sweat on her arms left her chilled in the cool evening breeze. His reaction was understandable; she'd probably have chased anyone who ran off with a telescope as fancy as his. "Oh."

She lifted herself off his things. Her palms and knees were skinned, fresh blood blooming. Glass on the ground glittered in the moonlight. A dark puddle of wine seeped out of the basket like a wound.

"I'm sorry."

Ryan lifted the telescope gingerly. "I think the broken glass is just the wine." He tapped the side of the scope and peeked into the eyepiece.

There wasn't enough moonlight to see if the shards were bottle-green or clear. The wind died and the distant ocean roar hushed.

On instinct, she looked up. Lyra frowned. "Huh. It wasn't cloudy earlier." Not a single star winked down at her.

"Our vision might need to adjust." He spun around, looking all over the sky. His fingers tapped a keypad on the side of the scope.

The longer Lyra stared up, the darker the sky appeared. No haze of clouds reflecting the city glow, no little dots poking through patchy cover. It was as though a velvet blanket had bound the earth.

"What the hell?" Lyra asked.

"My telescope isn't working. Crap. We need to do this on the beach."

"That won't make a difference." Lyra pointed at the sky, unsure why Ryan was so concerned about the beach. "The moon and stars are *gone*."

The ground pulsed like a beating heart. Ryan dragged her away from the tree line as the plants lurched, sinking into the damp, sandy ground. Trunks snapped with deafening booms.

They exchanged panicked looks.

"What's happening?" Lyra asked.

He shook his head. "We need another way to the beach."

"Am I imagining this? Are you not seeing the problem?"

"I see it. Beach. We need open water."

Both of their phones blared emergency alerts. Earthquake. Tsunami hazard. And a message titled "Miscellaneous" that read:

We are aware of the obscured sky. Seek shelter? Don't panic.

Another tremor hit. Lyra and Ryan grabbed each other and knelt on the asphalt. The rough texture burned her scraped knees.

A black wall crept toward them from the north. She pointed the telescope at it like a pirate's spyglass, but saw nothing.

"Strange. That's where Hercules should be," Lyra said. "You think what that professor saw is doing this?"

"Yes." He grabbed her with one hand and clutched the telescope with his other. "And it's going to kill us unless we make it to the beach. If we drive farther in, there's another trail."

Ryan whipped his keys out of his pocket, and they ran to his car. They drove south, but a tree blocked the road after less than a quarter mile.

Ryan slammed his fists into the steering wheel. He turned to the north, and Lyra followed his gaze.

The black wall had come closer. Much closer. The sense of being sucked into a giant, cosmic maw overwhelmed her. This wasn't the type of death she could fight against, and she was out of time. She'd wasted so much of her life worrying. Avoiding trips to foreign countries, turning down dates, and losing sleep imagining how she'd escape far-fetched kidnapping scenarios. So much anxiety for nothing. The most frustrating part of her impending death was that she'd never understand what killed her, and what she did wrong to get there.

"We won't make it," Ryan sighed.

Pitch darkness moved along the road, swallowing rows of overhead lamps.

Time to choose her last words. "I had a good date until the gator. Thank you, I suppose."

"I wish we'd made it to the beach." He hung his head. "Then I could have taken you with me."

"With you? Where?"

"My spaceship. I tried calling it." He patted the telescope on his lap. "It can only land on open water—that's why I needed the beach. Now, I waited too long; the Devouring Nebula already ate it. That's what I get for trying to collect a human last minute."

Utter confusion battled her dread for control over her emotions. Tears rolled down her cheeks. "The *what* Nebula?"

"I should say thanks on behalf of my people. Your galaxy's sacrifice means a lot."

"My *what*?"

The darkness devoured them.

STAR OF SAN LUIS

HOLLY RAE GARCIA

Malachi pulled back his foot and kicked, sending the coyote's bones clattering down Bluewater Highway.

"Ain't never seen no coyote at the beach before," he muttered.

"We used to have one for a pet, back when I was little," Bill said. "Maggie was the *best*."

"They're not bad eatin' either." Gideon looked at the scattered remains of the animal amid the broken, dusty chunks of asphalt. Moonlight glinted off sun-bleached bones. "Well…normally."

Bill shook his head and kept walking, followed closely by the other two men. Pet or not, he'd eat two Maggies at that point if it meant a full belly. They'd existed on nothing but dried strips of cat meat stolen from a street vendor in Dallas, and a few gallons of water bartered off a group in Houston. The water had cost Bill his grandpa's old Zippo lighter, half full of fluid. The thing only worked with every other swipe of the thumb but anything that worked even a little bit seemed to be a treasure those days.

Bill turned his head to the sky and frowned. A faint light crept up from the horizon, infecting the cool night. He scanned the dilapidated beach houses on either side of the road.

"Sun's almost up, we're going in that one." He headed toward a faded yellow house perched on stilts. It all looked as if it could tumble down with the slightest gust of wind.

"There?" asked Malachi. "Why? That blue one looks way better."

"Because, dumbass…that's where *most* people would stop."

"Yeah, 'cause it's *better*. Tell me again why we ain't going there," Gideon said.

Bill stopped and sighed before turning around to face the men, who still stood in the middle of the road. "Because that's where most people would stop. And if we don't want to be bothered *again* on this trip, we don't go where anyone else might find us."

"We ain't seen hide nor hair of anyone in three days," Gideon argued.

"We have to be careful. That little encounter almost cost us everything." Bill glanced at the packages.

"Oh," said Gideon.

"Yeah, *'oh'*, now make yourself fucking useful and help me carry this shit upstairs."

Bill dropped the rusted handle of the child's Red Radio Flyer wagon he had been pulling for the last few hours. Seemed like everyone suddenly forgot whose turn it was, so he had grabbed it just to get on the damn road. He rubbed the callouses on his hands before bending to retrieve a tightly wrapped bundle.

Gideon and Malachi picked up the remaining cloth-covered items and followed Bill up the stairs, through a door with a busted lock, and into the beach house.

As the men fell asleep, the sun rose.

When Bill opened his eyes, the sun and it's scorching rays were a hazy memory in the West, disappearing with each passing minute. Bill sat on the porch, holding a few gulps of water in his mouth. He tilted his head back, slipped a slice of cat jerky past his teeth and held it there with the water, hoping to bring back some sort of life to the poor excuse for food. It didn't work.

He swallowed the water and chewed on the meat as Gideon and Malachi joined him on the porch.

Malachi sat next to Bill and poured his own ration of water before leaning against the side of the house, licking his dry lips. "Is it up yet?"

Gideon stared off toward the night sky and rubbed his feet. The thin-soled shoes he found in a house near Pearland sat in front of him.

"Nope," Bill answered. "Not yet."

They waited.

Bill tried to imagine his life before everything happened, but he honestly couldn't remember a time when he wasn't staring at the sky and waiting for a star. Since he was a kid, his grandfather had told him about the new King and the Star of San Luis that would rise above his birth. The Child would save them all, ushering in a new way of life that didn't have them nearly starving, terrified to feel the sun on their skin. Over the years, the story had grown legs, and Bill was no longer sure how much of it was true and how much of it was them just wanting to be rescued by *anything*. Bill was now forty-five, much older than most men lived these days, and he felt every bit of those years in his aching bones and stiff back. But he would have traversed three times the distance they'd come if it meant seeing the prophecies fulfilled and being able to go outside during the daytime again.

Gideon and Malachi grew up with similar stories, and they had all found each other in a pub outside Oklahoma City. Bill sat at a table in the corner drinking a pint of hooch when Malachi walked in. Malachi was much shorter than whomever he had stolen his jeans from—they were rolled up at the ankles several times over. Everyone was thin those days, but Malachi was especially so. Looked to Bill like he wasn't much longer for this world. But he carried package wrapped identically to the one in the wagon at his feet, so they were stuck with each other. It wasn't but a few hours later when Gideon had shown up, wearing one-piece coveralls with long sleeves. He was a little more filled out than Bill, and looked like he hadn't suffered as much as everyone else. His grandpa used to say that meant he came from money, but in those days money was as useless as tits on a boar hog. Gideon must have come from one of the few remaining farms that had yet to be taken over by bandits. He carried the same wrapped package. Their pale, sun-starved faces reflected the lamplight flickering from the middle of the table where they talked over drinks, getting to know each other.

They were all following the brightest star in the sky, the Star of San Luis.

Bill pulled the wagon through the broken door and held the front, while Gideon grabbed the back end; they hauled it down the steps.

Bill dropped the wagon on the ground and walked to the road. He wasn't pulling that damn thing one more day. Let the other assholes help out. The prophecies never spoke of a leader among the three men, but Bill was the one with the least amount of screws loose, so they had unofficially appointed him their boss. He was fine with that, as long as they kept moving forward. Kept following that star.

As they walked, the wagon rattled against loose chunks of asphalt. The bad wheel that had threatened to pop off since Houston finally gave up the fight, nearly tipping the contents onto the road.

"We're close." Bill grabbed the package he had so carefully wrapped what felt like years before. "Grab your shit, we carry 'em from here."

Malachi and Gideon didn't hesitate before picking up their items and continuing down the road after Bill. The men made for a strange sight, walking single-file down a dusty, unused road in the middle of the night, but no one was around to see. They had encountered only a few people thus far, and had done what they needed to protect their mission. It was too important to get sidetracked by a couple of mangy thieves.

Ahead of them, the road ended in a jagged hole. Next to it, an old sign hung haphazardly on a pole.

"San Luis Pass." Bill read it aloud, the only member of the three who could read.

They stared across the water at the remains of an old bridge on the other side.

"What do we do now?" Malachi asked.

Bill looked up at the sky, at their star. It seemed to shift to the left as he watched, shining brighter than he'd ever seen before.

"We go that way." He pointed at the star northeast of them.

They followed a side road toward a grouping of houses in tight lines, with narrow canals connecting each line of houses to the waters of San Luis Pass. A clattering behind them in the distance rang out through the still night.

The men froze. There were those who would have followed them to the King, to put an end to His new life. His grandpa had said those men would be from the Devil. Bill hadn't seen any devils on the road, so he wasn't so sure about that part.

"Hurry, let's get off this road," he whispered.

They shuffled quietly into the overgrown grass and weeds until they came to the first row of houses.

"It's time," a woman whispered from above.

They jerked their heads upward and pulled their knives from their belts, ready for a fight.

"Oh, put that shit away," the woman hissed. "Do you want to reach the Child or not?"

Malachi and Gideon turned to Bill with eyebrows raised. Bill squinted into the darkness but saw only a large shape at the top of the stairs. Behind her, the star shone.

He turned to the others and returned his knife to his belt, gesturing for them to do the same.

"Smart," she purred from above them. "Below me, you'll find a boat. It ain't much, but it's been waiting for you. Take it to Moody Island."

"Umm..." Bill said.

"Right, you don't know what that is." The woman rolled her eyes.

She came halfway down the stairs, her features still hidden in shadow. Her robes fluttered on an otherwise still night, and her red hair splayed out like a lion's mane. The woman pointed to the waterway behind her house and spoke to them like they were children. "Get. In. The. Boat. Then follow the canal until you hit more water. Then just go straight until you hit land. Think y'all can figure that out?"

Bill sighed. The old woman wasn't who he had imagined as being the helper on this leg of their trip, but the prophets certainly worked in mysterious ways, so who was he to question them?

Without answering, Bill carried his bundle to the back of her house where the edge of a metal boat reflected the moonlight. The other men followed.

"What a bitch," whispered Malachi once they were out of earshot of the old woman.

"Yeah, fuck her," Gideon agreed.

Bill took a deep breath. "Whatever. Let's just go."

He clutched his package close to his chest and climbed into the rusted boat, careful not to step on the wooden oars on the floor. Bill perched on the middle seat and stared at the dark spots along the bottom of the boat. Gideon followed, climbing over Bill and settling on the front seat. He glanced down.

"What are those?" He pointed to the dark places.

"Repairs," Bill said. "Let's hope they hold."

Malachi took the bench in the back. Once they were all settled, Malachi pushed off from the dock. Bill set his package at his feet, picked up the oars, and rowed.

The canal wasn't long, and they soon emerged into the pass. The water rippled, shimmering and reflecting the light from the star above them. In the distance loomed a bulky shadow with no reflection.

"That must be the island," Gideon said.

The oars splashed as Bill rowed toward the darkness ahead. They spoke only in hushed whispers as the boat sliced through the water, drawing them closer to the dark space ahead. Finally, Bill stopped rowing and looked over the edge of the metal boat into the water below. He poked at the water with the end of the oar, pushing straight down until he met resistance.

"Malachi, get out," Bill said.

"What? Why me?"

"Because I said so. It'll only come to your knees, quit bitching. Get out and push us the rest of the way to the bank."

The boat rocked as Malachi stood. He looked down at Bill with his eyebrows raised.

"Put one leg over the edge, then your other leg," Bill said. "Just don't fucking tip us over in the process."

Malachi climbed into the water and somehow managed to not dump all of them out of the boat. Bill released his breath. He was so close. So close to never having to deal with these two idiots ever again. Once the tip of the boat hit the bank, Bill and Gideon carried the packages to safety on the sand before turning back and helping Malachi pull the boat farther onto the beach.

They may as well have announced their arrival with trumpets as they trekked through the thick underbrush to the center of the island, but it couldn't be helped. It was pointless to do anything else anyway, since the Mother already had to know they were close.

When Bill stopped, Malachi bumped into the back of him, and Gideon fell onto Malachi. Gideon cursed beneath his breath. It was like he was traveling with fucking idiots, but who was he to doubt who the Prophets had picked?

Before them was a circular opening about twenty feet across. In the center sat a mottled brown tent, zippered shut. In front of the tent were the remains of a fire, smoke still curling from the ashes. Empty tins of canned beans and soup lay in a pile off to the side. A soft glow emanated from the thin walls of the tent, highlighting a diminutive figure within.

Bill handed his package to Gideon and cleared his throat. He raised his arms and spoke the words he had memorized as a child:

"Holy Mother Mary, we have come to bestow gifts upon the Child. For unto us a Child is born, unto us a Son is given, and the world will be upon His shoulders and His name will be called Wonderful, Counselor, Mighty God, Prince of Peace, the Great I Am."

The shadow inside the tent moved, and the flaps opened as the purring from the metal zipper echoed in the small space. A woman emerged, bent over to clear the opening. As she stood, her long dark hair fell to either side of her face, and her ebony skin glowed in the moonlight. The Mother was small in stature, but faced the three men with her shoulders back and a fire in her eyes. A long sleeveless dress clung to her curves, not leaving much to the men's imagination. A small bulge revealed her stomach, still swollen from the recent birth.

Bill's jeans tightened. It had been a long while since any of them had seen a woman, especially one so beautiful.

"What is this? Why are you here?" Mary demanded.

Malachi and Gideon's eyes darted toward Bill. This wasn't the welcome they expected.

Bill, still standing with his arms outstretched, hesitated. His grandfather had not prepared him for this. He lowered his arms and clutched his hands in front of his swollen crotch.

"We, uh…" He took a deep breath to instill the wonder and holiness the moment demanded. "We saw the Child's star when it rose and have come to worship him. We have gifts."

Mary looked at the bundled package in Malachi's hand and the two in Gideon's. Her eyes rose to meet Bill's and she squinted, studying him.

"You're not gonna leave until you see Him, I guess," Mary said.

"No ma'am," Bill said. "We're supposed to give him this stuff. Then we'll be gone, I promise."

"Well, the tent's too small for everyone, so I'll bring him on out if y'all want to see 'im." Mary ducked inside the tent.

Bill turned to the others. "This is it." His voice raised a few octaves, shaking with excitement.

Mary emerged from the tent holding the Child against her chest. He was wrapped tightly in a blanket made from scraps of shirts and other fabric, creating a kaleidoscope of colors.

The men dropped to their knees with their heads bowed.

"Get up," Mary said. "We don't have time for this. He's hungry and y'all came right at dinner time."

Bill, taken aback by the lack of reverence, quickly jumped to his feet. He took his package from Gideon and gestured to the men to follow. They placed the gifts at Mary's feet, and each unwrapped what he had protected so fiercely along the journey.

In front of Bill, a block of solid gold.

Near Gideon, a small pile of Frankincense clumps.

Malachi revealed a packet of Myrrh.

They looked up to Mary—still holding the Child—and waited for her to receive the gifts on behalf of their new Lord and Savior.

She laughed. Long and hard.

Mary chortled as tears flowed down her face and she struggled to catch her breath. Finally, she managed to control her laughter. "What *the fuck* is a baby supposed to do with that shit?"

"Gold, for the King," Bill stuttered.

"And Frankincense, to burn in the sanctuary," Gideon whispered.

Mary sighed and turned to Malachi. "And you?"

"Um…it's Myrrh. For…" He hesitated. "… to symbolize the bitter times in the Child's life, to heal, and to—"

"That's enough. Yeah, we're good. But thank you for stopping by." Mary turned to go back into the tent.

"But, Holy Mother," Bill said. "Can we at least look upon his face before we go?"

Mary froze and turned around slowly, hands still clutching the Baby in her arms. She eyed the three men. Her shoulders dropped and she sighed.

"There's a stump over there by the fire. I'll set him on it and you can look if you want to."

Mary placed the Child on the hard wood and unwrapped the blanket from around his face.

The three men knelt in front of the stump and leaned forward to look upon the Holy Child. They gasped in unison.

"This isn't…" Bill said. "That…*thing*…"

Mary grabbed the Child from the stump and held him close. She glared at the men as she walked backward toward the tent.

"He's not a *thing*," she screamed. "He's a *baby*!"

Malachi and Gideon drew their hands to the knives at their waists and looked to Bill.

"It's an *abomination*. This isn't the Holy One," Bill yelled. "This is the False God. This is…the *Devil*."

At that, Malachi and Gideon drew their knives. They all knew what to do if this happened. None of them ever thought it would, they'd assumed those were old wives' tales, yet here It was, staring them in the face.

Mary backed into the tent and placed the child on a blanket inside, never taking her eyes from Bill.

"Mary, you know. You know what has to be done," Bill said.

Bill took a step forward. Mary's eyes darted around before landing on the closest thing at hand, a thick branch she had used to keep the edge of the tent down.

She swung it, connecting with the side of Bill's head with a loud crack. He fell to the ground, blood pouring from the split above his right ear. The knife in his hand dropped to the ground beside him. A lifetime of training flashed before his eyes, and all of it for nothing. He had failed.

Mary stared at the branch in her hands, then remembered the other two men standing in front of her. She swung again, but missed. Malachi jumped forward, shoving the knife into her swollen belly.

Mary looked down in shock and pulled the knife out. Blood poured onto her dress and hands.

Malachi pushed her to the grass then yelled to Gideon, "Hold her down!"

Before he could turn his head toward Mary, Malachi's neck spun around with a sickening crack. He fell on top of her. She struggled beneath him, her head pinned to the ground by his chest. She could see into the tent, could see the Child staring at them with knowing eyes. His small hand raised toward Malachi.

Mary wriggled free, grabbed the knife she had pulled from her stomach, and held it out in front of her toward Gideon.

"Don't move." She panted, growing weak.

To the side, Bill moaned as he tried to pull himself up.

Without hesitation, Mary threw the knife in her hand toward Gideon. It landed with a wet *schlep* into his neck. Only the alabaster handle showed against his pale skin. He fell to the ground.

Bill had climbed to his feet and stumbled, not toward her, but to the tent. To her Child.

Mary screamed and ran, eyes wild and hair flying behind her. She jumped on Bill's back, screeching and pawing at his eyes with her nails. He continued forward, blood spurting from his face and his head wound.

He ducked into the tent and raised his knife.

Mary dug her hand into the cut on his head and clenched her fist, gripping the blood-matted hair and open skin. She yanked back. He fell toward the Child on the blanket.

It was all going to be for nothing. The man would fall on the Child and surely kill him. Mary screamed as they fell together, never loosening her grip on the hole in the man's skull. They were inches from the Child when they froze.

Mary knew what was happening, the same thing that happened with the last group who tried to harm her Child.

The Child was fighting back.

Mary climbed down from the man's back while his body hung by invisible strings.

The Child gripped the edge of His blanket and giggled.

Mary grabbed him and ran from the tent. Behind her, she could hear the man's body hit the ground with a thump, then stillness. She sat by the remains of the fire, still holding the Child. A tug at her waist drew her attention to the ragged knife wound in her stomach. The surrounding skin pulled together and cinched tight. He was healing her. Again.

Mary picked Him up and held Him against her breast, pulling the top of her shirt down. He nuzzled against her, rooted around until He found her nipple, and began to feed.

He stared back at her with eyes as red as fire. The dark color had overtaken the white sclera so all that could be seen was a deep, blood red. He blinked and the sucking slowed as He grew tired.

Mary pulled Him from her breast with one arm and laid His blanket down on the grass with the other. She placed the Child on the colorful blanket and watched Him sleep until the first rays of sunlight crept through the dark. Mary pulled the sides of the blanket up and over the Child's arms and legs, covering the dry scales that consumed His skin.

"At least we'll have food for a little while." Mary eyed the bodies around them. "I'll take care of you. Always." She leaned down and nuzzled the Child before pulling away and smiling. "Until the last of the old prophets are gone."

She carried Him into the tent and placed Him on the floor. She rolled the man's body away from them and through the flap before zipping it shut.

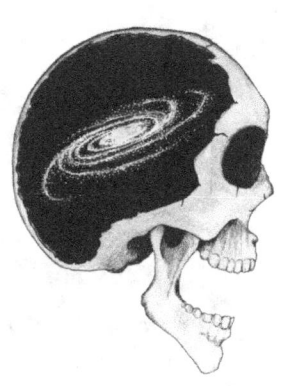

GAZING

AVRA MARGARITI

To watch the stars we have to pay
The lucky few in money
Others in kind
Favors, tithes, and pounds of flesh.

I offer the fingernails of my left hand
Ripped straight from the root
With stiffly rusted pincers
The scream wrenched from my throat
Replaced by a sigh—sweet anticipation.

I step into the meadow, bleeding hand
Clutched to my chest, my scarf
A makeshift gauze.
Armed handlers enter secret codes
The vaulted ceiling sliding back, a flap of skin
Unlocking a single stripe devoid of smog.
Black firmament, bright embroidery
Baroque frills of luminosity.
Castor, Pollux
Each diminutive distant star, an exit wound.

I watch and watch, ravenous eyes devouring
My mind filled with coppery wonder
As a timer counts down
The seconds in the background:

Sixty,
Fifty-nine,
Fifty-eight,

The handlers tightening their grips
Around their rifles.

I twirl in the night-washed meadow
Of my domed and blindsided city
Diamond blood dripping around me
Like shooting stars.

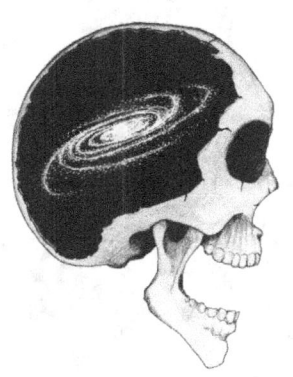

IN THE MOMENT

GRACE R. REYNOLDS

Carnage. Bloodshed. Total loss of human life. Why would anyone want to preserve such horrors; why would someone want to relive moments of malice caught in a series of photographs? When a person looks back on their life, they're supposed to think of specific moments in time. Moments captured frame by frame through a camera lens that should forever immortalize something important to them: a feeling, a place, or people they love.

Why did Alma Krpan take those photos? The Jackson, Wyoming police department were stunned when they recovered the SD card from her Canon EOS Rebel T6 after the decade's most extraordinary celestial event. What they found surpassed their wildest fears and haunted them.

No one told Alma how terrible cell phone service at Grand Teton National Park would be. Holding the phone toward the sky proved effortless. Even if she could get a signal, it wouldn't matter. The thousands of park visitors would inundate the network with social media posts throughout the day.

Alma felt Derek's eyes on her as she doom-scrolled through her outdated newsfeed, hoping the timeline would refresh. She knew what he wanted to say; she should tuck the phone away and be present with him. A part of her desperately wanted to do that, but the itch would still be there.

Like. Comment. Share. Repeat. Words of affirmation were Alma's love language. It was something that her 7,342 followers showed they understood in the comment section of her posts. Sharing amateur photography on the internet with strangers brought Alma joy. She made friendships, learned new techniques, and dreamed of a budding career in the industry one day— something Derek never understood or appreciated. Instead, screen time had become a point of contention between them.

The mood had shifted between them in recent months. Maybe they had fallen out of that so-called honeymoon phase. The way Derek stacked the dishes in the dishwasher thoughtlessly and chaotically seemed to suggest so. Or the way he chewed on his protein bars. Or maybe it was how Alma had grown tired of the performative acts of service that were seldomly returned now. Did Derek value her happiness the way he used to? She wasn't sure.

Maybe that's why she craved those likes, comments, and shares.

Alma tucked her phone into the cupholder of her foldable camping chair. She agreed to travel to Jackson to celebrate Derek's birthday that summer by going off the grid and hiking. Fate would have it that his birthday fell on the next total eclipse of the sun, and while Alma had no strong feelings about watching the eclipse, Derek did. So they carved out some time on their itinerary to find a good spot to sit and wait for the astronomical show to begin. Alma wasn't thrilled with sitting in a field for two hours without a wine cooler or a beer in hand, but Derek had bought her a solar filter for her camera lens. An act of good faith on his part, perhaps. Maybe he was trying to fix whatever was lost between them, too.

Alma did not have experience photographing the cosmos, but with the guidance of her friends and online followers, she learned astrophotography. Hours were spent watching instruction videos on YouTube. She toyed with the aperture settings and shutter speed. It wasn't until she properly photographed the full moon glowing in the night sky that she felt confident in her abilities to harness the beauty of the cosmos on their trip out west.

Taking a series of images chronicling the period the moon passed between the Earth and the sun would be an incredible feat. Maybe she could even learn how to combine the images to display a time sequence of the eclipse itself. She eagerly attached the camera to the tripod and pulled out the shutter release controller she'd bought online. A smile bloomed across her face as she thought of how the photo would garner thousands of likes on her profile. Validation was so addictive.

"I don't know why you're fussing with all of that." Derek bit off another bite of his protein bar. "If you're focusing on capturing the perfect shot the whole time, you'll miss it yourself. You gotta be in the moment, babe."

"You're the one that bought me the special filter for my camera."

"Yeah, but I thought it would be something you tape on and leave alone. You know?"

Alma nodded and focused on attaching the solar filter to the lens. Tears welled in her eyes, and she struggled to suppress the lump growing in her throat. Couldn't Derek support her in this without complaint?

"I brought a shutter release controller so I won't be glued to the camera. I promise." She grimaced. Alma checked the camera settings again before sitting next to him.

Thousands of visitors surrounded them in cars, campers, and chairs. How far have they traveled to get there? Were they wearing cheesy t-shirts, too, like Derek, who proudly sported his *It's My Eclipse Day Birthday!* shirt he'd bought for himself. Watching him rock back and forth with anticipation, while also wearing those flimsy solar glasses, made her smile. For a moment, a glimpse of the goofball she had fallen for three years ago shone through. Had they really become so dissociated that she could forget how he used to be?

Other than checking the clock on her phone, the only way Alma knew totality was approaching was the timer on her camera's shutter going off. She'd have to thank her online amateur astrophotography community, again, for teaching her how to set the shutter release controller to take photos in automatic intervals.

Shadow bands of light rippled gently across the plains, leaving only a thin crescent of sun remaining visible to the eye. "Five minutes! Get ready, Alma! Make sure you have your glasses on." Derek squeezed her hand, and to Alma's surprise, she squeezed back.

Alma closed her eyes and leaned in to plant a kiss on his warm lips. A flutter of butterflies tickled somewhere in her belly.

"Happy birthday, Derek." She pulled away and saw the gleam in his eyes. Alma knew what he was thinking. She even welcomed the idea of his hands tracing the curves of her body as her thighs squeezed together instinctively. How long had it been since they were intimate with one another?

Anticipation of the eclipse was palpable in the air, and the crowd started to cheer as tenebrous dusk crept its way across the plains. The song of nightfall lulled the crickets to sleep. Birds stopped chirping. Even the wind grew silent. They were in the penumbra now, shifting between the veils of light. Goose flesh prickled Alma's arms, and she wished she hadn't left her pullover in the car.

"Hey, check it out." Derek nudged Alma's shoulder and pointed past her periphery. An older woman swayed rhythmically toward the sky as she chanted premonition into the ether.

"Humanity has waited patiently for the cosmos to return us to the primordial wretchedness we once were! We thank it for this generous gift of allowing us to enjoy the pleasures of the flesh! Let us bask now as day turns to night in the eternal glory of the stars, and may we submit ourselves to the eclipse's awe-inspiring and terrifying presence!"

Alma fidgeted in her chair, unnerved by the woman, and now keenly aware of their vulnerability in their macrocosm of existence. Out in the open, they were exposed and waiting. Dread hovered like a cloud, and Alma caught her breath.

"Sounds like someone is in totality already, if you catch my drift." Derek chuckled, unfazed by the woman's eerie divination.

Alma shook her head and checked the clock on her phone. Sixty seconds remained.

"I'm going to check the camera one more time." Alma's knees began to shake. She had to adjust positions to calm her nerves, otherwise she was sure she'd fall over in her chair.

"Come on, Alma, you always do this. Forget the screens and be here with me!" Derek begged.

"I will, I promise…right after I get this shot!" She should have felt guilty, but it didn't stop her from getting up to adjust the tripod before Derek could protest further.

"Ten…nine…eight…" Alma tuned out the eclipse gazers who were dazzled by the brilliance of the last sliver of sun creating a diamond ring effect. She spent those final moments prepping her camera, checking the time for the shutter release. It was set to go off every thirty seconds, just as planned.

"Five…four…three…"

She was going to capture this moment. Like. Comment. Share.

"One!"

The park erupted in whistles and clanging of cowbells. Alma's eyes were glued to the display screen on the camera, assuaged by the timely shutter of her camera. Her focus had been crystal clear; the screen showed that she had indeed caught the moment the moon blotted out the sun. It was the best photo she had ever taken. She couldn't help but beam with pride.

She took a step back to look up. An obsidian orb hovered above with tendrils of white light undulating and illuminating the sky. It permeated omnipotence and absolute submission. It was as the woman said it would be: awe-inspiring and terrifying. It didn't take much for Alma to see how someone could get lost in the caliginous beauty of the umbras' influence.

Alma thought about the sky's transformation and a pang of guilt stabbed her gut; she should have been squeezing Derek's hand, counting the seconds in those last moments. Alma wouldn't blame him if he didn't forgive her for missing their own relationship's window of totality.

An agonizing scream broke her trance. She turned around to find Derek on his knees, hunched over in a child's pose. A guttural howl burst from his chest as he dug his nails into the fresh soil beneath him. Bile spilled from his lips into the grass, and he moaned in anguish. Without pause, without hesitation,

Alma rushed to his side.

"Derek! Are you okay? What's happening?" She reached out with trepidation, unsure how to help but hoping she could try.

Derek's gaze shifted, and he met Alma's stare. A steady stream of ichor oozed from his blackened eyes, scintillating the halo of light from above.

"R-r-run!!!" Bubbling clots of blood gargled in Derek's throat as he collapsed under the pressure of the outlandish influence that overcame him.

Alma gasped as Derek mutated into a grotesque new form. Bones cracked to create sickening pops. His spine snapped, and his skull caved in. He became inhuman, a pulp of flesh that resembled dripping sludge with limbs and serrated teeth. His flesh bubbled under what looked like radiation burns, decaying before her eyes. Alma could not find the sound to scream as the Derek she knew vanished. The monster he became shredded sinew from muscles to expose the ulna and radius of his arms.

Alma stumbled back, unable to fathom what was happening. The frantic cries of park visitors echoed across the valley as they, too, succumbed to the violent phenomenon.

What was she supposed to do? Where would she go? Even if she made it out of here alive, who would believe anything she had to say?

Alma glared at the inky specter in the sky. Though she could not explain it, she knew the eclipse had something to do with this phenomenon. The orb flared solar rays back as if in affirmation.

How much was stolen from her in those last moments that were supposed to be full of bliss? And Derek—she'd never know whether they could have repaired their relationship. She'd missed her last moments with him because she focused on taking the perfect snapshot for her followers. Overcome with rage, hot tears streamed down her face.

Screw the likes, comments, and shares. Derek's death would not be in vain. Somehow, she'd show the world what had happened to him, even if that meant sharing her photographs postmortem.

Alma snatched the Rebel T-6 off the tripod and ran straight into the writhing mound of bloodlust. Teeth gnashed at flesh. Bodies recoiled and entwined with one another. Limbs flew overhead and landed at Alma's feet, only to be snatched for consumption. She inhaled the fetor of decimation and knew it was only a matter of minutes until she, too, would be devoured by the gelatinous mound of malice.

Alma was in awe of the gore. Despite the horror of it all, somehow, this was the closest she'd ever felt to truly living. Maybe it was the thrill of terror rushing through her veins, but the high of existing in the space between life and death was invigorating. Addicting. It was validating, even. A spurt of crimson red splashed across her body and the camera lens, but she continued to photograph the slaughter anyway.

Alma never felt the horde of undead pull her down under the weight of their masticated limbs. Even amid the butchery, adrenaline prevented her from feeling any pain. Shutter after shutter, she captured the carnage, hunger, and gobbets of flesh and tendons as they were stripped from her bones.

Only when the bloodthirsty throng ripped the Rebel T6 from her hands did Alma's psyche rejoin her body again. The intensity of her suffering overcame her. Pain pulsated in the gaping wounds of her limbs and torso as a haze of teeth and nails sunk into her flesh.

Her eyes dilated, and she fixed her gaze on the sky. The crushing weight of the bodies above made it impossible for her to breathe. The black orb flared at her once more. Underneath the agony and sound of her screams, Alma was finally present and living in the moment—just as she promised.

DON'T LOOK UP

EMERSON SEIPEL

"Alright Elena, I'm heading out!" I called up from the base of the stairway. My voice echoed along the old wooden panels lining the walls, magnifying and carrying it throughout the tiny house.

"Marco, wait!" she called back, running down the stairs to meet me. Her face was flushed, and she panted slightly as she looked up at me, worry creasing lines into her forehead. "Do you have to go?"

"Yes, little sister," I said in the most patronizing tone I could muster, reaching a finger out to flick her on the nose. "Even in the Apocalypse, we still have bills to pay, and I have to go to work. People still get sick, and until the world actually ends, it's my job to take care of them."

"Don't talk like that," she scolded, and for a moment the fear in her voice actually made me feel bad. "You don't think the world is actually ending, do you?"

"Nah." I shook my head with what I hoped was a nonchalant smile. "The world will be around long after humanity is gone."

"Marco…" A pout furrowed her brow and she poked out her lower lip.

"Listen, we're fine until we're not. And until that moment comes, we're just going to keep on keeping on, business as usual, right?"

"But it's dangerous at night," she said. "Can't you switch to a day shift? Or get a different job?"

"Listen." I bent down slightly to look into her eyes. The golden flecks in the deep brown orbs caught the light like so many stars in the sky I could no longer see. "The night shift pays better. It's just you and me now, so we need all the money we can get."

"I could—"

"No." I cut her off before she could get too far down that line of thinking again. "Like you said, it's dangerous out there. I work, you study, that's the deal, remember?"

"I should be doing more to help." She looked down as she shuffled her feet, wringing her hands as though she could squeeze out every drop of guilt.

"You *do* help. You take care of the house. You cook the food. You keep me grounded," I said. "I would be lost without you, Elena. Just like one of those Gazers out there."

"Okay…" She still sounded unsure.

"Now, listen…" I said, pulling on my hoodie and grabbing my keys from the hook by the door. "You remember the rules. Lock the door behind me. Don't answer it for anyone while I'm gone. Keep the curtains shut tight and the TV off." I leaned forward and planted a gentle kiss on her forehead. "Do your homework and get some good rest."

"And you remember your rules," she chided, the only figure of any real authority in my life. "Keep your hat on and your hood pulled up. Don't talk to strangers. And don't look up."

"I won't look up," I promised, taking her hands in mine and giving a gentle squeeze. "I'll be home in the morning. Call me at the hospital if you need anything." Another quick peck on the head, and I pushed her back toward the stairs. "Turn around until you hear the door close, then lock it and go back to your schoolwork. Goodnight, little sister." I pulled my hood up over my ball cap and ducked my head, heading out the door and into the world beyond.

I shoved my hands into my pockets as I heard the door click behind me, Elena sliding the deadbolt securely into place. My feet beat a staccato rhythm against the pavement as I made my way quickly toward the hospital. I wasn't necessarily scared out here in the growing dark, but I wasn't stupid enough to stay outside any longer than I had to, either.

It had started as a star, an extra notch appearing in Orion's belt late one night in mid September. Astronomers, professional and amateur alike, were initially excited about the sudden appearance of a nova in the night sky. They turned their telescopes toward it, and that was when the problems first started. They peered into their eyepieces and looked at their computer screens, and simply never stopped looking. They lost all motivation to do anything but stare at this mysterious new celestial body. As the object grew in the sky, appearing earlier and earlier, more people began to take notice, stopping whatever they were doing at the time, simply to stare off into space.

Pictures, telescope images, videos of the phenomenon were all dangerous, all captivating unsuspecting people right out of their daily lives. We called them Gazers, because once they caught that first glimpse, that's all they were anymore. Mindless zombies, staring at the night sky.

When morning came, and the stars disappeared, they raged and thrashed, tearing out their hair and clawing at their own bodies until their hearts stopped beating. Incoherent and mournful screaming filled the air in every corner of the city as the Gazers breathed their last breaths, tearing themselves to pieces at the loss of their beloved star.

The street lights flickered as I made my way toward the hospital, but my path was well lit. Whatever it was that haunted the night sky now shone brighter than the moon, providing enough light to see clearly as I neared my destination. Temptation pulled at me, curiosity whispering in my ear as I walked, and I hunched my shoulders against it.

Just one peek, it lilted in the back of my brain. *A quick flick of the eyes can't hurt. Just to see what all the fuss is about...*

I collided with something hard and heavy, cursing under my breath as I fell to the ground. Instinctively, I curled in on myself and covered my eyes, waiting for my death. *Did I see it? Did I look?* The seconds ticked by as I mentally checked myself for injuries or psychological trauma. No, I was still functioning. I didn't inadvertently catch a glimpse of the alien body stalking all of humanity.

I hopped back to my feet, keeping my head lowered. I dusted myself off before looking around to see what I had so gracefully crashed into in my distraction. A man stood on the sidewalk, tall, muscular, and utterly still. His eyes were glazed over and raised toward the heavens. He seemed completely unbothered by the fact that another human had run into him, as a line of drool collected at the corner of his mouth, dribbling down his chin. His eyes sparkled in the sparse night light, reflecting something huge, a massive, glowing ball of—

No. I quickly averted my eyes.

Don't look.

I wasn't sure if catching the reflection of the thing in his eyes was enough to doom me to share his fate, but I didn't want to take the risk. I reached out toward the Gazer and took his wrist in my hands, my fingers pressing firmly over his pulse point. His heart beat steadily under my fingertips, a calm but constantly burning ember that I knew would be extinguished when morning came.

I took a breath to steady myself as I let the man's hand drop back to his side. There was nothing I could do for him now. The Sweepers would pick him up eventually and take him to wherever they kept the Gazers. The news claimed that they were sedated for their own safety and held in a government facility, but I had my doubts. As the number of Gazers grew, and the rest of humanity dwindled, it seemed more ethical to euthanize them.

Cynical, Elena always called me. As though my views on the world at large were somehow a negative. I generally preferred the term *realist.* If we wanted to live, we couldn't look at the thing in the sky, couldn't study it. Everyone who tried, died the same terrible death. And if we couldn't study the thing, we couldn't figure out how it was affecting people. We couldn't find a cure for the Gazers. Keeping them alive was a waste of manpower and resources. Better to put them, and everyone else, out of their collective misery.

"Hey, Marco!" A voice called to me as I stepped onto the tile floor of the Emergency Department. The astringent scent of disinfectant burned my nostrils, and I wrinkled my nose against it out of habit. "You look like you've seen a ghost!"

"Might as well have." I removed my hat and hoodie and stashed them under the desk at the center of the room. "I had a run in with a Gazer."

"You didn't see it, did you?" Randy gripped my chin in one hand and shined a penlight into my eyes with the other. "You didn't get a look at the thing in the sky?"

"If I had, I wouldn't be here…" I shoved him away, batting his hands off me. "I'm fine. Just wasn't looking where I was walking, and I bumped right into him."

"Was he already gone?" His tone took on a grim quality that I wished I didn't understand.

"Yeah," I said. "Dead to the world and everything in it. Everything except for the star."

"You know that's no star, right?" Randy leaned in and whispered, one eyebrow cocked.

"Alright, genius…" I rubbed the back of my head. "What do you think it is?"

"Aliens, my dude," Randy yelled in a whisper.

"Aliens," I deadpanned.

"Yeah, they're catching people with their light, hypnotizing them and robbing them of all sense. Then the Sweepers collect them all through the night and hand them over to the extra-terrestrials to study."

"Ahh," I said, nodding in a knowing gesture. "That explains why you haven't been caught yet. They're looking for intelligent life."

"Hey!" He punched my arm in mock offense. "Well, they haven't caught you either!"

"Yep," I said, putting on a show of solemnity. "You're right. One of these days, you and I will be the only two dumbasses left on the entire planet."

"Then we just need to find a few dumbass ladies to repopulate Earth with us." He winked.

I laughed at the ridiculousness of the statement. "Yes, they would have to be dumbasses to fall for the charms of the likes of us." I snickered. "Then we'll have a whole planet of dumbasses and the aliens will leave us alone."

A shrill scream interrupted our jovial banter, and Randy and I both rounded the desk to meet it.

"Help!" A woman cried as she stumbled down the hallway toward us. "Somebody please, help me!"

As I ran to the woman, I could finally see the source of the shriek echoing through the hallway. She held desperately to the thrashing, flailing form of another woman, a younger woman, howling bloody murder.

"My daughter!" she screamed at me as I arrived. "Help her, please!" She relinquished her hold and the struggling young woman collapsed gracelessly into my arms. She screeched into my face as her fingers clawed at her own, rending deep gouges into her cheeks. Her eyelids flapped uselessly, tattered pieces of skin falling around her face as blood pooled in the sockets where her eyes used to be. The viscous crimson liquid spilled over and smeared down her cheeks as she fought against my hold.

"Gazer!" I shouted to Randy as I attempted to restrain the violently thrashing woman.

He pulled the older woman off to the side as I picked the younger one up and hauled her toward a gurney.

"Get me the Midazolam, now! We need to sedate her!"

The woman howled and flailed on the bed, snapping her teeth viciously as I held her wrists, trying to keep her from harming herself further. Randy ran toward us, uncapping a needle as he approached, pushing her dress out of the way and jamming the syringe into her thigh. The woman jerked violently as he pushed the plunger and administered the sedative. She continued to thrash and shriek as the minutes passed, the sedative showing no signs of slowing her down.

"How much did you give her?"

"Six milligrams!" he yelled over her screeching. "That should have knocked her out cold!"

The woman curled her body, planting a foot against my shoulder and kicking with more power than a person her size should have been able to wield. I crashed back against the wall, the breath knocked violently from my lungs. My feet slid out from under me, bringing me to the ground with a hard thud. Gasping desperately for air, I crawled back to the gurney as the woman returned to clawing at her face.

"Addison!" The older woman reached out a hand toward her daughter, but remained glued against the wall where Randy had put her. "Addison, stop! Why are you doing this?"

As the screams died down, a choking, gurgling noise was the only response this woman would ever receive from her daughter, the death throes of a young woman lost to the world for the sake of a pretty light.

Blood ran in rivulets down the sides of her neck as her throat was flayed, torn open by her own fingernails. Randy and I continued our due diligence, attempting to stop the flow of blood from her wounds, to keep her heart beating as long as possible. But in the end, the girl was just another Gazer, forfeited to self-destruction.

"She said she was only going to look for a second," the old woman murmured to herself. "It wasn't supposed to hurt her. She was only going to look for a second…"

"Apparently that's all it takes." Randy patted her back and steered her toward the waiting room chairs. There would be paperwork to fill out for all three of us, but for now, the sudden stillness of the Emergency Department wrapped around us like a wet blanket, suffocating and stifling.

The rest of the shift passed as any other did these days. Mostly minor wounds and illnesses, one heart attack and a few broken bones. We delivered a baby in the ambulance bay, the new mother too enraptured by the celestial sight above her to be bothered by the pain of contractions or to even greet her child as it took its first breaths. We shielded the child's eyes from the sky above and left the mother in the street to be picked up by the Sweepers, knowing there was nothing more we could do for her.

As twilight crept over the horizon, I donned my hoodie and ball cap and headed out into the streets again. Walking back to the house, I thought about Elena, about the family and friends I had already lost, and the little sister who survived, waiting for me to arrive home. I wondered what was so compelling up there in the sky that people would risk losing everything just for a glimpse, even knowing it would be their last.

It must be something really amazing…

My feet stopped moving of their own volition, and before I knew it, I was standing still in the middle of the street, buildings rising on either side of me. I probably couldn't see anything right now if I looked anyway.

A single, tentative step, and I found myself frozen again. The sun would be rising soon. I would miss my opportunity if I didn't look now…

No.

Even a quick glance would result in a violent death by my own hands within the hour. No sight was worth that risk. Elena was home waiting for me. I should make her pancakes for breakfast. Blueberry pancakes, because they're her favorite…

I shook my head to dislodge the thoughts, then I forced my feet to continue their journey back home. The niggling curiosity pulled at me, a siren's song calling out as I floated adrift in the sinking ship that was humanity.

I felt myself slow to a stop again as I approached our house, one foot on the stairs. I screamed in my head, forcing myself to keep moving, don't stop, don't turn around. One slow step after another I climbed the stairs until I stood on my own front doorstep, staring down at the welcome mat.

Just a peek. The sun was cresting the horizon. I probably wouldn't see anything anyway. Curiosity finally got the better of me and I turned, raised my eyes to the sky, and I looked.

The light shining in the air above was huge—far bigger than any star, bigger than the moon at its fullest phase. The glow was a soft blue, pulsing and oscillating as though it were alive, breathing in rhythmic time to the beating of my own heart. Smokey tendrils of pinks and violets swirled out from the source of the light, stretching across the sky and sparkling like glitter spilled against the canvas of twilight.

Distantly, I thought I heard my name, felt a tug on my hand, a push against my chest, but it didn't matter. Nothing mattered except for this celestial spectacle. I couldn't believe that I had waited this long to see it.

"It's beautiful," I said to no one in particular. My words were unimportant. The way that this heavenly body dominated the sky, the whole world would see it eventually. "Gorgeous," I whispered, as though afraid my own voice would ruin the spectacular sight.

And as the sun swept across the sky, fading this beautiful masterpiece away into nothingness, I knew in that moment that I couldn't bear to live without it.

NOX INVICTUS

ROSE STRICKMAN

There are no windows anymore. There are black mirrors, reflecting only what's within and revealing nothing of what's without. Even with the electricity gone, candlelight alone is enough to turn a window into a black, reflective pit.

Before the Darkness, I never realized how much of the night scenery—what we saw outdoors at night—was defined by *light*, not darkness. The stars, the moon. Lighted windows, streetlights, the flash of cars. Chains of colored lights at Christmas. The faint stain of dusk or dawn, lightening the sky. Even reflective lights on bicyclists' vests. All those lights are gone now. The night is as featureless as it is endless.

I sit on the bed I shared with my wife, wrapped in a blanket against the cold, facing away from the black mirror of our window, and drink from a flask—I think it used to be my grandfather's. It's full of bourbon now, the last of the alcohol we brought up. I sit and I drink and I wonder if my wife will return from downstairs and, if so, will she be changed?

It was subtle at first. No one really noticed, aside from toddlers and the insane. The sun still rose and the days continued their accustomed lengths, but the shadows grew larger, longer. Darker. I remember one ordinary day at my office, squinting at a corner where we kept the printer and realizing that I couldn't actually see it. That there was nothing there but shadow.

Then the nights, too, grew darker. Streetlights burnt out and weren't replaced. Even the headlights on cars didn't seem as bright or as far-reaching as they had before. Every night, there were fewer lighted windows, as people stopped staying up late and kept curtains closed in their houses and apartments. There was no public outcry, no official alarm—not yet—but people went out at night less and less. We'd lie awake, listening to strange sounds in the night: barks and yelps, growls where such sounds had no right to be, where before there had been only traffic and the sounds of humanity.

Then people began disappearing.

I'm almost out of bourbon. I could go downstairs and get some more— I'm fairly certain most of our booze is still there, untouched and unchanged— but the Darkness has filled the basement to capacity and my wife still hasn't returned from the ground floor. When I crane around to see the stairwell through our open bedroom door, I don't see the reaching fingers of shadows. But who's to say they aren't gathering at the foot of the stairs even now?

I should go downstairs and check on her. I should take the flashlight, grab the knife we brought with us upstairs, and go find her, like a good husband. But it would do no good. No flashlight beam can penetrate the Darkness, and human weapons are of no use against it. Or what humans become when immersed in it.

The first reports were dismissed as campfire stories. Bipedal creatures with claws and fangs, stalking our streets—what had these homeless people been smoking? But too many people disappeared, and too many bodies piled up: ripped, bloody corpses, left half-eaten on street corners. Too many people saw these monsters—and too many people recognized the monsters they'd seen. The twisted remains of those they'd loved, or hated, or bought a house from, or accepted coffee from at Starbucks. Real people, made monsters by the encroaching Darkness.

Already, we were calling it the Darkness, with the capital D. It filled up neglected corners, turned basements and cellars into quiet, restless lakes of shadow. Lights wouldn't turn on in such places; shining lamps or flashlights into them grew progressively less effective. Flashlight beams extended less and less into the gloom, and lamp glow grew frailer, until both stopped altogether. You'd turn on the flashlight, you'd see its glow—but it wouldn't beam out or cut into the Darkness. Night reigned supreme and unchallenged where the Darkness invaded.

Soon, even the most hardened skeptics were frightened. Clearly *something* was happening—and on a global scale, too. Reports flooded in: jungles in Asia were now impenetrable, the trees dripping solid shadows even during the brightest tropical day. No one dared enter the oceans, on any coast; they were nothing but vast plains of Darkness now, and the marine creatures had grown bloodthirsty and savage. At the polar regions, spring didn't come; the winter night went on and on, with no dawn. People moved to lower latitudes, leaving the tundra to wolves and formerly human monsters.

There were a thousand theories, ranging from climate change to God's wrath against unbelievers, to a North Korean conspiracy. Scientists and government agencies around the world set themselves to solving the mystery, capturing monsters and trying to cure them, trying to analyze the Darkness, to find a light source that could penetrate it. But the Darkness soon invaded their labs and offices, and drove them all out, freeing the monsters, leaving only the computers behind to flicker and fade into death.

Of course, there was also plenty of religious hysteria. Members of all faiths gathered in prayer circles and desperate ceremonies, enacting prayers and rituals meant to atone for their sins, to call down God's mercy. But the Darkness knows no god, and seeped into churches, synagogues and temples, smothering crucifixes and altars in shadow, and sending the faithful out into the lengthening nights to seek shelter or fall prey to the monsters. Or become monsters themselves.

I hope the believers are wrong. I hope there is no God. Because if there is, then He has surely abandoned us. Or proven Himself far more terrible than we ever imagined.

My wife and I stopped going to work around the same time that most other people did. We stockpiled supplies: food, batteries, matches, candles and blankets. Cities set up supply depots for anyone to come and get them, but it was growing more dangerous to go to such places. The Darkness invaded all buildings, seeping up from basements to fill ground floors, silently lapping up to the ceilings. I remember accepting a bag of rice from a girl at a supply depot, and as I took the bag from her hands, the Darkness snatched her backward, and she disappeared without a single cry. That still seems the most terrible thing of all: she went without the slightest sound, no protest against her fate.

My wife and I holed up in our house, along with other survivors. Islands of humanity, cut off from one another. The sorry fact is that we had as much to fear from each other as from the Darkness or its beasts; people always turn on each other in times of desperation and terror, and this was no exception. There were murders, rapes, and plenty of looting. My wife and I hammered boards across our doors, blocked the windows. Still, we were attacked. I remember hiding in the closet with her, listening to the looters smash their way through the barricades and trash our living room, looking for valuables. It made us smile a bit, even laugh, because why were they still so intent on stealing our stuff? Why, at the end of the world, do greed and veniality persist? What did they think they were going to *do* with our television and silverware, our electronics and appliances?

We were lucky they didn't come upstairs, didn't find us. We lived to see another day—another *night*, rather. The days were still coming then, but they grew ever shorter and more fleeting, chased across the surface of the planet by the moving fronts of night. Constellations appeared outside their proper seasons, crowding the sky in brilliant multitudes. Indeed, we'd never seen the stars so clearly before, unblotted by artificial illumination. My wife and I used to lie on the roof, studying the celestial patterns, the burning planets, all held together by the scattered silver dust of the Milky Way. Below us, the Darkness seethed like a hungry ocean, howled with the cries of the monsters, but the lights of space still shone clear.

"Look at that," my wife said. I remember her voice so clearly, as though she's talking in my ear. "Almost makes up for everything, doesn't it?" And she laughed, and I laughed, cracked and miserable and ironic, because it *didn't* make up for anything, nothing at all, but still it was our only pleasure: to lie on the roof and gaze at an unreachable galaxy of stars.

My wife sat up then, to gesture at the impenetrable ocean of Darkness lying around us, stretching to the horizon, broken by only a few islands of light. "The Darkness has taken over the Earth," she said. "Do you think it will go on from here? Will it fill the entire galaxy, snuffing out the stars?"

I stroked her hair, still soft and smooth. "I don't know. Maybe."

We sat there, listening to the cries of the animals and the monsters below, and we said no more, but continued to gaze at the stars.

The Darkness is reaching up the stairs now. I can see its first stealthy fingers, inching their way up the walls and steps. I don't know why it still feels the need to be sneaky and subtle. The world is awash in Darkness, the Earth's surface clutched tight in its grip. Why doesn't it just charge up the stairs and break over me like a great crashing ocean wave? But I suppose that isn't the Darkness's nature.

"What do you suppose it is?" my wife asked me once. We'd just finished making love, and were still sticky and sweaty, lying wrapped around one another in our bed. She waved a hand at the black mirror-window. "Maybe it's not real. Maybe all those crackpot conspiracy theorists were right when they said it was a mass hallucination generated by the Russians."

"The North Koreans. And, even if it is, it's still real enough, isn't it? If everyone in the world is just lying around hallucinating, then we've all starved to death by now and we're all in Hell."

"So, this is Hell?" She huddled closer. "I thought there'd be more flames. Demons torturing sinners and things. Not just Darkness, swallowing everything."

I hugged her hard, as though that could protect her. "I don't think this is Hell." Hell, after all, is a very human concept, and there's nothing human about the Darkness.

A fire's been lit, miles away, at the top of a building, I think. I watch it through the window, as that's better than watching the Darkness creep up the stairs. I think I can see thin little figures dancing around it, hear their cries over the miles of empty blackness. Someone's throwing one last bonfire party, I guess. Those became popular as the Darkness advanced. People would build a huge fire and drink and feast and dance around it, whirling so close to the flames their clothes trailed showers of sparks and they sustained angry red burns that went unnoticed in the drunken haze and despairing euphoria. My wife and I attended a few ourselves; we danced wildly around the flames, losing ourselves in movement and music and wine, and, most of all, in staring into the flames, into the dancing points of light and heat.

I shiver now, drawing the blanket around my shoulders. It's been so long since anyone has been warm. Why don't we all freeze to death? Why don't we slip into icy sleep, one by one, instead of sitting and waiting for the Darkness to come?

But I suppose that would be too easy. That's not what the Darkness is after.

The fire's too large, too bright now. It's raging out of control, turning the top of the far-off building into a torch. I hear a few cries, but somehow I don't think the revelers are trying very hard to flee from the flames. Even at the beginning, people set themselves aflame, preferring to die in the agony of extreme light and heat, rather than wait in hopeless despair for the Darkness or the monsters to finish them off.

I nearly did so myself, once. We were at a bonfire party, and a rising tide of anguish came over me. The world was ending, and there was no escape from the Darkness. Save one. I danced closer and closer to the fire, tears running down my face, and I felt its heat sting my skin, singe my clothing. Another step, and I would become a living torch, a final defiance against the Darkness—

"No! Stop!" My wife's hand drew me back, away from the circle of heat, back into the coolness. She slapped me, glaring, her own tears shining. "Snap out of it! You're not going to die that way! You're not going to leave me!"

I said nothing. Half of me was grateful. The other half hated her.

And look what's happened now. I didn't abandon her, but she's abandoned me, heading out alone into the Darkness. It would have been better for us both to have thrown ourselves into the flames.

There are some monsters at the base of the house now. I can hear them sniffing around and growling. They probably won't get in; we boarded up the windows again after the looters left, and the monsters don't seem bright enough to break into secured homes. For a while back then, there were efforts to stamp them out, when it became clear they couldn't be saved: government-sponsored eradication programs, sharpshooters, that sort of thing. But the monsters quickly overran any attempt to kill them, especially after things unraveled completely, and governments of all kinds foundered and failed.

It's horrible to think they used to be human: men and women and children. But a part of me envies them, despite their savagery and viciousness: they belong in the Darkness, and can survive in it. I wonder how the Darkness chooses whom to transfigure and whom to kill. I wonder what the monsters will do for prey when the last of humanity is gone. I wonder if that's my wife I hear out there.

"Are you crazy?" I hissed when she announced she was heading downstairs. "You'll be killed!"

"We need more food. More candles. We've still got some downstairs." She was very calm, and there was a strange, flat look in her eyes which disturbed me. She moved around purposefully, collecting a pillowcase to carry supplies. There was an odd quality to her movements: they were single-minded but dreamy, like she was sleepwalking. "I'll be up in just a second. You worry too much."

"Are you listening to yourself? The *Darkness* is down there!"

Her glazed eyes pierced through me. "It's up here, too."

"Which is why we should stay together—"

"It's fine." She leaned up to kiss me on the cheek, a soft warm peck. "I'll see you soon. I love you."

"No—wait—"

But she was gone, darting down the hallway and down the stairs, before I could stop her. I heard footsteps, and the sound of her tuneless humming. Then nothing.

I wish I had said *I love you* in return, when I had the chance.

The Darkness has pooled up the stairwell and is lapping at the hallway carpet. Its fingers crawl forward, questing. I could close the door, I suppose, hide in the closet. But somehow, I don't want to. I want to sit here, drink the last of my bourbon, and watch it come.

I don't believe the Darkness is a mass hallucination. I don't think it's a result of climate change, or of a shift in the Earth's rotation. I don't think it's divine judgment, or even the advent of the Elder Gods. I think the Darkness is something much simpler than that. I think it's *rage*. I think it's punishment. I think it is the vengeance of Night, brought down on humanity, who have slaughtered its creatures and lit its darkness and disproved its myths and drowned out its stars and even dared to set foot on its moon. I think the Darkness is the ultimate revenge of Night on all who have defiled it, on puny humanity who dared to set itself up as a rival power. On humanity, who dared to face it without fear.

The Darkness is almost at my bedroom door now.

I stand, shrugging off my blanket and putting aside the flask. The last of the bourbon glugs out, staining the bedspread. "You may seek revenge," I say to the Darkness, to Night. "You may conquer the world and destroy humanity. *Nox Invictus*. But I can make one last light." I pick up the candle from the bureau. It burns tall in my hand. "One last fire."

I turn with the candle. Tilting its flame, I set fire to the paper lampshade, grinning as it goes up. The bedspread is next, the spilled bourbon spitting a tall flare, and, opening my closet, the clothes in their ranked files. The room fills with flames and choking smoke, with heat and blaze and *light*. It's not enough to hold off the Darkness, but it singes it, slaps back those first few tendrils.

Heat blistering my skin, lungs full of smoke, I laugh. "Come on!" I spread my arms wide, and the fire climbs onto my sleeves, turning me into a blazing angel, the last sentinel before the victorious army. One last fire, one last defiance. "*Nox Invictus*! Come and get me, Darkness!"

No more hiding, no more fear. I've had enough of both. My wife went out facing the Darkness, and so can I.

Still laughing, trailing my cloak of fire, I fall forward, into the embrace of Night.

ABOUT THE AUTHORS

ALAN BAXTER

Alan Baxter is a multi-award-winning author of horror, supernatural thrillers and dark fantasy liberally mixed with crime, mystery and noir. This Is Horror calls him "Australia's master of literary darkness" and the Talking Scared Podcast dubbed him "The Lord of Weird Australia." He's also a martial arts expert, a whisky-soaked swear monkey, and dog lover. He creates dark, weird stories among dairy paddocks on the beautiful south coast of NSW, Australia, where he lives with his family and other animals. Find him online at www.alanbaxter.com.au. You'll also find him spending far too much time on Twitter.

TIFFANY MICHELLE BROWN

Tiffany Michelle Brown is a California-based writer who once had a conversation with a ghost over a pumpkin beer. Her fiction and poetry have been featured in publications by Black Spot Books, Jolly Horror Press, Cemetery Gates Media, Fright Girl Summer, and the NoSleep Podcast. Tiffany lives near the beach with her husband Bryan, their pup Zen, and their combined collections of books, board games, and general geekery.

DINO PARENTI

Dino Parenti is a writer of dark literary and speculative fiction. He is the winner of the first annual *Lascaux Review* flash fiction contest and is featured in the Anthony Award winning anthology *Blood on the Bayou*. His short-fiction collection, *Dead Reckoning and Other Stories*, is out with Crystal Lake Publishing. He lives in Los Angeles.

PAULINE BARMBY

Pauline Barmby is a Canadian astrophysicist who believes that you can't have too many favorite galaxies. When not reading or writing, she runs, knits, and ponders the physics of curling. Her fiction has appeared or is forthcoming in Tree and Stone and Martian magazines and the Compelling Science Fiction anthology from Flame Tree Press. Find her on Twitter @PBarmby.

ZACHARY ROSENBERG

Zachary Rosenberg is a horror writer living in Florida. He crafts horrifying tales by night, and by day he practices law, which is even more frightening. His forthcoming debut novella will be published by Brigids Gate Press, and you may find his works released or forthcoming at Air and Nothingness Press and Nosetouch Press. You may follow him on Twitter @ZachRoseAuthor.

ZIGGY SCHUTZ

Ziggy Schutz (she/him/he/her) is a queer, disabled writer who is at all times looking for ways to make his favourite fairytales and horror stories reflect people who look a little more like her. You can find more about his writing on Twitter @ziggytschutz.

INARA ENKO

Inara Enko feels rooted in the night sky, as a steady source of familiarity in a life that has been filled with international moves. She comes from a mixed cultural/racial/ethnic background and has always been interested in star-lore from around the world—particularly from the Arabian Peninsula, where she spent most of her childhood. She will also talk your ear off about astrolabes if you're foolish enough to give her the chance. You can follow up with her creative work at www.retepunk.art.

JEREMY MEGARGEE

Jeremy Megargee has always loved dark fiction. He cut his teeth on R.L

Stine's *Goosebumps* series as a child and a fascination with Stephen King, Jack London, Algernon Blackwood, and many others followed later in life. Jeremy weaves his tales of personal horror from Martinsburg, West Virginia with his cat Lazarus acting as his muse/familiar. He is an active member of the West Virginia chapter of the Horror Writer's Association and you can often find him peddling his dark words in various mountain hollers deep within the Appalachians.

VANN ORCKA

Vann Orcka is a UK-based professional designer and former comic book artist who spends his mornings and evenings writing horror. His stories often explore childhood trauma, grief, and religion.

PATRICK BARB

Patrick Barb is an author of weird, dark, and horrifying tales, currently living (and trying not to freeze to death) in Saint Paul, Minnesota. He is the author of the dark urban fantasy novella *Gargantuana's Ghost* (Grey Matter Press), *Turn* (Alien Buddha Press), *The Nut House* (currently serialized in Cosmic Horror Monthly), *Helicopter Parenting in the Age of Drone Warfare* (Spooky House Press), and the collection *Pre-Approved for Haunting* (forthcoming, Turner Publishing, Summer 2023). In addition, he is an Active Member of the HWA and a Full Member of the SFWA. For more of his work, visit patrickbarb.com or follow him at twitter.com/pbarb.

JUSTIN MORITZ

Justin Moritz (they/he) is a non-binary writer of queer horror, ranging from grotesque camp to societal filth. Raised on true crime and horror movies from too young of an age, their work tends to explore the terror of living as a queer person in modern times, while adding a speculative twist. After completing their MFA in Screenwriting at the University of Texas-Austin, they hope to diversify queer representation in horror by pursuing a career as a screenwriter while working in film development. They've been featured in

Sci-Fi and Scary's *Twisted Anatomy* body horror anthology and are currently writing and producing several short films. You can follow them on Twitter at @jeepers_justin.

MATTHEW CONDELLO

Matthew Condello lives in Jersey City with his incredible husband of 22 years. He's a bookworm, singer, actor and huge nerd currently working the nightmare world of retail! He loves horror, sci-fi, and fantasy and is absolutely thrilled to be sharing his writing with the world for the first time after years of keeping it to himself. He wants to dedicate this story to his three old pups, Simon, Cody and Chip, who sadly all passed away this year, but whose inspirational cuddles while he wrote this made it what it is.

M. RICHARD ELEY

Richard Eley writes Sci-Fi, horror, fantasy, creative and instructional non-fiction, and is a member of SFWA. His publications include: Issues in Science and Technology magazine (SF story "Hot Dogs and Corn Flakes"); the Owl Creek Press SF&F anthology *Cabinet of Curiosities*; the Third Flatiron SF&F anthology *Brain Games*; and a forthcoming Fahrenheit Books SF&F anthology *Automobilia*. His nonfiction has appeared in the Virginian-Pilot newspaper, several writing craft articles for Hampton Roads Writers, and several dozen articles for various corporate clients. Four of his short stories have won awards and prizes in multiple writing contests.

MADISON MCSWEENEY

Madison McSweeney writes horror and dark fantasy from Ottawa, Ontario. She is the author of the horror-comedy *The Doom That Came to Mellonville* (Filthy Loot), the Short Sharp Shocks! novelette *The Forest Dreams With Teeth* (Demain Publishing), and the poetry collection *Fringewood* (Alien Buddha Press). She blogs at madisonmcsweeney.com and tweets from @MMcSw13.

BERNARD MCGHEE

When not writing fiction, Bernard McGhee works on the editing desk of a busy newsroom, which provides a constant source of inspiration for horror and other stories of unusual mayhem. He was raised in the New Orleans area but has lived all around the country. He currently lives in the Atlanta area with his wife and son and is looking ahead to the next death metal concert. You can follow him on Twitter at @BMcGhee13.

ELIZABETH DAVIS

Elizabeth Davis is a second generation writer living in Dayton, Ohio. They live there with their spouse and two cats—neither of which have been lost to ravenous corn mazes or sleeping serpent gods. They can be found at deadfishbooks.com when they aren't busy creating beautiful nightmares and bizarre adventures. Their work can be found at *After the Goldrush*, *Woman Unbecoming*, and *Troublemaker Firestarter Vol 2*.

LINDSEY RAGSDALE

Lindsey Ragsdale (she/her) is a writer from Chicago, Illinois. Two of her stories appear in the anthologies *Howls from Hell* and *Howls From The Dark Ages*. She loves reading, writing, cooking, and long walks by the lake. On Twitter, find her @Leviathan15.

JACOB STEVEN MOHR

Don't buy the hype: Jacob Steven Mohr was not raised by wolves. Feral children are capable of many things, but weaving wild words into flesh and fantasy isn't one of them. Lucky us. If it were, we'd all be speaking Wolf. Mohr's work has previously appeared in *Summer Bludgeon*, *Night Terrors Vol. 20*, and *I Cast You Out!*. His work has also been featured on the Scare You to Sleep Podcast. You can follow him online @jacobstevenmohr.

TONY LOGAN

From a very young age Tony Logan was obsessed with the horror genre. Kruger, Jason, Myers, Audrey Two, and Jerry Dandridge were his heroes. An active member of both Hampton Roads Writers and Tidewater Writers. He's had multiple short stories for Crystal Lake's *Shallow Waters* anthology, *Scary Snippets* anthologies, and *Black Ink Fiction* Anthologies, as well as having a story featured on the Tales to Terrify Podcast. When not helping people find the best fruit-forward Pinot Noir or buttery Chardonnay, he's breaking up fights between his hellcats, Stoker and Belmont, or walking his hellhound Achilles.

KIM Z. DALE

Kim Z. Dale (she/her) writes plays, stories, and essays. Her plays have been performed primarily in her current and previous home cities, Chicago and Pittsburgh. Her other writing has been published in anthologies and textbooks. More information about Kim's work can be found at kimzdale.com. Follow Kim on Twitter and Instagram where she is @observacious.

AI JIANG

Ai Jiang is a Chinese-Canadian writer and an immigrant from Fujian. She is a member of HWA, SFWA, and Codex. Her work has appeared or is forthcoming in F&SF, The Dark, PseudoPod, Prairie Fire, Hobart Pulp, The Masters Review—among others. Find her on Twitter @AiJiang_ and online at http://aijiang.ca.

C.R. BEIDEMAN

C.R. Beideman writes from Butte, Montana. His fiction appears in: *The Saturday Evening Post*, *Gray's Sporting Journal*, *MetaStellar* and yadda . . . He won a master's degree at a carnival. He's branded cattle and broken the same leg four times. In addition to skiing and fly fishing, these days he's into gardening.

SALVADOR AYALA

Salvador Ayala is a PhD Candidate at Rutgers University, where he works on twentieth-century U.S. and Latin American literature. He was born in Mexico, grew up in Los Angeles, and resides in New Jersey. He has had an interest in astronomy ever since taking part in the Academic Decathlon in high school.

KATE OTA

Kate Ota has a short story published in *The Kitsap Writers Anthology* (2020). She's a member of Tidewater Writers, Kitsap Writers Group, and the Pacific Northwest Writers Association.

HOLLY RAE GARCIA

Holly Rae Garcia is the author of *Parachute, The Easton Falls Massacre: Bigfoot's Revenge*, and *Come Join the Murder*. Her short fiction has appeared in numerous places online and in print, including the recent anthologies *Slash-Her* (Kandisha Press), *Generation X-ed* (Dark Ink), and *Dancing in the Shadows: A Tribute to Anne Rice* (Yuriko Publishing). More information can be found at www.HollyRaeGarcia.com.

AVRA MARGARITI

Avra Margariti is a queer author, Greek sea monster, and Rhysling-nominated poet with a fondness for the dark and the darling. Avra's work haunts publications such as Vastarien, Asimov's, Liminality, Arsenika, The Future Fire, Space and Time, Eye to the Telescope, and Glittership. *The Saint of Witches*, Avra's debut collection of horror poetry, is available from Weasel Press. You can find Avra on twitter @avramargariti.

GRACE R. REYNOLDS

Grace R. Reynolds is a native of the great state of New Jersey, where she was first introduced to the eerie and strange thanks to local urban legends of a devil creeping through the Pine Barrens. Since then, her curiosity with things that go bump in the night bloomed into creative expression as a dark poet, and horror and thriller fiction writer. Her debut collection of horror poetry *Lady of The House* was released in December 2021 by Curious Corvid Publishing. Connect with Grace on Instagram or Twitter @spillinggrace.

EMERSON SEIPEL

Emerson Seipel is a queer writer from the bowels of hell, also known as the American Midwest. He has been lost between the pages of one book or another since early childhood. Currently his work in speculative fiction is overseen by a masterful team consisting of his dog Talulah, his tarantula Ophelia, and his snake Laveau.

ROSE STRICKMAN

Rose Strickman is a speculative fiction author living in Seattle, Washington. Her work has appeared in anthologies such as *Sword and Sorceress 32*, *Nightmare Fuel*, *UnCommon Evil* and *Gilded Glass: Twisted Myths and Shattered Fairy Tales*. She has also been published in several e-zines and has self-published novellas. Please see her Amazon page at www.amazon.com/author/rosestrickman.

EDITOR: RED LAGOE

Red Lagoe grew up on 80s horror movies and carried her paranoia of slashers and sewer creatures into adulthood. Her stories can be found in various horror anthologies and within her short fiction collections *Lucid Screams* and *Dismal Dreams*. She worked as a staff writer with Crystal lake Publishing on their *Still Water Bay* dark fiction series, and is a member of the Horror Writers Association. When she's not writing, you might find her in the inky black of night, stargazing. Find more about Red at www.redlagoe.com.

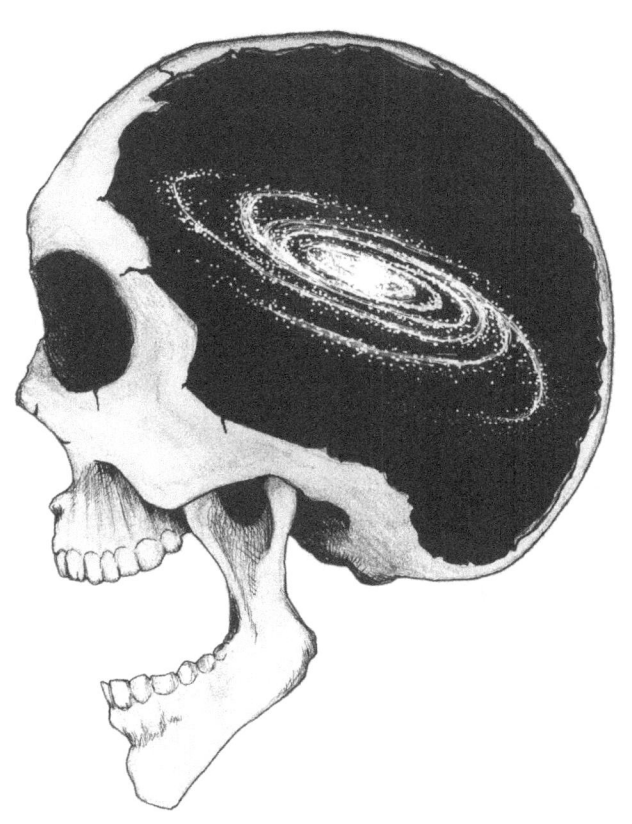

CONTENT WARNINGS

The stories and poems in this anthology are works of horror fiction which contain dark content that may be triggering to some individuals. Several stories contain instances of graphic violence, death, and gore. Please read with caution. Authors have offered the following warnings:

Stargazer, by Tiffany Michelle Brown:
    death, self-mutilation, mutilation of a corpse

Infinite Focus, by Dino Parenti:
    animal death

The Ravenous Empyrean, by Zachary Rosenberg:
    apocalypse

By the Hand of Sorayya, by Inara Enko:
    human trafficking, child abuse, violence, death of a family member, implied sexual abuse, dismemberment, non-consensual drug use

Horoscope of a Toxic Union, by Justin Moritz:
    domestic violence

Into the Great Wide Open, by Madison McSweeney:
    missing child

The Center of Everything, by Elizabeth Davis:
    suicide

Gazing, by Avra Margariti:
    body horror

In the Moment, by Grace Reynolds:
    graphic violence

Nox Invictus, by Rose Strickman:
    monsters, suicide